CLAIR *de* LUNE

ALSO BY JETTA CARLETON

The Moonflower Vine

CLAIR
de LUNE

Jetta Carleton

HARPER ◐ PERENNIAL

NEW YORK • LONDON • TORONTO • SYDNEY • NEW DELHI • AUCKLAND

HARPER ● PERENNIAL

FIRST EDITION

Designed by Michael P. Correy

Library of Congress Cataloging-in-Publication Data is available upon request.

ISBN 978-0-06-208919-9

12 13 14 15 16 OV/RRD 10 9 8 7 6 5 4 3 2 1

Moonlight

Your soul is a chosen landscape
Where charming masked provincials go
Playing the lute and dancing and almost
Sad beneath their fantastic disguises.

All singing in a minor key
Of conquering love and fortunate life
They do not seem to believe in their happiness
And their song mixes with the moonlight.

The still moonlight, sad and beautiful,
Which makes the birds dream in the trees
And makes the fountains sob in ecstasy,
The tall, slender fountains among the marble statues

—Paul Verlaine
Translation by Ann Patty

CLAIR de LUNE

One

Allen Liles is a fictional character. I made her up. Her story is made up too. But not all of it. Part of it's mine, handed on to her, altered to fit.

It's an old story. You've heard it before, any number of times. But I wanted to tell it again, as it happened in a time and a place where something existed that, nowadays, it seems to me, is in short supply: innocence.

Innocence, of course, can lead to error, and error led to the expulsion from Eden. Or so it is generally considered, although as far as we are told it was the end neither of Eden nor of the garden. It was the end only of the sojourn there of its first inhabitants. Evicted for the error of their ways, they were forbidden to return. Angels and a flaming sword were set to guard it at the east.

Nothing is mentioned of the other boundaries. Nor is it written that the garden was destroyed. We are left to assume that it still exists. As of course it does, as a creation of the mind, as it has always been. And it is known for a fact that now and then the garden is rediscovered—here or there—and a way in found. (Perhaps from the west.) None are granted citizenship there. But there are those who enter, on sufferance of the angel, and choose not to know that after a short, blissful time, they too will be driven out.

And so it was with Allen Liles, one spring a long time ago when the world was more innocent than it will be again and she was younger than her years.

Spring came early that year, before winter had officially ended. In the streets of that Ozark town the wind blew catkins along the sidewalk, and maple wings and the dark seed clusters of elm trees half as old as the town. People walked out in the dusk, sniffing the weather, paused to chat under streetlamps, or strolled home slowly from some casual errand, stopping to buy ice cream in paper cartons, reluctantly going inside. Doors were left unlocked.

Their lessons done, children played hide-and-seek in the dark angles of house and yard until they were called in to bed. On Center Street the two motion-picture houses were dark by eleven. By eleven thirty the local buses had returned to the barn and the lights were out in store windows. Only the bus-station cafe, where the lone attendant was dozing at the counter, awaiting the arrival of the last run south from Kansas City, was open. Except for a few passing cars, the streets were deserted. Stillness settled over the town, over the bus barn and the railroad tracks, the schoolyards and the eighteen churches. The great houses rose tall and secret along dark streets. And except for certain nights when the moon was high, the expansive, hospitable park lay silent.

If facts are required, the great houses would be scattered and fewer, not all together on one grand avenue. The park on the west would not be so spacious, the town not arranged in quite this way. But it is remembered this way. A street and a house from another town may have moved in, a different park slid southward to become this park. Memory fits everything into place. And memory is truth enough.

The fact of the matter is southwest Missouri, on the edge of the Ozarks. The fact is 1941. And there is a war in Europe. It hangs like haze in the distance, like the threat of violent storm or heat wave. But it may go around, as they say in those parts; it could miss us. It is far away.

It was an orderly town, bred of the mines, nurtured by agriculture and some manufacture, a blend of Southern gentility and Western enterprise, firmly set in the conservatism of Middle America. Once rich and rowdy, it had fallen into meager times and respectability. It had survived the one, if not the other, and as the worst years of the Depression waned, the town of some forty thousand souls looked forward to new prosperity. Its banks were sturdy, its civic clubs active, and its churches filled on Sundays. Nine tenths of the population listened to the indisputable word of the Lord and asked His blessing on their endeavors.

He had not failed them. While Spaniards destroyed one another, while Britain rearmed and negotiated, Roosevelt, in Fireside Chats, condemned war, and in that hilly corner of Missouri the business of recovery went on, peacefully, if slowly. By the spring of 1941 there was talk of a new chemical plant. Members of the country club had refurbished their clubhouse. In Chisdale Park, which adjoined the country-club grounds, the lake was dredged and the tennis courts resurfaced. The junior college, only three years old, had enrolled almost three hundred students.

Miss Liles taught there. Miss Allen Liles, Master of Arts, who had arrived fresh from the university, with her brand-new diploma, *cum laude*, and letters of recommendation, her innocence of the outside world still more or less intact, and her virtue only a little less so (slightly flawed one summer night by an educational incident that took place between a fraternity house and a hedge). She was a lively, friendly sort—small, eager, and grateful as all get-out that they had given her a job.

She had not won it without first having to endure the inquest of office, an interview with Mrs. DeWitt Medgar, the female member of the school board. Seated at a parlor table, the application, résumé, and letters of recommendation before her, the stern-looking lady had studied both letters and candidate with a skeptical eye.

"I see by this that you are twenty-five." A severe glance across the table. "You look younger."

There was nothing much to say to that.

The lady eyed her a moment longer. "And you have two years of teaching experience? In a high school?"

"Two years, yes."

"Merely a scratch on the surface. Most of our people come to us with ten or fifteen. This is a college, you know, not a secondary school. You would find it quite different."

"I'm sure."

Another glance at the application. "How were you allowed to teach two years without a degree in education?"

"I was given a special permit."

"By whom?"

"The state board of education. I had a bachelor's degree—"

"—in arts and science, major in English." Mrs. Medgar read from the résumé and looked up, waiting.

"They had hired a new teacher for the high school, but she resigned at the last minute, and they needed another one in a hurry. I had been a substitute teacher there one winter when I couldn't go back to school—"

"Why was that?"

"My mother couldn't afford to send me."

Mrs. Medgar nodded.

"So the superintendent got me a permit and they hired me."

"I see. Well, I hope you aren't expecting a special permit for this position."

"No ma'am."

"Then how would you expect to teach here without a degree or some special—"

"I believe they consider my two years of actual experience the equivalent. That and my master's in English."

"Which you have not yet received."

"I will at the end of the summer, when I hand in my thesis."

"I see." Mrs. Medgar flipped through the letters and returned to the application. "You state here that in your last position—" She was interrupted by a sound from somewhere within the house, a windy sigh or a moan, so faint that Allen heard it only in retrospect as the lady rose. "Excuse me," she said and left the room hurriedly, closing the door behind her.

Allen leaned back, as she had not dared do in Mrs. Medgar's presence, and had a look around the room. It was smaller than it had appeared at first. A writing desk stood against the opposite wall—across one corner, a black settee with a horsehair seat, its uncompromising back carved to resemble a lyre.

The parlor table stood in the middle of the room on a patterned carpet, above it a ceiling fixture with three bare bulbs. Lace curtains hung at the two windows; on the wall, one picture (still life with roses). Not a book, not a knickknack, not a cushion; except for the painted roses, not a hint of softness. It was not a room sat in often. But there was one thing, overlooked on first inspection, that didn't quite fit with the rest—a framed photograph of a young woman, a man, and a child of perhaps three or four—whether a boy or a girl it was hard to tell by the clothes and the cut of the hair. All three were smiling. The photograph stood on the desk, but even from across the room she could make out the lace edging on the woman's dress, her piled, heavy hair, and the man's large, dark, intelligent eyes. The rest of the man's face was less appealing; a heavy mustache camouflaged what might be a weak mouth. She was still studying the photograph when Mrs. Medgar returned.

"I'm very sorry," the woman said tersely. Without looking at Allen, she bent over the papers on the table.

Her hair was gray, thick and coarse, with a slight wave and pinned at the back into a heavy coiled knot. Allen cast another glance at the photograph.

"Now then . . ." Mrs. Medgar looked up.

What had happened to harden that other face into this one?

"Your application says that in your last position you taught a class in modern dance. Just what is meant by that?"

Allen hesitated. A definition acceptable to Mrs. Medgar wouldn't come off the top of her head. "Well, as an undergraduate," she began, "I had taken interpretive dance. That's one of the regular courses in physical education—"

"Yes, yes, I know that. But modern?"

"You might call it a form of interpretive," Allen said, groping. "It's somewhat different. More of an art form. The great modern dancers, like Martha Graham—" She saw that this was not the right approach. "It's wonderful exercise!" she assured her. "So I asked if I might start a class—in addition to my regular classes, that is. It was quite a good class and we—"

"Have you considered starting such a class here?"

The idea had not occurred to Allen and she felt she had better say so.

"Well, I certainly hope not," said Mrs. Medgar. "This is a serious college. Our emphasis is on academic subjects and our standards are high."

And so on and on for another ten minutes. And just after she'd been dismissed, and was rising to leave, there was one thing more. "Your name is Ellen, I believe? Here it's spelled with an A. A typographical error, I assume."

"It's not a typo. My name is Allen, as it's spelled there. With an A."

Mrs. Medgar looked up with a hint of disapproval.

"I was named for my father. He's dead," she added, as if that explained everything. "My full name's really Barbara Allen. After the song, you know? My father used to sing it to me. But nobody ever called me anything but Allen."

Mrs. Medgar studied the résumé for another moment, tapped the papers neatly together, and looked up. "Well then, Miss Allen Liles, I must thank you for your time and assure you that your application will be taken under consideration . . ." etc., etc.

Allen left in despair. She had had such hopes, and so had her mother. Positions such as this didn't open up every day, not to her, at any rate. She might as well face it: in spite of her Phi Beta Kappa key and all the warm recommendations, her teaching credentials were flimsy. (If her mother's reputation hadn't burnished her, and if her mother hadn't made a special trip to see them, the state board of education wouldn't have bent the rules to allow her to teach in the first place.)

As it turned out, however, she had not failed. She was given a contract, whether over Mrs. Medgar's dead body or not.

Two

She had not intended to become a teacher. She became one by force of breeding, through a long line of women—aunts and great-aunts, her own mother— who entered classrooms for lack of alternative, except to marry; who married later and, perhaps, returned in their widowhood to teach again. Some of necessity, some also out of love; there were those, like her mother, called to it as to fate.

But Allen felt herself to be the variant, the break in the line. Though subject to the same necessity, the same narrow choices, she had other ideas, like many others of her time. She wanted to live in New York City and write books. Not a very practical longing. She was country bred, awed and bewildered by even Kansas City. She wrote poetry, and one of her stories, sent by an English professor to a national contest, had won an honorable mention. But you didn't live on poetry unless you were Edna St. Vincent Millay, and honorable mentions didn't pay the rent. She had student loans to repay and a loan from her brother. She could not think of any possible way to earn money and live in Greenwich Village, which at this point was much, much farther away from southern Missouri than it measured on the map. She would get there someday, she promised herself. She wanted to be where books were published, among other writers and actors and painters and musicians, all of them trying as hard as she and some who had already got near where they were going. Three years, five at the most, and she would take her place among them. Meanwhile, she must earn the fare in the only way she knew. She must teach.

Moreover, her mother insisted on it. Mother often insisted, and Mother was usually right. Or at least she thought she was. "You will be a very good teacher," she assured Allen, "and I just know you'll love it as much as I do." Mother had taught her whole life, except for those ten years after her brother and then Allen were born.

"And you enjoyed it too, didn't you, honey, those two years you taught in high school?"

"Yeah, I guess I did. More or less." Allen sat in her mother's kitchen with the Daisy churn between her knees. She had come home for the few weeks between the summer session and her new job at the junior college. She was now in possession of an official master's degree.

"I know you always talked about doing something else, writing or acting and all that." Mother laughed. "Oh, you had your head in the clouds, all right. Just like your father. Always fancied what was far away, never saw much glory in what was before his nose. But I always knew you would see that teaching was for you, same as it was for me. You come by it naturally. And you're a good teacher. I could tell, that time you substituted up here in the high school. That was a bad winter, when we couldn't send you back to school. I was dead set on it, but there just wasn't enough money."

"Don't feel bad about it, Mother. Those were hard years."

"Still are, in some ways. But not as bad as it was in 'thirty-six and 'thirty-seven. Anyway, I got you through school, and now you have a wonderful new job in a college. What more could a girl hope for! We've done well, haven't we?"

Mother paused with the measuring cup in her hand and beamed with such pride that Allen looked away, feeling guilty. "Yeah, I guess we have."

"I was sorry not to go with you when you went to your interview last spring, not to drive you down there in the car."

"I didn't mind the bus."

"I hated to think about you down there all by yourself, having to be assessed by all those people."

"But Mother, you couldn't have gone with me to the interviews anyway."

"Why not?" She paused, as she often did when she was reminded that her daughter was now a grown woman. "No, I guess that wouldn't have done, would it? Anyway, you did just fine without me. But I would have taken you down there, if it hadn't been so near time for the baby to come." The baby was her new grandson, second child of Allen's brother Dalton and his wife, who lived on the family farm. "I wanted to be here to help Gwennie. And see to it that they didn't give him some outlandish name." Mother laughed again, her big cheery laugh. "'Course, they did it anyway."

"What's so outlandish about Terence? I think it's a lovely name."

"Oh, it's all right, I guess. But there's never been a Terence in our family, nor any other around here that I know of. Someone your dad knew up in Liberty. Don't you think it sounds a little uppity?" she sighed. "Well, at least I got his grandfather's name in there. Terence Edwin sounds nice; I've always liked the name Edwin."

"Howdy, folks." Allen's brother walked in through the back door. "Here's your mail."

"Oh, thank you."

"Long as I was at the post office, thought I might as well pick it up." He hung his big farm hat on a chair knob and scrubbed a hand through Allen's hair. "How you doin', Curly, workin' hard?"

"Can't you see me sweat?"

Mother was picking through the envelopes. "Oh, here's a postcard from Violet. From Greeley—no, it's from Estes Park. Doesn't it look pretty! 'Dear Sis and family, Up here for the day with Mamie and Ted.' Mamie's her friend she used to teach with. She married some fellow from Denver. Guess they drove her up there. 'Summer school's fine,' she says. 'So am I. Hope all of you are too. Love, Violet.' Well, I'm glad to hear from her again."

Mother handed it over and laid the rest of the mail on the table. "How's my little Edwin, that sweet, cute thing?"

"Terence gained a pound since you were out the other day. If he keeps on like this, he'll be lifting feed sacks by the time he's two." Dalton took a jar of cold water out of the refrigerator. "Boy, it's hot out there."

"And always hotter downtown," Mother said. Downtown was a single long block with a scatter of stores on either side, a filling station at one end, the post office at the other, and Chalfont's

Feed Store around the corner. "There's some of that cherry pie up there in the cupboard."

"Thanks. I could use a piece."

"Put some of that heavy cream on it. In the blue crock in the icebox, second shelf. You want a piece, Allen?"

"Not right now."

"What's the matter," Dalton said, "afraid it'll ruin your girlish figure?"

"Never has yet. No, I'm going to have a glass of fresh buttermilk."

"That sounds good too."

"Well, you can have some," Mother said. "Allen, get one of those big ice-tea glasses off the top shelf. It's an awful good pie. I could always make good pies. These are some of those cherries Gwennie picked this summer. Sure was nice of her to bring us so many. What's she doing today?"

"Picking pole beans, when I left."

"Out there in all this heat? That Gwennie!"

"She feels fine. Nanette's out there helping her, or thinks she is." Nanette was their first child.

"She's a baby doll, she is. Tell 'em we're coming out and see 'em this afternoon."

"Not me," Allen said. "There's some reading I have to do."

Dalton said, "Shakespeare again, I reckon?"

"Uh-uh. A book about words."

"What is it, the dictionary?"

"It's a book about language—word derivations and usage and why we favor certain words over others."

"Sounds like work to me."

"Oh, she enjoys it," Mother said. "Don't you, honey? Just like me, you love to think about language. Every teacher does. Maybe you can read me some of it after supper. I wouldn't mind learning more about it, myself."

"Why don't you-all stay for supper with us?" Dalton said. "I might even talk Gwen into making ice cream."

"That would be nice. And I'm putting a cake in the oven right now. I'll bring it along. And we'll pick up the ice. If you take it now it'll melt before we can use it."

"Okay, if it isn't too much trouble. Thanks for the grub." He picked up his hat and grinned at Allen. "You're in good practice with that churn—we'll let you turn the freezer."

"What a thrill."

"Well, I better be gettin' on back. I'll tell Gwen you're coming."

"We'll be there," Mother said. "And tell her to use that recipe of mine for the ice cream. It always turns out best. Remind her."

Dalton said he would and winked at Allen as he went out.

As soon as lunch was over and the dishes done, Allen went into her room and read a couple of chapters of her book while Mother had a nap. Later they packed up the cake and drove down to Chalfont's Feed Store, where they bought the ice. With a fifty-pound chunk wrapped in a gunnysack in the trunk, they set out for the farm, four miles away. The rest of the afternoon they snapped beans, watched the baby sleep, and hung diapers on the line. Toward sundown Allen and Nanette wandered off to the creek. Allen held the child on her lap and told her a story about a princess who lived with her kind father on an island, with good fairies all around. The little girl sat very still. She might, Allen thought, hear the music creep past them on the waters.

The child said, "There's a bug on my nose."

The story changed then to a tale of a tadpole who lived under a rock.

"What's his name?"

"Roddy. Now Roddy was a rather tiresome tadpole who didn't know how to laugh. Till one day—"

"I know how to laugh."

So they had a giggle contest till it was time to go back.

Then there was supper, with ice cream and cake, and Mother and Allen drove back home through the late dusk.

They sat in the backyard, as they often did, talking into the darkness, sometimes comfortably quiet, each occupied with her own thoughts. This night, after they had sat for a while, Mother said, "I do love to be out like this on a summer night. And it's so much nicer when you're here with me. I'm always sorry when you have to leave. I do miss your company. But I know you have to. And your accomplishments give me such pleasure."

"They don't amount to much yet."

"But they will, I haven't the slightest doubt. You are my great joy, little Allen."

"Thank you, Mother."

How much longer must she go on calling her "little Allen"?

She looked up at the stars. They were very bright tonight, millions of them and billions more beyond the reach of the eye. "Remember when we were little," she said, "how we used to lie out in the yard on quiet summer nights and you would teach us the constellations?"

"Do you remember that?" her mother said, pleased. "I didn't know much more than the Big Dipper and the Seven Sisters—that's not even the proper name but that's what I called it."

"We thought it was fine. And Halley's Comet, you used to tell us about the time you saw it."

"Yes, and you always felt sorry for the comet because it had to keep going always and never could stop to rest."

"I remember." She still had to remind herself that a comet was an insensible thing with no need of compassion. But what a journey it had to take to get wherever it was going and back! She tried to bend her mind around the magnitude of the circuit, the boundless extent of the universe. And where beyond that was heaven? No one had ever been able to say. Yet there was always a heaven of one sort or another, some celestial muster in the sky, where the true believer, earthly senses intact, would exist forever. And ever and ever. Eternity, time going on and on. The very thought of it scared her out of her skin.

She brought her mind down to the congenial finitude of the earth and the sound of the crickets sawing away in the grass. The night was filled with their anxious summoning.

It seemed urgent, as if they sensed the coming on of the cold and must hurry. From her mother's garden the scent of tomato vines, released by the evening damp, drifted across the yard. To-morrow they would can tomatoes again. Barring frost, the vines would go on bearing into October. And Gwen was coming in with tomorrow's crop of beans. "Will we have to can those too?"

"Can what?"

"The pole beans."

"Yes, Gwennie's coming in tomorrow, isn't she? Yes. I suppose we will. There'll be a good many. She says the vines are outdoing themselves this year."

"Ho-hum."

Mother laughed. "You never cared much for canning, did you? It won't take long, and you're good help."

Because she was expected to be. They were disciplined children, she and Dalton, both of them required to help with the chores. Well, they had to do—by the time Dalton was twelve, Dad was gone and he was the man of the house. Some of the chores Allen quite enjoyed: gathering eggs in the morning, gathering kindling for the big cook stove, helping in the garden. As long as she was outdoors she was happy.

Choring or playing, she was outdoors a good part of her childhood and often allowed to run loose. When she was old enough not to drown herself, she spent hours at the creek, paddling about, wading, catching crawdads in the shallows. She climbed trees, stole watermelons with the kids from the next farm out of their own father's patch, and chased turkeys around the barn lot, making them scatter and squawk. In winter she and Dalton and the neighbor kids coasted down snowy pasture slopes on the wash-boiler lid.

Their mother often read to them in the evenings, and both of them learned early to read for themselves. Allen took to it better than Dalton. There were times when she'd rather read than chase turkeys. She read in bed, in the hayloft, in the crotch of an apple tree, upstairs, downstairs, pretending not to hear when called.

But Mother never fussed too much about it; she was a reader too.

"Have you finished the book yet?" Allen said. Mother was reading *The Grapes of Wrath*.

"Two chapters to go. I had to put it down last night. I just couldn't read any longer, it was so terrible. Those poor souls."

"That man can write, can't he?"

"He makes it so real. And it was real, that's the worst part. All those families forced out of their homes and no place to go. And the dust! Remember the dust? You couldn't breathe for it. And it was worse in Oklahoma. We had some bad times here, but nothing that bad. I thank the good Lord we didn't lose the farm. Your father bought that farm with his hard-earned money and I was determined to keep it." She heaved a sigh, as if some great task was over and done with. "We were lucky," she said.

"Yes." But Allen knew well enough that it wasn't all luck, but her mother's resolve and hard work.

"And we're still lucky. I'm so thankful I can keep on teaching. And Dalton and Gwennie are doing right well. And now you're going to be a college professor!"

"I'm a long way from that."

"You'll get there."

The hell I will, Allen said to herself, rebelling. But then, maybe I will. "Did you always want to be a teacher?" she said. "Didn't you ever want to fly an airplane or dig up mummies in Egypt or travel to Italy or anything like that?"

Mother laughed. "Mercy no! Girls didn't do those things in my day."

"Some of them did."

"Nobody I ever knew. No, I just wanted to teach school. That's all I ever cared about. Until I met your father."

"You find him or did he find you?"

"Well." Mother chuckled. "I saw him before he saw me. Saw him in the post office one day and made up my mind right there that he was the one I was going to marry."

"Simple as that."

"It was, in my case. And we were happy together. We had a good marriage."

A firm, insistent pronouncement. But it was a good marriage, Allen thought. As far as she knew, though she knew little enough firsthand. All she remembered of her father was that he sang to her and made her laugh and sometimes danced her around the kitchen on his shoulders. They said she looked like him. Sometimes, when she was younger, she'd tried to find him in the mirror, to summon him back.

"I never told you, but he left me once."

Allen turned her head sharply. "Who did?"

"Your father. For a little while."

"Why?"

"Oh, we had had some problems. Nothing that couldn't have been worked out. That's what I thought anyway. But Dalton and I came home from church one morning, and he was gone."

Allen murmured in sympathy, and in surprise at this new view of her father. "Did he leave you a message?"

"There was a letter. Said he was sorry. But he guessed he couldn't worry too much about me. Said I could run the farm as well as he could. And some other things."

Allen stared into the darkness. Why was her mother telling her this, after all this time? Her father had left her. Why? "But he came back?" she said.

"Um-hum," Mother said. "I went and got him."

"Oh."

She had a good idea where she'd find him. Down in Cape Girardeau with his brother Woodrow. "So I went down there—I waited two or three days, then I got on a train and went down. We had a long talk. And then—well, he came home."

Allen said, with a little shake of the head, "You must have said all the right things."

"I don't remember now what I said. But I remember . . . I cried. I didn't mean to!" she said defiantly. "I'd made up my mind I wasn't going to cry and carry on like some silly little goose. But when he put me on the train and he didn't get on with me, I was crying. I couldn't help it! And then . . . I guess it was two days later, he came riding in home one morning. He'd come in on the morning train and caught a ride from town with one of the neighbors, who was in there with his wagon."

Allen listened in silence, embarrassed almost by this confessional, as if she had stumbled in on something private that she wasn't meant to hear.

"I guess he'd never known me to cry before. I don't let myself do it very often. But that time . . ." She paused and said, like a child admitting guilt, "I loved him and I wanted him back."

Allen hadn't often heard her mother use that tone, maybe never. Her mother seldom talked about her feelings, much less about feeling vulnerable. And what had she done that made Father leave? Allen could imagine—her always being right, always knowing what's best. Her father was a dreamer, that's what Mother always said about him. Just like her, she said. Mother didn't set much store by dreaming, but she loved him, and he had come back, and soon enough Allen had come along.

Mother said, with a little chuckle, "And you can bet, after that he went to church with me every Sunday!"

And then he died in a cyclone. Struck in the head by the barn door hurling through the air like a leaf as the barn went down. Allen remembered that, though she was only three. Remembered the roar and the quiet and the long scream as her mother ran through the yard. And after that, how still the house was, how she went about on tiptoes so as not to disturb, with a feeling she would recognize years later as a kind of exaltation. Her father's death was something precious handed to her, that made her older and wiser, different from anyone else. It was something to be borne like a sacred vessel, with gravity and great care.

In the comfortable darkness, Mother said, "There was always something about him that I couldn't quite get at. He always seemed a little bit lonely. Oh, he was jolly, always laughing, making jokes. But a part of him was sort of far away . . . where I couldn't reach." She drew a long breath and let it out. "Well, I think I'll go in." She rose, emitting the faint, clean, talcumy scent of a plump woman careful of her bodily habits. "I want to read another chapter. You coming?"

"In a minute."

"Don't stay too long. Good night, honey. Mother loves you."

"Love you too. G'night."

The screen door closed. Light from the kitchen fell into the yard. Mother would be pouring herself a glass of water. Then that light went out and another came on in Mother's bedroom. Allen stretched her arms, stretched her bare legs, and kicked off her slippers to feel the cool grass under her feet.

She listened to the myriad muted sounds of the night and wondered about the nature of love. Wondered about the difference between loving and being loved, and which was more desirable in the long run. But then she'd known neither. And Mother? Loving, it seemed, for her.

She stood up and yawned and stretched. Tomorrow was another day. And after that, only nine more days before she must leave. She was ready.

Three

So here was Miss Liles, instructor in a junior college, proud of her position, hopeful, determined, a little scared. Nevertheless, bored stiff at faculty meetings, where she sat like a good child, younger by ten years than most of her colleagues, by twenty or thirty than others.

The only exception was Miss Maxine Boatwright, who was about the same age. Miss Boatwright, along with Mr. Delanier, was the music department; the two of them divided their time between college and high school. Mr. Delanier handled the orchestra, Maxine the choral group. She was tall and pretty and nice as pie, with a smile for everybody and a laugh that ran up the scale, skipped a couple of notes and wound up on something like B flat. They might have become good friends, Allen thought, except that Maxine was always so busy. She had grown up in town and lived at home and had a busy social life. She taught piano lessons on Saturday mornings and poured tea at frequent receptions at the Episcopal church. On Sundays she sat demurely in the family pew with her parents and a younger brother. The family was remarkably handsome, self-assured, and a little haughty, as became the aristocracy.

Maxine was also kept busy by her gentleman friend. His name was Max. ("Max and Maxine!" they said in the faculty ladies' lounge. "Isn't that the cutest thing!?") He was tall and gorgeous, an officer in a bank, and Episcopalian, like Maxine. From all reports it was Serious. ("Made for each other," the Ladies said in the lounge. "They call each other Max!")

In spite of her schedule Maxine did try. "Listen," she would say almost every week, "we've got to get together and have lunch!" There followed the usual qualifications. "I've got to go to Kansas City this Saturday, right after my lessons. But maybe next." Or as soon as tests were over, or right after the music teachers' convention.

They did manage it once, one Saturday in October. They went to the Bonne Terre Hotel. But they hardly had a chance to get acquainted. People kept stopping by the table to say hello to Maxine, who was kept busy introducing Allen to all and sundry. After a polite "Happy to know you," Allen was roundly ignored. Then, right after the fruit cup, Max joined them. They behaved as if it hadn't been arranged, but she had a notion it had been. She had gone home feeling sorry for herself. They were pretty together, Max and Maxine. Being in love looked very attractive. She thought about crying but lost interest and went for a walk instead.

With anything beyond the school she had very little contact. There was not much time for activities out in the town, and few opportunities. The country-club set led a life of its own, out of the reach of schoolteachers, who were considered a lower, though necessary, order. (This did not apply to Maxine, whose credentials were unassailable; her family had always belonged.) She went to church, of course; one was expected to. Raised Methodist, she had drifted to the Episcopalian, drawn by the Gothic architecture of the churches and the pageantry of the service. But although the priest was a good deal more literate than the usual run of preachers back home, she found herself gathering wool during the sermons and more and more wondered why she bothered attending. She no longer adhered to the true faith, having devised a theology for herself, somewhat at variance from the one here prescribed. (If you believe in eternal life, Alice went down a rabbit hole.) She tended to pantheism, a little lower than Tennyson's, perhaps, but comfortable to her.

She joined the American Association of University Women and attended several meetings, discussions of New Deal economy or isolationism on campuses. The others seemed to know all about it, the older members and all those compact, doll-chinned young marrieds with husbands in business and children in kindergarten. They were hellishly efficient. She sat, for the most part, tongue-tied among them, with the sense now and then of dizzying alienation. What had all this to do with Tennyson and Eliot and Blake, and the death of kings and the rite of spring and Dancing in the Chequer'd shade? Later she would begin to see a connection between the two. But for the moment she neither saw nor too much cared. And she crept away quietly, guilty but relieved.

She was too recently emerged from the dim light of libraries, where Agincourt was louder than Dunkirk and fallen Lucifer more real than Haile Selassie. In colleges one lived considerably in the past—that being the means of education—to study as much as possible of what went before. Though she had picked up a thing or two from the past, she failed in the next step—to relate it to the present. Except as it concerned her immediately, she gave little thought to the issues of the moment. They seemed to come at her out of left field, and had little relevance to her daily life for all she could see.

Moreover, she was weary of serious pursuits, having worked steadily and yearlong, winter and summer, and having finished her thesis only weeks before her job began. And it seemed there would be no respite now. She had to work hard—she was teaching four classes—and she was willing. Nonetheless, secretly, she wanted to dance and flirt and drink beer, as she had done so little in her student days. In spite of her tomboisterous childhood, she had been a shy, studious adolescent, awkward around boys, and had never quite outgrown it. But she'd had a few tastes of pure frivolity and looked with longing at the country club, where they had an orchestra and danced and played golf and gave dinner parties.

The closest she came to that crowd was a ballet class to which they sent their daughters. She was small, and among the thirteen- and fourteen-year-olds did not stand out too glaringly. And even that class, taught by a white-haired mistress of impeccable character, she'd had to give up. It was made known to her by discreet suggestion that such a pursuit was inappropriate for a teacher; ballet was for children. After twelve weeks in the intermediate class, she regretfully bowed out. Early on, she had given up the idea of joining the Little Theatre. A remark by a colleague let her know that the Little Theatre was considered a "fast crowd" and was frowned upon.

For diversion she turned to the poets. And she scribbled lines of her own. Haltingly, feeling her way along, she began to set her lines down in a notebook. Sometimes they became paragraphs, whole passages, which might be, she thought, the germ of a novel. She worked away at it, sometimes for nights in a row, and at intervals, the words came in a rush—images, ideas, flowing from the tip of her pencil, always to her astonishment.

Then she would walk out in the dark, announcing soundlessly to each house, *Tonight I have written this line—this page—I have written this!* Afterward, sobered, she'd go upstairs, wash her dishes, eat an apple, press a dress, brush her teeth, turn out the light, stand at the window awhile. Go to bed.

Four

She lived in a great brick house on the western side of the town, well away from the stockyards and the railroad yards and the factories producing shoes, sewer pipe, and smokeless powder. Those stood to the east and north. Farther to the north was the section known as Jackroad, which took its name from the old road that used to lead to the mines. There, ore was roasted, reduced, and turned into zinc. Zinc and lead, drawn out of sphalerite and galena, out of the chert and limestone that underlay the region. For half a century, mine tailings, heaped gangue, had risen into massive cones.

But all this was on the far north end of Center Street, which ran south from there into the business district and beyond into open country, headed for Arkansas. The older residential section lay to the west. Here, before the turn of the century, the very rich had built their mansions. Over time, lots had been divided and lesser homes sprouted among them, but a few of the mansions stood as they always had, commanding whole blocks. They were massive structures of brick and native stone, set on deep lawns. Retaining walls of gray limestone supported black iron fences that ran the length of the front yards. Mermaids thirsted in fountains long gone dry.

Far back on the lawns stood the carriage houses crowned by cupolas, in turn sporting weathervanes that had lost all sense of the weather, or martin houses that might or might not be tenanted come summer. Gabled, slate-roofed, mullion-windowed; housing a Buick, a Pierce-Arrow up on blocks; their attics full of bound journals; wicker rockers; half rolls of flocked wallpaper; croquet balls and rusted wickets; blue glass jars, half-gallon size; dead dolls, spiders, and the smell of camphorate. Below, the wide doors opened onto broad graveled alleys, grass-grown down the middle. By day, no refuse disgraced the premises. Trash bins, tightly covered, and such articles as a broken chair or cast-off picture frames appeared discreetly only at dusk on the eve of trash collection. These genteel corridors ran west to east for seven blocks, lined on either side by a tangle of vegetation: snowball bushes and honeysuckle, small mulberry trees, japonica, rose of Sharon, and thickets of forsythia gone wild. Bridal wreath, unpruned, drooped across the fences. In their season the scent of viburnam and old lilacs lay on the air.

One of the mansions was a museum now, seldom open. In others, the lingering remnants of old families hung on, their presence known by the raising or lowering of a window blind, or a light in an upper room. Some said an old crazy woman lived in one of the houses. A corner house, its original symmetry distorted now by odd rooms and porches added on, had become an apartment house. In this one Miss Liles rented an apartment, tacked onto the existing roof rather like a martin house. She preferred to think of it as a penthouse. To reach it, one turned in from the side street, proceeded a few steps into the alley, and climbed an outside stairway three flights. From the rooftop landing, one entered the apartment through the kitchen and thence into a sitting room with a couch for a bed. A bathroom adjoined the kitchen. A somewhat shabby little place, but it came cheap, and the kitchen had an electric refrigerator.

This was her first apartment. At school she had always lived in a dormitory or a certified rooming house for young women. Mother, who had driven down with Dalton to bring Allen and her belongings, had been dubious when she saw it. "It's too secluded," she said, "way up here away from anybody. You'd be a lot better off in a nice rooming house with a landlady."

"For Pete's sake, Mother, I don't need any fussy old landlady poking around. Anyway, we've looked at four places today with rooms for rent, and I couldn't stand any of them. Neither could you."

"Well, we can just look some more."

"I like it here. It's sunny and quiet and roomy. I can spread out all my stuff and work without interruptions."

"Well, yes," Mother said. But there were more arguments before she would give in. "Well, all right," she finally said grudgingly, "if you're determined. But you behave yourself, up here so private." She shook her head. "That long, rickety stairway is a mighty peculiar way to get into a place. How's your brother going to make it up all these steps with your things?"

"I'll make it." Dalton appeared on the landing, suitcases in hand.

To Allen the three flights of steps were one of the attractions. Like climbing to the top of a tree or up the ladder to the barn loft. Much better than being earthbound. From the landing at the top of the stairs you could look over roofs and treetops and see the Presbyterian steeple, two blocks over, pointing the way to heaven. The steeple chimes rang sweetly on the quarter hour. She sat there often during the fall, under yellow moons in foggy Prufrock nights, far away in her thoughts.

When we are young, particularly when young and lonely, we imagine a future and dwell in it, as later we dwell in a past we also have imagined. So, on those fall nights, she dreamed herself forward into Italy as she knew it from the English poets, and the Paris of Hemingway, and the New York City of Katherine Anne Porter. It was a rich improbable future, made up of other people's pasts. Such fantasies were her entertainment, the pageants of a thoroughgoing romantic, and she invented within them, projected and plotted course, until the steeple clock, striking the late hour, brought her back to reality and the grudging acknowledgment that, far as she was from Paris or New York, she had a job and she could damn well be contented. As Mother said, she was lucky.

And after a time, as she got into the work, she had to admit that she almost liked it. Though her colleagues were a colorless lot, they were pleasant. Faculty meetings were tiresome and, as far as she could see, useless. But college classes were no harder to teach than high school and a lot more fun. It was very gratifying to teach Shakespeare in some depth and be able to dwell at length on the English poets, Romantic and Victorian, with a little modern thrown in now and then if she took a notion. She even enjoyed grammar and composition classes. And she liked the students. They were bright kids, most of them, happy and alert and funny. All of them were polite. There were a few who were older, working men in their twenties, enrolled late in college. Like the others, they came regularly to class and sat, attentive, faces tilted respectfully. Fertile, orderly rows, and hers to hoe. Here and there was a blank face and inevitably a squirmer, and two or three who were bored within an inch of their lives. Still, they made a pretense of learning and that made it easier for her.

And there was something else: she recognized it slowly as a sense of power. She saw that this had infected all the teachers, some more than others. Older than their students, with more learning, and with vested authority, they assumed more superiority than perhaps they possessed. A treacherous condition. It could lead to complacency, as indeed it had in some of them. Still, the sense of power, dangerous though it might be, was a heady thing, and she had to admit that she found it extremely pleasant.

It gave her an assurance she had not felt before, a sense of herself, and the courage to exert that self (within the bounds of propriety) and depart a little from the norm. No one seemed to mind that she wore to school what she had worn as a student—sweaters and saddle oxfords, like the rest of the girls; nor that now and then between classes she ran up the street to the hamburger shop where the kids hung out and had a Coke. Dr. Ansel went there for Cokes and candy bars, so it had to be all right for her to go too.

Dr. Ansel, being a Ph.D., was chairman of the English department (which consisted of him, her, and an unobtrusive little man named Hudgin). His dissertation had been titled "The Teaching of English in the Missouri Public Schools: 1895–1925."

"I only took this job because of Mother," he explained to her one day. "I could have got in over at Springfield if I'd tried. But Mother doesn't want to live in a big city. She doesn't even like it here very much. But I can't teach and stay on the farm. We've got a place down south of Pierce City, you know? Quarter section? I go down there to see about it every few months, take Mother. She gets awful homesick."

"Why doesn't she stay down there?"

"I tried to get her to, but she won't. She thinks she has to be here to look after me." He said drolly, "She thinks I'm going to be the dean someday."

"Here?"

"After Dean Frawley goes."

"Do you want to be the dean?"

"Umm," he said with a nonchalant glance out the window, "I suppose I have to expect something like that. Frawley's not getting any younger. They'll have to find *somebody*. And as long as you're right here and qualified . . . After all, if you're a man you can't stand still in the academic profession."

"How about women?" she said.

"It's not so important for them. Women get married."

"So do men."

"Yes, but men can go on teaching."

"So can women."

"They can now, but school boards aren't too keen on it. Most women don't want to anyway. Women want to get married and have kids."

"Not all of them do."

"Don't you want to?"

"Not necessarily. Not for a long time anyway."

"How long do you plan to teach?"

"Three or four years, maybe five, till I'm out of debt."

"What are you going to do then?"

"I'm going to go to New York and I'm going to be a writer."

"You sound mighty sure of yourself."

"I'm not a bit sure. But that's what I want to do. I'll probably have to start as a typist at some magazine or publisher and work my way up. But I'm going to be a writer."

"Yeah, well, I'm going to do some writing, myself. Matter of fact, I'm working on a paper right now—'Solecism and Correct Usage: Utilization of Regional Speech as an Aid in the Teaching of Grammar.' Sort of an unusual approach, I think. Ought to be just the ticket for one of the scholastic journals."

Dr. Ansel was an indefatigable researcher. In his spare time he liked to dig through the files of the local historical society and the county courthouse. Not all his biographical research involved dead history. He was good, as well, at the living. He seemed to know all about every teacher on the staff. Mr. Pickering, for instance, had tried to get into the army air corps and failed. Miss Gladys Peabody had once been married to a gentleman who turned out to have two or three other wives. And so on. You couldn't believe half what he said. On the other hand, he always seemed to have documentation. And he wasn't mean about it; he was just interested.

Dr. Ansel had a small blotch, roughly the shape of Iowa, over his left eyebrow, which tended to turn red whenever he got into an argument. It was an exercise to keep her eyes off it.

He could be tiresome and he was a little smug, being the only one among them with a Ph.D. But he wasn't entirely awful, and they had a few interests in common. Which was more than she could say for Mr. Pickering, who taught economics and looked indigestive, or Mr. Lord, the chemistry teacher, who had four or five kids and was always trying to flirt with her. Dr. Ansel was tolerable. He wasn't handsome, but not altogether ugly either. He was middlin'. Medium-tall, almost good-looking, fairly bright. Middlin'. That's the best she could give him. Well, he wasn't fat. And he had good posture.

Sometimes after school they had long discussions about Orson Welles or the teaching of Shakespeare or what the novel was coming to. It amused him that she had read *Ulysses* and looked into *Finnegans Wake* (loaned by one of her professors), while Ansel had scarcely heard of them. It riled him so. He always came back at her with the American Frontier or the novels of Harold Bell Wright. According to Ansel, *The Shepherd of the Hills* embodied the key ideas of the entire Western movement.

"It's okay," she said, "for the kind of thing it is. Romance and sanctimony." She added, just for the hell of it, "When he starts preaching and gets sentimental, that's when I run for Faulkner!"

That always got him up on his hind legs. He hated Faulkner. And they had a fine invigorating argument. At least you could argue with Dr. Ansel and talk about something besides which restaurant served the best lunch for the money.

Now and then they branched out onto Rooseveltian policy (Ansel was against it) or Hitler and how things were going in Europe. But Allen preferred their literary conversations.

One day in October, classes were cancelled, long tables set up in the gym, and the faculty, charged by the Selective Service Board, registered students, those over twenty-one, for the draft. Allen had quite enjoyed it. It was like a holiday, overlaid with a not-unpleasant sense of the gravity of it all, which none of them was quite convinced of.

"Roosevelt has said that no American boy will be sent overseas to fight."

"And I think he'll stick with it, unless he wants to lose votes."

Over a sandwich at noon, she and Ansel had had a solemn discussion of the implications. He leaned toward the isolationists.

"Look at it this way: we made the Declaration of Independence. We are absolved of any allegiance to the British Empire."

"Well, I don't know," she said and tried to defend the protection of British shipping.

But this was self-conscious talk and neither of them was on sure ground. In general, the Federal Theater and *Henry V* were as close as they came to politics and war.

On occasion they argued the merits of the Federal Writers Project and the effect of the Depression on the arts. At the time of the crash, she had not yet turned fifteen. Dr. Ansel, though he didn't come right out and say so, must have been all of twenty-five. He remembered the early Depression better than she did. But both of them bore the stamp of those years—a seriousness of purpose, the drive to achieve, born of necessity. They lived scared, knowing by observation the perils of joblessness. With much in common, the two of them got along well enough.

It was nearing Christmas when Ansel came to her room one afternoon with his feathers all ruffled.

"So!" he said, "Miss Liles is going to conduct a seminar next semester!"

"Not a seminar," she said, "just a discussion group, reading and discussing. But I suppose," she added (the term had a fine ring to it), "you could call it a seminar."

"What's it on?"

"The modern American novel. We're going to read three or four that I consider important and discuss them."

"Well, if you ask me it sounds like more work. I'm glad Frawley didn't ask me to do it."

"He didn't ask me. I asked him."

Ansel looked blank. "How come?"

"I'd been thinking about it for quite a while."

"You mean it was your idea, this seminar, discussion group, whatever you call it? You never said anything about it."

"I didn't think I should till I talked to Mr. Frawley."

"Yeah, well, it sounds like a lot of extra work."

"I think it'll be fun. And it's only for six weeks. Tuesday and Thursday, four to five."

"Aren't many of these kids going to show up after four o'clock?"

"I don't expect many. Five or six at the most. But I've got a few kids in my classes who are really bright, who ought to be reading Hemingway and Fitzgerald—"

"And Faulkner," he said with a sniff. "I suppose you think they should read him."

"Sure I do."

"Wait'll Dean Frawley finds out about that!"

"He's already found out. I showed him my list and he approved it."

"Bet he doesn't know what he's getting into. Bet he's never read Faulkner."

"You want to bet? We had a good talk about him. He drew the line at *Light in August*, but I wasn't going to use that one anyway."

"Hm. Well . . ." Dr. Ansel's blotch was quite red. He stuck his hands in his pockets and made a couple of paces past her desk. "Who's going to pay for the books? How many of these kids can afford—"

"The school's buying them. We've already got them ordered."

"Well! I'm surprised he's lettin' go of the money. He's so tight with it."

"He thinks it's a good idea. It's an experiment. If it works, he says maybe next year we can do one on Greek drama. I'm going to bone up on Sophocles and Aristophanes this summer."

"Well, good luck."

"Thank you."

She didn't tell him it was her mother's idea. It had come up at Thanksgiving, when she was home for the holiday. "You know, I've been thinking," Mother said, "there must be some way you could distinguish yourself in this job. Oh, I know you're doing fine, I don't doubt that for a minute. But I don't want them to think of you as just another competent teacher. I want you to be noticed. Let them know you're somebody special. And I think I've got just the thing!"

"What do you want me to do?" Allen said with some apprehension.

"Why don't you start a discussion group!" Mother reared back from her pie-making with the rolling pin in her hand.

"You mean a community thing?"

"No, at school, as part of your job. A little discussion group after school in the afternoons."

"Discussing what?"

"Well—*something*. We can work on that. Something that would interest enough of the students, add to their education. Your dean—what's his name?"

"Mr. Frawley."

"He ought to be impressed by that, if he's as dedicated as you say he is."

"He is. He's a wonderful old man."

"Well, then, I'll bet if you went to him and talked it over, he'd help you set up a discussion session. It wouldn't be too much extra work, would it?"

"Well, it would be some, but I suppose I could handle it."

"Something you know a lot about. My goodness, that could be anything!"

"Now Mother, what do I know a lot about?"

"Don't be so modest, Barbara Allen. Where's your self-confidence? You read a lot of books, there's got to be something you know more about than your students do."

As a matter of fact, there was, and the more Allen thought about it, the more attractive it seemed. A discussion group wasn't such a bad idea, after all.

But maybe she *should* have told Dr. Ansel whose idea it was. It wasn't quite fair to take all the credit herself. Oh well. Her mother would never have suggested the subject she'd chosen.

With the exception of Dean Frawley, Dr. Ansel was the only man on the faculty whom she rather enjoyed. The dean was a scholarly old gentleman of great courtesy and an air of genuine kindliness. Now and then he dropped in on one of her classes and sat for a while, observing. This was his practice, as some of the other teachers explained. And all of them agreed that, rather than making them nervous, his presence was somehow reassuring.

During their friendly chat about her proposed seminar, he had told her that he was very pleased with her work. He felt it was his obligation to encourage young teachers, he told her. The conversation moved easily into their philosophies of education, and back and forth from teaching methods to favorite books, from primary sources as opposed to textbooks chosen by committee. A fine, satisfying talk. She went away well nourished and feeling quite scholarly.

The only other male of whom she took special notice was the men's gym teacher, coach of the basketball and football teams. He was blue-eyed and beautiful, without a perceptible brain in his head. But in his presence she went all over self-conscious and gawky, a state easily changed as soon as he left the room.

He reminded her of a boy from her undergraduate days who had sat next to her in Sociology II—a blond sonofagun with a lazy grin who copied her answers and called her "kid." She had longed for him till she feared she was giving off fumes like a Bunsen burner. He never so much as noticed, until one summer night when she ran into him on the way home from the library. He said "Want a Coke?" and after that, strolled her over to his fraternity house, now largely deserted during the summer session, and on through to the backyard, where they sat in the dark and he told her how she had affected him in sociology class. Even if she didn't believe a word he said, it was nice to hear him say it. Then he started fumbling around till she decided she wasn't so crazy about him after all. She figured that, since she had a few things to learn, this was as good a time as any to start. A halfhearted start, not quite consummated, but instructional all the same. And though that put an end to her crush, she thought of him now and then with a certain gratitude.

It seemed it was often the good-for-nothings who attracted her. The rotters had most of the charm. There was a long precedent for that, going back to Satan. Since Genesis, when he appeared as a serpent, very few (not Milton and not Goethe) who cast him in human form had managed to make him wholly repulsive. Wholly evil, of course—of repulsive deed—but magnetic in himself, seductive and clever, "more knowing than any man," according to Burton (who, being a clergyman, must have known quite a lot about Satan).

It was doubtful that the coach could "perceive the causes of all the meteors and the like," but he was a bit of a devil and he sure as hell was magnetic. Trouble was, he was not often present. Since, like Miss Boatwright and Mr. Delanier, he divided his time between college and high school, he skillfully avoided meetings. It was a rare occasion when he showed up for anything except gym classes twice a week.

He had danced with her once, at the Halloween party. She was a chaperone, along with Miss Peabody and Mr. Lord and Dean Frawley, and chaperones, providing they knew how, were allowed to dance with the students. She was having a jolly time with a freckled freshman when the coach cut in and put her in such a dither she went into instant aphasia.

"How's it goin'?" he said, not giving a damn.

"Fine." Well, that was one word.

He danced her around, looking over her head.

"I didn't know you were here," she said.

"Just got here. Got to show up once in a while and keep Frawley happy. You come to these bops very often?"

"Oh yes! I'm nearly always here."

"Zheesh!" he said in condolence.

"They're not so bad—I mean, it's only the kids, but—"

He was grinning down at her lazily out of one side of his mouth.

"Well, somebody has to," she said, "somebody has to chaperone. It's just one of the duties. And I really don't mind it too much. I'd rather be doing this than—" Oh, shut up. Whatever she said wouldn't change it. She came to these dances because nobody asked her to any others. She danced with the kids, and what's more, she enjoyed it.

"You like the fights?" Coach said idly.

"The fights?"

"Prizefights."

"I don't know, I've never seen one."

"You haven't?"

"Do they have them around here?"

"In this burg? Kansas City's the closest place."

"Do you go up there to see them?"

"Sometimes," he said, adding offhandedly, "May go up to-morrow."

Was he asking? She thought he was. She waited, dry of mouth.

But he danced her along in silence as if he'd forgotten that she was there at all. She might have been a coat slung over his arm.

"I'd love to see one sometime."

Now *she* was asking and she could have cut her throat. She turned with relief as one of the bright boys from her English class cut in.

"Digadoo," said the boy, straight-faced.

"Hello, George." She smiled, grateful for being rescued and ashamed at having to be.

"Hammertoes," he said with a jerk of his head toward the coach, who was going out the door. "He dances like the Scottish Rite Temple." And with a tidy maneuver he twirled her around and spun her the length of the gym like silk off a spool.

So there went the coach and any glimmer of hope. Only Dr. Ansel was left, and the three Ladies who, except for her and Miss Boatwright, were the only faculty women. They were a homogeneous clutch, maiden and graying, their buttocks disciplined by girdles, their lives lived out in classrooms and rented bedrooms.

Miss Gladys Peabody taught French and Spanish. She was a large woman with bright black eyes and a wide smile that sometimes threatened to extend right off her face. Plump little Mae Dell Willette, the art and education instructor, had in her youth been blonde and pretty, and the manner was still there, the wide-eyed sweetness gone a little wistful now with her beauty fading. And there was Miss Ingersoll, Verna, of the business department, a brisk little body who marshaled the rest of them into line and saw to it that they wore their galoshes.

They were good women, gabby and friendly, ready to help if she needed help, and as keen to their small pleasures as they were numb to the scarcity of them. She could laugh with them in the faculty ladies' lounge and share their jokes. They lunched together in cafeterias, and sometimes on Saturdays they took the bus to Kansas City and went shopping and saw a play at the Music Hall.

Weekdays they did their work, Miss Liles as diligently as the rest. She graded papers, made lesson plans, attended meetings, and in January began conducting her seminar. She was punctual, cooperative, courteous, and conscientious, teaching her heart out as she was expected to do.

This was Miss Liles by daylight, all that fall and winter.

Five

*B*ut the night, as Thoreau reminds us, is a very different season. And it was a different creature who—on those spring nights when spring had barely appeared, so shivering and dissembling that only the very prescient could tell it was there at all—ran down the steps from Miss Liles's apartment, leaving behind the trappings of the day. Down through the alley, past the fairy-tale houses with their catwalks and turrets mysterious in the dark, and on to whatever adventure beckoned.

She did not go adventuring alone. She had found some friends, two of them, who came often at nightfall, when the order of the evening was books and serious discourse. As the evening progressed, earnestness of purpose diminished as the laughter and merriment grew, till at last, overcome by their native high spirits, they left their books and ventured out into the night.

They might foray beyond one of the wrought-iron gates and snoop around an old house, or run to the bakery for a delectable something, fresh-baked. They might explore an unfamiliar street; on moonlit nights they might haunt a graveyard or take a hushed promenade through an empty church, in those times left unlocked. And after some of their explorations they'd have a beer or two at Sutt's Corner, a dingy saloon down by the stockyards.

There was so much fun to be had in a world transformed by darkness. And Miss Liles, transformed from her daytime self, could find fun everywhere.

Had teaching been uppermost in her mind, had she found the friends less agreeable, and had she not lived in a neighborhood of half-deserted castles, she might have been more mindful of her actions. But she lived where she did; she had found kindred spirits; and in her heart it was foreordained that one day, not long away, she would depart from academe and embark on her intended life.

Meanwhile, life had become very pleasant indeed. She was comfortable with her new friends—these two bright, well-behaved boys—as with her brother. They were both intelligent, and seemed as interested in books as she was. And they were more good plain fun than anyone else she had ever met.

She had even begun to enjoy her work, especially the seminar. Now and then it crossed her mind that if she worked hard enough and stayed with it, she might become a teacher like a few of those memorable ones who had taught her. Scholarly, at ease with their learning, and skillful at passing it along.

All the same, she looked forward to the nights.

It had come about so seamlessly that they were friends before they knew it. The boys had walked into her room on an afternoon in January to enroll in her seminar—lanky, limber, happy-go-lucky George, along with Toby, who was not quite as tall as George. He was dark haired with a hint of a scowl and a wary look in his eyes. Second-year students, both had been in her English poetry class in the fall; both were good students, full of ideas and argument. George was quick to grasp and remark, Toby more deliberate and questioning. George was a prankster, Toby more serious, but the two seemed inseparable. There were only three others who enrolled in the seminar, three girls, one of whom, Maggie, seemed to be there solely to bask in George's presence. After the second session on the modern novel, the boys talked Allen down the hall and down the steps to the door. After the third they, along with Maggie, talked her all the way home. They stood on the landing, voicing opinions on this and that, until she was blue with cold. It was early February and already dark.

Finally she asked them in.

"Is it okay?" they said, hesitating.

"Why not?" She knew well enough why not. She was a teacher and young and alone. If it were known that she had invited male students into her apartment, well, there were those who would raise an eyebrow or two, at the very least. Mother, for one. *You behave yourself now, up there so private.* Well, let her. It was cold on the landing and the talk was good and they hadn't finished yet. "Of course it's okay. Come on in, I'll make some tea."

And she did, as the wives of professors used to do when the Honors group met in their homes. Tea and polite little cookies, never enough. Soon the boys were in her kitchen every afternoon after class, sitting at the table with tea and cookies and talking about anything and everything. After two afternoons, Maggie, though she was cute and bright and very respectful of Miss Liles, didn't continue to join them after class. She hadn't quite caught the tune, and, in spite of Allen's efforts she was somewhat left out. She began leaving class promptly with some excuse or other.

George never mentioned her, but Allen suspected she was not happy about his continuing to come to her salon, as she now allowed herself to think of it.

Toby read the newspaper assiduously and listened to news on the radio, much concerned about what was going on in Europe. He had wanted to join the Lincoln Brigade after he graduated high school, but his parents would have none of it. Instead he had been a counselor at Scout camp. "That was my last time at camp," he said. "My folks made me go every summer and I never did like it much. First time I went, I made up my mind I never wanted to join things. The Lincoln Brigade was different. You weren't tying silly knots all day or parading around with your hand on your heart. You were driving dynamite trucks through the mountains at night."

George whooped. "Rover Boy in Spain! You just wanted to be Robert Jordan!"

"Go to hell."

Like all students, they discussed their courses (none of them hers, except the seminar) and commented at length on the teachers. They were particularly entertained by Dr. Ansel, the Holder of the Third Degree, as they liked to call him. That, or the Phud. They talked about chorus class (conducted by beautiful Miss Boatwright) and the orchestra, and mostly, of course, about themselves.

George lived on the east side of town, he and his mother and a sometimes-married sister who was in and out. His father traveled, selling pianos. (Not very successfully, she gathered. These days there wasn't too much money around for such refinements.)

Since he covered territory from Wichita to Chicago, he was away most of the time and turned up home whenever he had a mind to. His mother worked nights in the telephone office. On alternate Saturdays George worked in a neighborhood store.

Other Saturdays, he took the bus to Kansas City for his music lesson. George was a gifted pianist. He intended to study at the Juilliard School in New York. Meanwhile, he would settle for the music school in Kansas City. Just like her, he longed for the larger world of the arts, but was making do with gathering his resources where he could. With the help of his teacher in the city and Mr. Delanier at the college, he had applied for a scholarship. It had looked very promising, but he couldn't expect to hear anything before April or May. "If I don't get the scholarship, I don't go. Even if I do, I'll be livin' on beans. My Dad says he'll help, but I don't know what with." Even so, he was hopeful and practiced four hours every morning without fail before his college classes began. George wanted to play in Carnegie Hall. He and Allen sometimes fantasized their future lives in New York City, where musicians and writers abounded.

Toby didn't know what he wanted to do. He only knew what he didn't want to do.

"Murdstone's got it into his head that I'm going to be a chemical engineer or some damn thing."

Allen said, "What does a chemical engineer do?"

"Hell, I don't know and I don't want to find out. Even if there is a great future in it. So he says. I'm not even sure there's going to be a future."

Toby lived only a few blocks away, in a big, square white house with green shutters and a deep front porch, screened in.

He'd lived there all his life. The man he called Mr. Murdstone was his stepfather.

Toby's parents had divorced when he was four years old. His real father went off to California, he thought, and after that to Argentina. "He was in the blood-and-guts business, one of those big meatpacking companies. He used to send me postcards, but then he stopped. I don't know where he is now."

She thought Toby a very sad young man. He seemed lonely and not optimistic about his future, though he was bright as could be, and as voracious a reader as Allen. He often borrowed her books, her precious *New Yorker* magazines (an extravagant and much-appreciated Chrismas present from her brother), and returned them with more ideas to discuss.

Toby's parents were quite social, and much more well off than George's. Murdstone worked as a research chemist for a mining corporation. "Something to do with munitions. He won't say much about it, but that's what I think. They've sent him to Washington a couple of times."

Nevertheless, Toby seemed envious of George, and his passion and talent for music.

When she asked Toby what he might want to do, he said, "I don't know. Read books, I guess. Be a reporter. Or a whiskey drummer. I know I'll end up being called up soon, one way or another."

Allen insisted that they weren't going to get into the war, but Toby was better informed than she, and insisted they would, and he would go.

"Maybe it won't be so bad," Allen said. "Maybe you'll get sent to Italy, Even as a soldier, wouldn't it be wonderful to walk on Italian soil and smell Italian smells and taste Italian food? I've always wanted to go to Italy. Don't you?"

"Not now I don't," Toby said.

"Not *that* Italy. The *real* Italy," said the Romantic. "Where the Brownings went, and Shelley and Keats."

"It's gone," he said.

"It'll come back."

After her seminar ended, in early March, the boys began to drop in some weekend evenings after supper. Sometimes the three of them went to the movies and back to her place afterward for scrambled eggs. They listened, with questions and many comments, as she talked about books and art and other enchantments of that nature, even of the philosophers—Spinoza, of whom she had read a little; Nietzsche, of whom they had read a little; Plato and the ideal form; and Aristotle's *Poetics*. She had learned enough in her time to know how much was left to learn, but it surprised her that she knew as much as she did. The boys seemed to draw it out. Perhaps because she wasn't intimidated by them. She had the upper hand—she was the Teacher. A little authority and a salary gave one a heady sense of oneself.

But the boys knew a thing or two, themselves. Both of them read, though Toby had the wider range. Reading haphazardly— Conrad or Thomas Wolfe, Francis Parkman, Melville, Darwin— he had covered a good deal in his nineteen-going-on-twenty years. And George knew so much about music, educating her to the excellence of Mozart, the strict form of the sonata, and the unexplored pleasures of more modern music. He had introduced her to Debussy. She allowed herself one new record out of every other paycheck, and on George's recommendation, had bought "Clair de Lune," which she listened to over and over again.

The three of them settled into a pattern. The boys came after school some days, some weekends after dinner. They brought each other presents: limericks, passages from books, records to play on her phonograph. Having recently read *For Whom the Bell Tolls* in her seminar, the boys frequently obscenitied in the milk of something or other. Such as chemistry tests or Wednesday morning assemblies with speeches by local dignitaries. They disapproved of the Selective Service draft. But she assured them they needn't be so suspicious of it, that they had nothing to worry about.

"After all, you are not twenty-one."

"We will be."

"Yes, but by that time—"

"They'll lower it to eighteen!"

"No they won't."

"They did last time."

"And should have learned their lesson," she said. "They won't do it this time. Roosevelt said—"

They obscenitied in the milk of what Roosevelt said.

She changed the subject. "I've got a new paragraph. Shut up and listen."

She did not write many new paragraphs these days, but she read them passages from her notebook, written during the fall, and they discussed them. Other times she read Eliot or Yeats or choice stanzas from Blake and Tennyson. Sometimes they read

Shakespeare together. Innocent as she was of disaster, and stubborn in that innocence, she persuaded them that nothing was wrong with the world that poetry couldn't cure. Though George was inclined to believe her (he felt the same way about music), Toby was not persuaded.

Under all this ran the steady obbligato of music. She owned only a few records, but they played the same ones over and over: "Clair de Lune" and "Nights in the Gardens of Spain," a Rachmaninoff concerto and one by Tchaikovsky, and two or three others by Mozart and Beethoven that George had brought. She also had a few dance records, Glenn Miller and the Dorseys and Artie Shaw, and whatever they heard over the small radio her brother had loaned her. On their nights together at her house, there was always music. And there was incessant talk. Around the kitchen table, under streetlamps, on their runs through the alley, the words poured out, their colloquies a mix of book learning and native wisdom, silliness and sense. They spoke maxims and great truths, pronounced upon the world and found it hilarious. They were brilliant, those nights—witty, profound, and wildly funny. Or so they seemed to one another.

Six

*T*here will be a meeting of the staff this afternoon in Room 102 at one fifteen. Your atten-
dance is urgently requested."

She laid the note back on her desk. She didn't know who
had put it there—faculty meetings were usually posted on the
bulletin board—nor why they should meet upstairs in Mr.
Pickering's room and not downstairs in the usual place. When
she saw Dr. Ansel in the hall, she asked if he knew anything
about it.

With a look that told her he knew everything, he said it was a
special meeting. "A few items that need to be brought up. Seemed
like this was a good time to do it."

"Why in Pickering's room?"

"I guess that's where he wanted it. He's chairing."

"Pick? How come Mr. Frawley—"

"He's over at Jeff City today."

"Oh."

"Some deal the board wanted him to go to. He and Souder
went over." Mr. Souder was the president of the school board, a
banker with a square face and teeth like Teddy Roosevelt's.

It sounded suspicious. And indeed, as she discovered shortly after 1:15, the meeting was more or less clandestine. Its purpose was to send Dean Frawley packing.

"He's too old." Mr. Pickering told the assembled teachers. "He should have retired five years ago."

Allen was not wholly surprised. All year she had heard grumblings, mostly from the men: the dean was out of step with the times, he wasn't progressive, he didn't push hard enough, he didn't raise money. One thing and another, to which she paid little attention. She admired the old man, even if others didn't.

"They should never have made him dean in the first place," Pickering said, "and they wouldn't have, except that Souder wanted him. He's too slow, he's too conservative, his ideas are outdated—"

"They're Souder's ideas anyway," said Mr. Lord. "He's the one with the eastern education."

"Well, they're Frawley's ideas too, wherever he got 'em, and he carries them further. It may be Souder who wants Greek and Latin like he had back east, but it's Frawley who's pushing for 'em, along with the music and art and all that folderol. No disrespect meant," he said to Mae Dell, who taught the one art course, "or to Miss Boatwright." Maxine was not present. Neither was the coach.

"If I may put a word in here—" Dr. Ansel rose from the back of the room. Everybody had to turn around to look at him. "What we must understand," he said in his best Speech Class diction, "is that Mr. Frawley is a nineteenth-century educator. Having some knowledge of that period myself, I, for one, have a great deal of respect for the classical program—as well as for our dean, I might add, as I'm sure we all have. Times change. It is my contention that our institutions are called upon to keep pace. It isn't enough that we offer languages and philosophy and the creative arts, valuable as they are. Our schools have to adjust to the values of contemporary society. We have to meet the demands—"

"Kids gotta earn a living!" said Pickering, coming to the point.

"I can agree with that!" said Verna of the business department.

"I don't say we shouldn't give 'em the basic stuff, English and history and all that. But we don't have to go overboard in that direction. It's enough that we offer 'em French and Spanish." Pickering gave a nod to Miss Peabody. "They aren't going to earn a living with Latin and Greek."

"And they don't need to expect me to teach it," Gladys said, looking around. "It's all Greek to me." She laughed through her back teeth with a satisfied hissing sound.

"We all know," Pickering went on, "that what they get here is going to be all the college most of these kids will get. The ones that can afford it go to Springfield or the university. But we're bound to get the rest of 'em and what they need is practical training. I'd like to see more stress put on the teacher-training program and on business education."

"I could sure use some new typewriters," said Verna.

"I'd like to see us put in some courses in the agricultural sciences."

Mr. Lord said, "They could improve things if they supported the science they've got. I'm desperate for equipment. I'll bet there would be twice as many kids in these courses if we could build up the department, give it a little more importance in the curriculum."

"That's what I mean!" Pickering put his fist down. "We need to reorient the direction of this school. The mostly scholastic program does not serve the needs of this community. If I had my say—"

"I agree!" Dr. Ansel rose to his feet and everyone had to turn around again. "I heartily agree with my colleague here, that the needs of this community should be served. But there is more than one way to serve them, a great variety of ways, if you will. Now as we all know, this is a community of intelligent, progressive people. They've made this new college possible, they support a series of concert performances brought in from outside. Many activities of that sort."

"Did you go to that last one?" Mae Dell whispered to Allen. "It was so *good*!"

"And it is my feeling that the college is not doing enough to cooperate in those particular interests that are so manifest among the townspeople. Now, I don't say the humanities don't serve a purpose. But I do say there are more practical applications to which they might be addressed—and immediately, sooner than might be done under the present administration. For example, an active flourishing dramatics department would be of great benefit, I believe, to both community and student body. That's one of the first things I feel should be done as soon as—"

"Well, I don't know," said the sociology teacher, and everyone shifted back around, "I don't know much about playacting. But a good football team would sure do a lot to serve *my* needs—like bringin' in some money so they could raise my salary!"

There was a chorus of agreement.

"A healthy athletic program could do more to stimulate support than just about anything else at the moment." Mr. Pickering said. "I wish Coach were present—I sent him a notice. But I'm sure he supports us in this movement."

Ansel said, "I don't see that athletics and dramatics should be mutually exclusive."

Pickering ignored him. "So what we need is a reorientation toward practical education, so these kids can walk out of here better equipped to hold down jobs." There was a significant pause to let that sink in. "And we all know we will never get that out of Frawley." Another significant pause. "Is there any further discussion?" His tone of voice said there had better not be. "If not—"

But Dr. Ansel rose again. He had some more things to say, and Pickering said more because Ansel had and the other men got a word in here and there. Mae Dell spoke up bravely on the subject of art in the schools.

"Now, I think it's important. Naturally I would, since I teach it and I enjoy it. And if I may say so, I think the students find it enjoyable too. I think it means a lot. Of course, that's just my opinion. I know they're not any of them going to go out and get a job with it, but—" She smiled, lifted one shoulder, cocked her head, and sat down.

"Anyone else want to say anything?" Pickering gave them three seconds. "We have a prepared statement here to present to the school board. It says about what we've been saying here, how the faculty feels about the direction of the college and the reasons that we don't think the dean is heading us down the right path. I've got carbons here, so you can read it. I'll pass them around so you can all have a look. Miss Ingersoll, would you . . . ? Thank you. It says about all we've been saying today. And I'd like to get it into the hands of the board before their next meeting. That will be week after next."

Verna handed the copies around.

"I don't want you to expect a miracle," Pickering said. "Souder's going to go to bat for his man, and he swings a heavy club. We all know that. But there's some on the board don't care much for his dictatorial ways either. And one of these times . . . It may take a year or two before the old man can be eased out. And it may not be very pleasant for us till he is. But we wanted to get the process rolling. . . ."

"There's just one other thing I want to say." He waited for the doodlers to stop doodling and for everyone to look up. "And that is that all of us have to sign this statement. Unless all of us sign it, none of us can. It's got to be the whole staff. Four or five of us sign it, they'll fire us. But they can't fire the whole bunch, not without a whole lot of trouble."

"Safety in numbers!" Gladys said, with her usual zing.

"If there's anybody still hesitating, maybe we can discuss it further. How do you feel about it?" He looked out over the group. "Anybody not prepared to sign it today?"

There was an awkward silence. No one met his eyes, instead everyone looked at the floor or the blackboard.

"If there's anybody not ready, would you please hold up your hand?"

Allen hesitated, then held hers up. Timidly, Mae Dell followed. And there was one other hand raised somewhere in the back. She didn't dare turn to see whose it was.

"Well!" said Pickering, sitting down with a thump. "I see there are a few of us haven't made up their minds yet. That right, Miss Liles?"

"I think it's made up," she said in a small voice.

"But you don't want to sign. Is that it?"

"I'd rather not."

"She'd rather not. Would you care to give us your reasons?"

"Well, I think Mr. Frawley knows what he's doing, and I guess I think it's the right thing."

"Yeah. Well, I'm not surprised you'd feel that way. He let you have that course you wanted and money for the books."

"That's not the only reason."

"I don't know what you wanted with more work but . . . how about your reasons, Hudgin?"

Meek little Mr. Hudgin spoke right up and said he thought a good basic education was more valuable in the long run than specialization, and a small two-year college could not offer both.

"I thought we'd been through that." Pickering smoothed out the petition and twisted his neck over his collar a time or two. "I was hoping to get this thing settled today."

Somebody else said it wouldn't hurt the three of them to sign as long as the rest of them did. Allen figured it would hurt Mr.

Frawley, but she didn't say so. She didn't say anything. While Pick went over the arguments again, and Verna put in her two cents' worth, Allen was thinking of the blacksmith she'd seen in church, now and then, as a child. Sometimes on a Sunday night, under the sallow lights, while the choir sang "Jesus Is Calling," the preacher came down from the pulpit and whispered in the smithy's ear, while the poor devil stood red and hangdog and stubborn as a post, refusing to be saved.

"Aw, you just like being the dean's pet," said the sociology teacher.

There was more good-natured ribbing and a good deal of laughter, which irritated Pick half to death. Then Dr. Ansel stood up and said he agreed with Miss Liles heartily, but went off on a long spiel that proved he didn't, and said that if they would all sign the petition and listen to him the school would turn into the University of Chicago.

The meeting finally broke up for lack of consensus. Pickering packed up his petitions and stomped off, leaving the rest of them to straggle out and make their peace with each other.

Mae Dell hooked her arm through Allen's. "You sure got us in trouble!"

"Gladys and Vernie are mad at us, aren't you?"

Verna shrugged. "It's your business. You can do as you please."

"I just didn't think it would be nice to do that to poor Mr. Frawley."

"Look what he's doing to us," Gladys said, grinning.

"What *is he* doing?" Mae Dell said. "I just don't understand all this."

"Then you should have kept your mouth shut," said Verna.

"Don't be mad at me, Vernie. Please?"

"Oh, come on, let's go eat and forget about it. It wouldn't have done us any good anyway. You comin', Allen?"

"Not this time. I've got a lot of work to do."

"Well, you asked for it, starting that extra class."

"But she *wanted* it," Mae Dell chimed in. "Didn't you, Allie?"

"I wish he'd let me have something I wanted," said Verna.

Allen said, "Maybe if you asked him—"

"Oh phoo. He doesn't want anything practical."

"Well, what's practical," said Mae Dell, "about a football team? Would somebody tell me that?"

"It brings in money," said Gladys, "so they can raise our salaries."

"I don't see what that's got to do with it. I just don't understand—"

"Get your things and come on," said Verna. "We'll explain it. 'Night, Allen."

"'Night," she said and went home unregenerated.

Seven

*I*t was terrible!" she said, giggling. "Pick turned purple."

The three of them, bundled in sweaters and jackets, sat on the landing. Though official spring was only a day away, there was still a distinct chill in the twilight. Allen wore slacks. In the house it was warm, but outside, a planet as big and bright as a silver dollar hung in the cold blue sky.

George said, "He's just mad because you won't help him be the dean."

"Wonder which one will win," said Toby, "him or the Phud."

"Probably neither." Allen laughed again and bit into an apple.

"I'll lay my nickel on the Phud."

"Why?"

"Pick's the militia. He'll go into the army." Toby always brought things around to talk of impending war.

"I don't know why he'd do that. If he wants to be the dean, he'd better stick around."

"He may not be able to," Toby said

"Why not?"

"He's national guard—they can call them into regular service."

"For what?"

"The war, for chrissake. Don't you know there's a war on?"

"Not here," she said, spitting a seed.

"So we'll go there." Toby assured her

"We will not. The president said no son of an American mother—"

"In a rat's reticule," said Toby. "We've got a draft, haven't we?"

"It's a peacetime draft."

Toby snorted.

"Well, that's what they call it, don't they?"

"This isn't peacetime," said Toby.

"We are *not* at war!"

"Give us time."

"Oh, shut up and eat your apple." She slammed into the house, dropped her apple core in the garbage, and came back. "Honestly! You are the most pessimistic! You'd think you *wanted* a war."

"Like hell I do," said Toby.

"Then why are you always talking about it?"

"Because I'm scared."

"Nonsense. You don't have to be."

"Like hell I don't."

"You said that before. Oh dear. I don't know who to believe."

"Whom," said George.

"Not in the vernacular." She leaned back against the wall and, resorting to poetry as she always did, looked up and said, "'In the high west there burns a furious star. . . .'"

"Wonder what it's so mad about," said George. So much for Wallace Stevens. "Want to ride the bike?" They were giving her lessons on George's old hand-me-down, which he now left in her apartment.

"Not much," she said. "I fell off three times the other day. My knee's still sore."

"How come you never learned to ride a bike?"

"Bikes cost money. We rode plow horses."

They leaned back comfortably and listened to the steeple chimes ring twelve times.

"Quarter hours are unresolved," said George. "They leave you hanging."

"Quarter hours," Toby said, "are a warning."

"How so?"

He said solemnly, "Your hour is coming."

"Well, let's improve it then." Allen stood up. "Want to tackle Nietzsche again?"

"Nah, it's Friday night," said George.

"What's that got to do with it?"

"Who wants to be deep on Friday night? I'd rather tackle Judy Garland. Let's go up to the Osage and see her. I've got thirty-five cents. How much you got, Tobe?"

"Half a buck."

"I've got some money," Allen said. "Let me run in and get it."

"We got enough for popcorn?" George said as they went down the steps.

"We'll manage."

They detoured across a lawn, and took a shortcut through a lot where a house had burned down long ago. Jumping onto the stone foundation, they followed-the-leader all the way around and back to the street, toward town. As they turned onto Center Street, George stopped in his tracks.

"Smell that!" The bakery was only two blocks away. "I'm starved."

"You're always starved," said Allen. "Didn't you have any supper?"

"We didn't have any dessert. Let's go get a pie."

"Can't," said Toby. "Not if you want to popcorn with Judy Garland."

"A pie—a big, sloppy goddam pie. Breathe in!"

The mingled odors of butter and yeast, cinnamon, warm sugar, lemon and clove. Judy Garland hadn't a chance.

At the back door, which always stood open, the warmth from the bakery kitchen drifted into the alley. Inside, pastries fresh from the oven lay in rows on the long tables—cakes and sweet buns, thin brittle cookies, and muffins fat with raisins and nuts, cherries and apples steaming through lattice crusts, and cream pies hidden under gold-tipped meringue. The vote went for banana cream. Holding it carefully in a white paper sack, they carried it out to the curb.

"Let's take it to the park," said Allen.

"Too far," said George. "We could drop it."

"Hey," said Toby, "how we gonna eat this? We can't cut a pie with our fingers."

"Use your pocket knife," said Allen.

"I lost it."

"George?"

"I got a pocket comb."

"We should have bought cookies. Maybe we can trade it in."

"Over my dead body."

"Then we'll just have to go back to my place."

"That's too easy."

Toby was scowling down the street. "Follow me."

They followed him back downtown and into a side street. The lights of the bus station glimmered through the plate-glass windows. Leaving George with the pie—"And don't eat it!"—Toby and Allen crossed the street to the lunchroom. The waiter sat at one end of the counter, reading a newspaper. He rose as they came in. "Hy're you folks tonight?"

They said they were fine and slid onto the stools.

"Yawl want to see a menu?" he said, filling water glasses.

Toby said they did. They studied them as they drank the water.

"Yawl from around here?"

"Just passin' through," said Toby. "How's the trout tonight?"

"We don't have no trout tonight."

"No trout?"

"'Fraid not."

"Doggone. I'd heard you could get real good trout in this town."

"Maybe you can some places. We don't ordinarily have it here. Have catfeesh sometimes. Don't have none tonight."

"Well, golly. I'd been looking forward to some good trout. Hadn't you?" He turned to Allen.

"Had my mouth all set."

The waiter grinned. "You kids serious about this?"

"No hay!" said Toby. "We come from over in Kansas where there's not such good fishin'. Maybe we could get some trout on down at Neosho."

"Ever'thang'll be closed down there, time you get there."

"Guess we'll take our chances."

The waiter said, "If yawl expectin' to catch a bus, it don't go there."

"Nah, we're drivin'," Toby said. "Left the car around the corner. You ready?" he said to Allen. "Guess we'll be on our way then. Thanks for your trouble."

"Yeah, thanks," she said.

They sauntered out, taking their time till they were well beyond the light. There they broke into a run. George caught up with them in the next block, and they ran out of breath in front of the Scottish Rite Temple.

"Did you get it?"

Toby shook a fork out of his sleeve. "If they'd a-had trout, we'd a-been up a creek."

They sat on the steps between two sphinxes that supported the clustered lamps. In the dim yellow glow they finished off the pie with the relish of lucky thieves. George scraped the plate clean with his finger.

Leaning back on their elbows, they listened to the bleating of frogs somewhere in a grassy ditch.

"'Last night we sat beside a pool of pink,'" said Allen, letting the rest go unspoken. Stevens's bright chromes and booming frog were familiar enough; they could finish the lines for themselves.

"What are you reading?" she said, pulling a book out of Toby's pocket. "Oh, that again."

Toby had borrowed her copy of A *Portrait of the Artist as a Young Man* and never given it back.

George said, "How many times have your read it, for crine in the bucket?"

"Four, more or less, since we read it for the class."

They laughed.

"Well, I like it," he said. "There's always something I didn't get before, something you can sink your teeth into. Listen to this." He flipped through the pages and began to read from the fifth chapter.

> —*Look at that basket—he said.*
> —*I see it—said Lynch.*
> —*In order to see that basket—said Stephen—your mind first of all separates the basket from the rest of the visible universe which is not the basket.*

He read on through the passage on perception, apprehension, and esthetic image; the three forms—lyrical, epical, dramatic—into which art divides itself; and Stephen's questions on the theory of the esthetic: Was a finely made chair tragic or comic? If a man carves an image of a cow, is the image a work of art, and if not, why not?

"Is a sonata pathetic?" said George.

" 'That's a lovely one,' " Toby said, reading. " 'That has the true scholastic stink.' "

"Never mind him," said Allen. "Go on, Toby."

—The artist, like the God of the creation, remains within
or behind or beyond or above his handiwork, invisible, re-
fined out of existence, indifferent, paring his fingernails.—
—Trying to refine them also out of existence—said
Lynch.
A fine rain began to fall from the high veiled sky and
they turned into the duke's lawn, to reach the national
library before the shower came.

He closed the book, and they sat for a moment, thoughtfully hugging their knees, lost in the Joycean weather—mist, fog, rain, and evening.

"I don't get it," George said.

Toby beat him over the head with the book and they laughed, relieved of a tension congenial but not to be held too long.

"Now," said Toby, taking up the paper plate that had held the pie, "regard this plate. In order to see this plate, the mind separates the plate from the rest of the universe. Which is not the plate. Observe it luminously. Is this finely made object tragic or comic?"

"Tragic," George said promptly. "It's empty."

"Bull's-eye!" said Toby, and sent the plate spinning into the street.

"Pick it up," said Allen. "Only white trash leaves white trash in the street."

Toby dutifully trotted across and retrieved the plate.

When he returned, he offered Allen a hand, pulled her up. "Regard this sphinx," he said. "Is it animal, mineral, or vegetable?"

"Two of the three," said George. "Mineral in the immaculate form of a lion and a woman, both animal."

"Head on," said Allen, "it looks something like Mrs. Medgar."

Having thus disposed of the riddle, they descended the steps and wandered on.

"They used to have a tiger out at the park," said Toby.

"When?" said Allen.

"Twenty, thirty years ago. Before my time."

"Where'd they keep it?"

George said, "There's a cave out there. We've passed it a thousand times. Didn't you ever notice it?"

"It's always dark."

"I'd have thought you could smell it."

"Does it smell?"

"It ought to, it had a tiger in it."

"Do tigers smell?"

"Of course they do."

"Why?"

"They just do, that's all."

"What happened to it?"

"I don't know. He died or something. Maybe ran away with the circus."

It was necessary then to go investigate the cave, and presently they were crossing the high bridge over the ravine that bounded one side of the park.

"Down this walk," said Toby, "and over there to the right."

A high fence guarded a sort of cave hollowed out of the limestone strata. They considered scaling the fence but gave up the notion and, after sniffing and snuffling along the bars, soon lost interest.

Cutting across to the swings, they pumped themselves into the air a few times and from there wandered on past the lake and down a long, easy incline at the far end of the park. At the bottom of the slope a footbridge led across the creek at a narrow point and on to the country-club grounds. The evening was young yet, by their time, and they lingered on the bridge discussing tigers and zoos and whether they were or were not ethical or esthetic and if not why not, until the moon, rising behind the trees, prompted George to sing.

> *Au clair de la lune*
> *Mon ami Pierrot . . .*

Miss Boatwright had chosen the song for the chorus, and the boys had learned it there. Toby picked up the harmony, more or less:

> *Prete-moi la plume*
> *Pour ecrire un mot.*
> *Ma chandelle est morte*
> *Je n'a plus de feu . . .*

The sound of their voices pleased them almost as much as they pleased Allen. They sang it all the way through. Then they worked out the words in English. A boy pretends to be the god of love and gains admission to a brunette's room, and they look for the pen, and for fire. "I don't know what was found," the song ends coyly, and closes the door on them.

"Ol' Miss Maxie has us singing a dirty song." George whooped with delight.

Toby smirked. "She probably has no idea what the words mean."

Allen was unsure, and their speculations about why Maxine had assigned that song, none too innocent, occupied them for some minutes as they strolled on across the bridge into country-club territory.

It was the very extent of the grounds that drew them on. Acres of lovely greensward—open, inviting, and forbidden. (After all, they were not members.) They stood on a low rise now, taking it in. The ground was mossy with moonlight, the gentle swells billowing off into the distance. In the tree-lined borders of the course, the light picked out the white trunks of sycamores, Every limestone outcrop had turned to rough silver.

"Listen!" Allen said. From the top of the hill, where the club-house glittered among the trees, came the faint sound of the band playing "All the Things You Are."

"They're having a party!"

George said, "Let's go up and crash it. Wouldn't that rattle their bones!"

"And get the dogs sicced on us too. Like Cathy and Heath-cliff."

"We'd get Murdstone," Toby said. "My folks are up there."

That tickled them so—Mr. Murdstone, nose to the ground, sniff-ing though the underbrush; Mr. Murdstone barking up a tree.

But the moonlight and the music in the distance overcame their hilarity. They could just make out the band playing "Fools Rush In." "May I have this dance, Miss Allen?" George asked with a debonair bow, and Allen moved into his arms and he began leading her gracefully around and around the lawn. George was a fine dancer—she remembered that from times he'd cut in on her at the college dances she'd chaperoned in the fall. Toby looked on until the song ended and George and Allen separated. Next the band struck up "Thanks for the Memories." Toby bowed gallantly and said, "Then I believe this dance is mine, mademoiselle."

And halfway through, George joined them and the three of them danced around in a circle twirling in and out of one another. They were out of breath when the music ended, and stood, almost shyly, giggling. The band did not strike up another song. Finally, Toby said, "I better get going now, before Murdstone beats me home."

Eight

*I*n the faculty ladies' lounge something was going on. It was noon, just after the last morning class, when the Ladies always met in a rush, with much hair combing and toilet flushing and soaping and rinsing of hands. For the last few weeks the petition had been the main topic of conversation; there were rumors that Mr. Pickering had some new scheme up his sleeve. But this noon there was none of that.

Allen had come in late (waylaid in the hall by Pickering himself, who wanted to twist her arm) and found them hived by the window with Maxine, of all people, in their buzzing midst. Maxine usually met Max for lunch or went home. She sat on the edge of the table, smiling, blotting her eyes with an absurd lace hanky, and looking happier than any girl had a right to look. The room was awash in sweetness. It was like walking into warm tapioca.

"Come in, Allie, wait'll you hear!" Mae Dell pulled her into the circle. "Show her, Maxine."

Maxine held out her left hand. There on the fourth finger was the diamond, big as a doorknob and flashing blue and gold like a soap bubble in the sun. The engagement, which surprised no one except, apparently, Maxine, was official.

Allen admired the ring. "When did it happen?" she asked.

"I can hardly believe it—I've been engaged for almost four weeks!"

"And you didn't *tell* us?" Mae Dell said.

"We thought we shouldn't announce it till we set the wedding date. And we had to wait till—well, I didn't want it to spread all over school just yet. You know how news travels."

"Especially romantic news."

Nothing would do Mae Dell until Maxine went through the story again.

"Oh, you don't want to hear all that again!"

"Yes we do!"

"Well . . ." It was the third week in March. It was the spring dinner dance at the club. "It was such a beautiful night, we just couldn't stay inside. So we went out on the terrace, and we were dancing out there in the moonlight. It was so lovely! And everything seemed—I don't know—so special, as if something wonderful was going to happen."

"And it did!"

"Stop interrupting," said Verna. "If you want to hear it again, let her tell it."

"Max looked so handsome that night. He always does, but that night—" She paused with a little smile. "It was just one of those magical nights. There was a full moon. . . ."

Past full, if she wanted to get it right.

And if she had wanted to, she could have seen three other dancers at the bottom of the hill. And suddenly Allen felt rather silly, dancing like a child with her friends, while Maxine was being proposed to. "And the band was playing 'All the Things You Are.' It's my favorite song and we were alone on the terrace." And she was the promised breath of springtime. And at that moment divine, while Allen and George and Toby danced around and around the lawns, Max slipped the ring on her finger and Maxine and Max were engaged.

"And that's how it happened." The lovely eyes filled again with tears.

"But what did he *say*?" Mae Dell crowed.

"Be quiet, Mae Dell, she can't tell you everything." Verna prissed up her mouth and handed Maxine a Kleenex.

"Thanks. You're a pal." Even Maxine's nose could drip. "I don't know why I'm crying. But it was just so beautiful!"

Mae Dell said she could cry too. Allen ducked her head to hide a red face and a grin.

Drying her eyes, Maxine said she wanted the girls to be among the first to know. "We're going to announce it formally at the club. You'll read about it in the paper. But I wanted you to know ahead of time, from me."

Verna said, "Does Mr. Frawley know?"

"I told him this morning."

"How'd he take it?"

"He was darling. He's the sweetest man. You're all so wonderful. I wish I could ask you all to the announcement party, the whole faculty. But there are so many people, my parents' friends and people from out of town—you know how it is. There are so many. But you will come to the wedding, won't you?"

Mae Dell clapped her hands. "We're invited?"

"Of course you are. I wouldn't think of getting married without you."

"You hear that, Gladys?" But Gladys had gone to the john.

Verna said, "You'll have to get married without me. My sister and her husband are going to Yellowstone Park on a vacation trip, and somebody has to look after Dad and Mama while they're gone. I'm sorry. I'd like to be there."

"But we're getting married on Saturday afternoon, the day after school's out."

"Oh well, then. I guess I could wait that long."

"And I want you all to come to the reception afterward at the club."

"The country club?" Mae Dell pounced on Gladys when she returned. "You hear that, Gladys? We're invited to the country club!"

"You will come, won't you? I know it's awfully short notice, but didn't know till last week that Max would have to leave so soon."

"Leave?" everyone said. Gladys said, "Why? Where's he going?"

"Texas!" Maxine wailed. "Fort Sam Houston."

"That's an army camp!" said Verna.

"He's joining the *army*?" Allen looked at Maxine, incredulous.

"He says everybody will have to, sooner or later, all the men."

"Oh, I don't believe that."

"Well, you'd better listen a little," Verna said. "If you ask me, we're going to get into it before we know it."

Maxine said, "I just can't bear to think about it, but I guess I have to. He says rather than wait and be drafted, he may as well get a jump ahead. So that's why he applied for a commission. That was in February, and it just came through, a commission in the army. He'll go in as a captain."

"Well, that's some help," Verna said.

"Yes, but he has to go for indoctrination the first week of June!"

"That's terrible," said Mae Dell. "Why would he want to do that—leave you, and a good job at the bank? Does he have to?"

"Well, it's probably for the best. Starting as a captain, he could come out with the rank of colonel, maybe even general. He'll be a wonderful officer, I know he will."

"And a wonderful husband. You're so lucky, Maxine."

"So's Max," said Verna.

"He certainly is. Oh, you'll be a beautiful bride. Tell us about your dress."

The dress would be custom-made, tulle and lace. She would wear her mother's bridal veil with the long train.

Mae Dell sighed with rapture and gentle regret. "I was engaged once."

"Yes, you've told us about that," said Verna, hitching a stocking up.

"I didn't know about it," said Maxine. "What happened?"

"I broke it off." Mae Dell said, "I was going to be an artist. My sister and I were planning to go to St. Louis to art school. But then Daddy got sick and we had to stay home and help take care of him. And after that there wasn't any money."

"Then you never got to art school?"

"No, but I took art courses at teachers' college. It wasn't the same thing, but better than nothing, I guess."

"Better than getting hitched," said Gladys. "You never know what you're letting yourself in for. Oh, I don't mean you," she said quickly, turning to Maxine. "*You're* not buying a pig in a poke."

"I think I know him pretty well," Maxine said, laughing.

"And you know his family. Well now!" The familiar grin stretched across Gladys's face. "I'd say she's picked a winner, and this calls for a celebration. How about it, girls? Let's take Maxine out to lunch. Shrimp cocktails and all the works. We'll go to the Bonne Terre!"

Amid a flurry of assent, Maxine wailed with regret that she couldn't go. She had a fitting this noon hour and Max was picking her up. "He's probably waiting out there this minute. I'm so sorry. You're so wonderful. I'd love to go. But I've really got to run."

She rushed off with thanks and apologies. As the door swung shut behind her, Verna picked up her pocketbook. "It's late. Let's go eat."

"Oh, who wants to eat"—Mae Dell sighed—"with all this excitement?"

"I do. And so do you."

"Can we still go to the Bonne Terre?"

"Without her? Mercy land! We've got to save that for special occasions. We better go to the Show-Me."

"We went there yesterday."

"I know, but it's closer. Take your bumbershoots, everybody, it's going to rain."

Nine

*T*he students bent over their desks composing paragraphs. Later they would analyze the structure of their paragraphs, discuss the logic and development of their ideas. They would, if she could keep their minds on it. It was the last hour of the afternoon, when the kids were leaning toward four o'clock. And they were the dullest of all her classes. After the bright bunch in her Shakespeare class, these seemed very low wattage.

She opened another paper, homework turned in at the beginning of class. According to Lindsey Homeier's paper, he had got through high school by "hard studding." It crossed her mind to throw the passage open to discussion. That would get their attention! But of course that wouldn't do. Nor would she do that to poor Lindsey. He had trouble enough. Impossible Lindsey, who had cropped up now in three of her classes. She circled the word in red, wrote "sp" in the margin, and let her thoughts wander back to the scene at noon in the ladies' lounge. Maxine with the ring on her finger, her blue eyes bright with happy tears. Maxine at the top of the hill, with kisses and diamonds, and down below Miss Liles of the English department with Toby and George. She looked down at Lindsey's paper and choked back a giggle.

"High school is not so interesting as college," Lindsey wrote. "In college you're more grown up."

Some of us are.

She closed Lindsey's paper and picked up another. But she couldn't get Maxine out of her mind. Pretty Maxine, a maiden pure of brow serene. Maxine was so . . . hygienic. Max too, from all you could tell. They were the couple on the wedding cake, forever garbed and garlanded, preserved in purity on tiers of sweetness. You could imagine them dancing and romancing and possibly some heavy breathing, but never anything as lowly as a roll in the featherbed. Max's going away only made it more properly romantic, the finishing touch of chivalry. Like Lovelace—"Loved I not honor more." Indoctrination for ninety days might not be all that chivalrous. All the same, from her chaste breast to war and arms he flew.

In a pig's eye.

"Yes, Lindsey?"

"I've finished my paragraph, Miss Liles."

"Already?"

"Yes ma'am. May I bring it up?"

"If you like."

Pear-shaped Lindsey wallowed forward and laid the page lovingly on the desk.

"Thank you. We'll wait till the others finish before we discuss it."

He lingered, smiling. The thick lashes over his gentle, slanty eyes made her think of butterfly wings laden with golden dust.

"Maybe you'd like to study your book while we wait," she said. "You might like to go over those passages again, about paragraph structure."

"Yes ma'am."

She glanced briefly at the tidy paragraph written in Lindsey's rounded purple backhand. "My topic is spring. Spring is my favorite time of year. The reason is because in spring you are supposed to make up poems to your lady love."

She laid it aside. How had the boy ever got this far? How did he get by at all? Because he was allowed to. You couldn't flunk Lindsey. That poor brain, that sunny temper, those dusty golden eyes, and all that hard studding. Lindsey tried. She picked up another piece of homework.

Through the big classroom windows she could see the rain coming down, as Verna had predicted. A hard green spring rain that bounced on the pavement and ran in streams along the curb. A cluster of kids stood in it, the Lord knew why, four or five of them crowded together under an umbrella with a broken rib. She could hear them laughing. George was among them, making some comic ado. George in his cracked yellow slicker and a poison green sweater, with his pants turned up at the ankle, the way the boys wore them. The kids stumbled up the walk and in through the side doors.

Doodling on a memo pad, she thought of Max again. Tall, manly, impeccably dressed. Max looked like an officer. And Maxine would be a proper officer's lady. She lost herself briefly in visions of waltzes and chandeliers, white gloves, sabers and gleaming boots, and glasses sparkling with champagne. But that was in another age and in the movies. And maybe Max would get no closer to the war than Texas. If the president meant what he said, he wouldn't. He would come home in ninety days and be promoted at the bank, and he and Maxine would settle grandly in a lovely house and raise lovely children and be upstanding citizens, pillars of the church, members of everything, a credit to the community and to the country club.

She scratched a big red X across the memo pad. She wanted no part of that. And yet, there was Maxine, creamy and clean and womanly and loved. And there was Max, manly and handsome and protective. She couldn't quite put down the feeling that she was missing something. (Nobody ever told *her* she was the promised breath of springtime.)

She stayed on after school, correcting themes, pausing now and then to gaze disconsolately at the rain and kids running through it toward home. Upstairs, the chorus drifted by fits and starts down Bendamere Stream, Maxine at the helm. During the frequent intervals her classroom seemed unnaturally still and lonely. Not even Dr. Ansel came in to chat. She stared at the work before her with distaste. Worn out words, lifeless sentences. How was she to explain the relation of sentence structure to life? How to make clear that verbs and nouns were common to Shelley and Popeye the Sailor (though perhaps not the same ones)? She heaved a great sigh and set her elbows firmly on the desk, bracketing her work. Holding the red pencil, she read on for several minutes before flinging the pencil down. It was no use. She was cross and unhappy, like a child left out of the game.

"Oh, *nuts* to Maxine!" She rose and went to the window.

The rain was tapering off but the sun had not come out. Still, it was spring and there was a luminosity in the air. In the pale sheen everything glowed—grass, green shrubs and masses of leaves, the black, wet trunks of trees and the red brick of the house across the street. She looked at it in despair. Such an exultation of light, and she with no urge at all to exult. What *did* she want?

She turned suddenly and walked out of the room. The sound of the chorus in her ears, she went up the hall and entered the rustling quiet of the library. Nodding to the librarian, fierce little Miss Pettit, she went into the stacks, down the rows of books, lingering on the way, her glance like a caress along familiar names—Chaucer, Donne, Keats, Milton. She took down a book and opened it.

Of man's first disobedience, and the fruit of that forbidden tree whose mortal taste brought death into the World, and all our woe, With loss of Eden . . .

The flesh on her arms tingled. She stood in the narrow aisle, secure in an environment beloved and comforting. Here, she was at home.

Many of the authors were among the books on her own shelves. Many were here whose acquaintance she had yet to make. She moved quickly back and forth, pulling down books. Shaw and Dante, John Donne, *Songs of Innocence*. Yes, and Voltaire, she must have that one too. How many would Pettit let her take out? Already there were more than she could carry. She put back Shaw and Voltaire.

Up front the door swung open, letting in the sound of the chorus. Engaged or not, Maxine was still hard at work. Allen reached for another book, feeling benevolent now, having found her way home again. This was her world. Maxine could have hers and welcome to it—husband, house, children and all. But she paused with her hand still on the book. What if Maxine were denied all this? What if Max did have to go off to battle and what if he did not come back?

She stood there guiltily, as if her envy alone could bring it about. Well, she didn't envy Maxine *that* much. And she needn't worry about Max. Somehow, Roosevelt would keep the country out of the war.

And yet . . . She stood for another moment, her arms full of poetry, then slowly put it all back.

There were other books that she had better read.

She tiptoed down the aisle and around to the history section, where she stood in bewilderment. What had she done when she studied such subjects? Memorized, that's what, just enough to get by. Memorized, and remembered nothing. She was as dumb in such fields as Mae Dell. And where to begin now? To understand Hitler's war she must understand the kaiser's. To understand that, then the wars before that, and the treaties and trade and conquests that divided the globe into separate kingdoms, and what led to what, and on back and back, until if you were to understand everything you had to start with Attila the Hun.

Well, she might as well be at it. She leafed through a few volumes and read tables of contents. Settling on three that seemed likely, she checked them out and, bidding Miss Pettit good night, carried them home through the soaked afternoon with a weighty sense of purpose.

Under the reading lamp the books looked plump and promising. She glanced at them with satisfaction as she passed back and forth at the evening chores—the wastebaskets, the sudsing, and supper. She had a bowl of soup, some lettuce, a cupcake and a glass of milk, eating slowly as she read *The New Yorker*. The door stood open to the landing, letting in the cool, damp rain-scented air. Leaving the dishes, she pressed a skirt and had a bath. Then in pajamas and robe she settled herself among the cushions and took the top book off the stack.

She read the title page and the preface, jumped up and put a record on and sat down again. Two or three pages into the text, she stopped and started over. After a time the words began to make sense. She plowed on doggedly through the first chapter, rereading, skipping a page here and there. She was well into the second chapter when there came a faint familiar sound from outside.

She looked up, listening. The sound came from the stairs, a light scuffle of feet, muffled laughter, then a tap at the door. The origins of the kaiser's war landed on the rug.

From the darkness of the kitchen she could see them on the landing, silhouetted against bright moonlight.

"Come with us," they said, "the sky is falling."

Ten

She went down with them to the alley, sinking waist-deep into clouds. Overhead the night glistened. The moon was full and the sky clear as ice. But the ground smoked with thick white fog, streams and billows of fog, rising from the rain-soaked ground. They waded through it down the alley, watched it wash around the great houses, their turrets and slate shingles obscured. There had never been such a fog, not in their lifetime. They called it foam and soup of the evening; hell had cracked, the smoke seeped through; they called it shaving cream and meringue. They groped through the fog, stumbling over the curb, and climbed to the door of the Presbyterian church, where they sat in the clear, watching the fog lap the bottom steps. The church spire shone in the sky like the samite arm.

"We're sinking into the sea!" said Allen. "It's Germelshausen. It's the froth of heaven!"

"It's cold air flowing over a warmer surface," said Toby.

"Spoilsport."

"Steam fog. The condensation of moisture around specks of dust. Or maybe it's radiation, when the air cools below a certain point, and heat radiates from the ground. The cold air falls and the warm air rises and fog forms where they meet."

"You makin' this up as you go?" said George.

"I read a book. About advection and cirrostratus and fracto-stratus and how weather forms in the upper air."

"You understand it?"

"Not all of it. But I like the sound of the words."

"They're good words," Allen said.

"I like weather. Clouds and wind currents and all that."

George said, "You and Dean Frawley ought to get together."

"We did—that time he called us in, remember, when we were raisin' hell in the hall? I don't know what he said to us—"

"He dressed us down a little."

"—because I was looking at all those instruments on his walls."

"All those thermometers and things," Allen said. "What does he do with all those?"

"Looks at them, I guess. I wish he'd call us in again."

"I think we could arrange it," George said.

"Oh, hey," said Toby, reaching into a pocket, "I brought us something." He pulled out a thin brown bottle.

"Vanilla!" said George.

"In a rat's reticule. Get a whiff of this."

"Wowzie! Old booze in a new bottle. Where'd you get it?"

"Out of my dad's quart jug. Siphoned it out with a soda straw, quarter inch by quarter inch. Been workin' on it for a month. Here, Teach—ladies first."

"Not here!" she said.

"Why not?"

"We can't get drunk on the church steps."

"We can't get drunk on eight ounces either."

"I don't care, I don't want to drink it here."

"Consider it the sacrament," said George, "and hurry up."

"I don't care what you call it, I won't drink stolen hootch on the Presbyterian steps."

"Baptist maybe?"

"We'll drink it in the park."

So off they went across the town, steering their way by trees and lampposts along the shrouded corridors. The fog was capricious. It shifted and melted and reappeared dead ahead, swallowing them whole, disgorging them then into the full glare of the moon. Prankish, a conspirator come to play in the night when all sane folk were abed.

Single file and holding on to the concrete rail, they made their way across the bridge. The fog boiled up from the ravine, enveloping street and bridge and gateway. A short way into the park they came out in the clear again at the top of a long hill that sloped down to the creek. The upper part lay in full light, the wet grass glistening. Below, the ravine was filled like a bowl with the dense white mist. It rose halfway up the slope.

They rested a moment on a bench. Then "Dive in!" said Allen, and disappeared into the whiteness. It was over her head. She could see nothing until, near the foot of the slope, the dim shapes of trees emerged, sycamores and willows, and the low tangle of underbrush along the edge of the stream. She could hear the boys coming down behind her. A few feet apart and they were lost.

"Where'd you go?"

"Here."

"Where?"

"Over here!"

They swam in it, ran up again into the clear, drank from the bottle, and plunged again into the white sea. They played tag, skidding on the slippery grass, tripping over one another, and rising to touch and dart away. Then abruptly the fog would tear, drift away in patches. And they climbed the hill to wait till it gathered again.

The moon hung directly over their heads. "In all my life," said Allen, tipping her head back, "I never saw the moon so bright."

"Neither did I," said George.

"If I climbed that tree, I could reach it."

"Leave it where it is," he said and he began to sing. "'Ah, moon of my delight who knows no wane . . .'"

Allen joined in and they sang their way through the tentmaker's garden, where the moon sought for one in vain.

"Perty," said Toby. "You make up the tune yourself?"

"Yep," George said.

"Nice." Toby leaned back on the bench. "Did you ever stop to think," he said, in that lavish improbable light, "that night is the true condition?"

"I can go for days without giving it a thought," George said. "What do you mean, the *true* condition?"

"The real one. Factual. Permanent. Light may be a fact, but it's not eternal. It comes and goes."

"The sun goeth down, but it cometh up again in the morning, by gum."

"Yes, and it by gum goeth down again that night. And there's the dark again, waiting to swallow us. Light is a temporary thing, a spot on the dark. And darkness is always there. That's what I mean, it's the true condition."

"But wait," said Allen, "you're saying permanence is the essential quality of truth. But doesn't truth change sometimes, in the light of circumstance?"

"No. Circumstance may show it in a different light. But that doesn't mean it's changed. That just means we didn't see it very plain in the first place. Truth is truth. It just *is*. It's there, whether we see it or not. Like the dark."

"Well, so is the sun," said George. "It's always there too, someplace, whether we see it or not."

"But it won't always be. It'll burn itself out one of these times."

"Don't wait up. Anyway, ours isn't the only sun. When this one goes, there'll still be others."

"They'll burn out too, no matter how many. Lights go out," he said darkly. "Darkness abides."

"You're a hard man, Tobe. You'd have made a good preacher."

"God forbid!"

"I think He did," said George. "Pass the jug."

They drained the last drops. Drawing his arm back, Toby flung the bottle far down the slope and dashed after it into the fog that filled the ravine again.

Allen ran after him, George close behind. "Tag!" she said, running into Toby.

"No fair, I was looking for the jug."

"Wait'll it clears again." She darted away. There was the sound of their running, the swish of their feet across the wet grass. But she could see nothing except the white drifts.

"Where are you?" George called.

"Here!"

He was somewhere above and behind her. Changing directions, she ran downhill toward the stream where the fog was thickest.

"Give a clue!" he shouted. He was closer, coming down the slope behind her.

She was among the trees before she could see them. The pale sycamores materialized in the dimness directly in her path. She swerved, missing a tree, turned, stumbled over a root, and fell smack into Toby.

"Oh!" she gasped, pitching against him. And before she could right herself, he pulled her closer and kissed her, quick and deliberate. She drew back with a little low laugh, then kissed him back and turned and ran, feeling her way until she was clear of the trees.

"Hellooooo!" from uphill. "Anybody there?"

"Here!" she called and darted off at an angle.

"Where?"

"Here."

They collided somewhere in the middle.

She rose from the slick grass, out of breath, laughing.

"Is that you?" he said.

"It's me. Is that you?"

"I think so. Let's get out of this muck and find out."

They trudged uphill into the clear. "Look at you!" she said. "You look like a dandelion. You're all frizzy—your head's gone to seed."

"So's yours. You look like the end of a mop."

"Anyway, I'm not wet to the skin." She flapped her sweater a couple of times. "My shirt's still pretty dry."

George flapped his shirttails and swung his arms back and forth. "Where's Tobe? King's X," he sang out. "All outs in free."

Toby emerged from the fog like a man walking out of water.

"What happened?" George said. "You fall in the creek?"

"I drowned."

"You look like a fish," Allen said, "all shiny."

He laughed, a small exultant laugh, and stretched his arms to the sky. "O glabrous noon!"

"That's *glaucous*," said George.

"Glabrous if I ever saw one. Bald as an eagle."

They shook themselves like wet puppies, keeping warm. Suddenly then they were hungry.

"Hamburgers!" said lean George. "Big, messy, ketchupy hamburgers on a greasy bun. Maybe the Grease Pit's still open. I'll race you to the bridge!"

They reeled through the quiet town, dizzy with laughter, a little crazy from the moonlight and a few mouthfuls of whiskey.

Eleven

She was late to school next morning. As she ran up the steps, the buzzer was sounding and the hall was full of kids scurrying to their first-hour classes. Toby came up the hall laughing with a black-haired girl, and they passed with only a nod. She felt suddenly pulled back into last night's fog. He had deliberately pulled her close and kissed her, and she had kissed him back. Was he parading this girl before her classroom to show her last night's encounter meant nothing? Did she want it to mean something? And how ridiculous she must have looked with her hair all frazzled and her clothes wet and frumpy. But already her classroom was full and she had to dispel the fog and get back to the task at hand.

It was a particularly busy day, and at 4:15, after the last afternoon class, there was a faculty meeting. Something to do with the debate festival scheduled for the following week. The meeting went on forever. She tried to listen, though everyone wanted to talk at once, and Pickering, who wasn't even in charge, kept trying to force Dean Frawley into Robert's Rules of Order. The dean was paying him no attention. They chattered away about the visiting teams and how to schedule them and get them fed at lunch and who would be the judges.

"We'll draw on the history department," the dean said, "and economics and English. That seems a good balance. Dr. Ansel will chair, of course."

Of all the varieties of human expression, academic debate, usually about economic or political issues, seemed to her the dullest. Debate was so terribly *earnest*. She hid a yawn behind her hand and ignored ol' Lordy, who was easily as bored as she was and trying to relieve the monotony by flirting with her. She wished he would wink just once at Mae Dell. Do her a world of good.

Her mind wandered back to last night's escapade. She had scarcely been able to think about it since the morning. Like a dream it had evanesced through the day, growing dimmer, harder to recall in detail. Except for that one moment when she had stumbled . . . well, it was only a lark, a midsummer-night's romp on a bright spring night, perhaps no more real than Titania and Bottom. And split three ways, there wasn't enough whiskey in that little bottle to get a bumblebee drunk.

"And now let's see—Mr. Gunther and Mr. Pickering, and we need a third. Would you be willing to serve, Miss Liles?" The dean was waiting for an answer.

"Oh—yes," she said, realizing too late that she had just agreed to help judge the debates. How tiresome. Now she would have to bone up on the League of Nations.

"Mr. Chairman?"

"Yes, Mr. Pickering."

"I assume Dr. Ansel will prepare grading sheets for the judges?"

"Well, I hadn't thought about that," said the dean.

"I wondered if you had."

"These are only high-school teams, you remember. What do you think, Dr. Ansel? It's only a matter of who has the best argument and the best delivery. We can pretty well judge by listening, can't we?"

"Mr. Chairman?"

The dean sat down wearily. "You have the floor, Mr. Pickering."

Pick stood up and delivered himself of the virtues of tallied points, much interrupted by Ansel and the others, regardless of parliamentary law. Allen's thoughts wandered again to last night. It was odd that all day no one had mentioned the fog. It was a most extraordinary fog. Surely others had thought it so.

"Do I hear a second?"

A chorus of seconds was drowned out by the scraping of chairs and the meeting noisily adjourned. She went off down the hall with the Ladies.

"My land, it's after five," said Verna. "You girls want to go eat right now?"

"I'd just as soon," said Gladys.

Mae Dell said she ought to go home first and freshen up.

"Aw, you look all right," Verna said, going through the lounge door. "You don't need to go home. You coming with us, Allen?"

"Might as well. I don't have a thing in the icebox but Cokes." There was some beer, which she kept for weekend nights with "her boys," but she didn't say that.

"I look a fright," said Mae Dell, fussing at the mirror. "Gladys, do something with my hair."

"What do you want me to do with it, sweep it under the rug?"

"Oh, you know what I mean. Curl it up in the back a little."

"Hand me your comb."

Waiting for them, Allen stood at the window, idly looking out at the street. "That was quite a fog, wasn't it?" she said.

"When?" said Gladys.

"Last night."

"Oh, yeah, I read something in the paper about that."

"Heaviest fog I ever saw."

"That's what they said."

"Who said?" said Verna, coming out of the John. "What are you talking about?"

"The fog last night."

"I noticed that, when I got up to shut my window. I went to bed with the window up, but there was a draft so I got up and shut it. It was chilly last night."

"Pretty, though," said Allen. "The moon was so bright and the fog so thick and white below it. It was low to the ground but sometimes it was over your head."

"Were you out in it?" said Mae Dell.

"I mean, it looked like it was over your head. You could see it from the window."

"That's where I saw it," said Verna.

"I saw the moon," Mae Dell said. "I don't remember any fog."

"Your mind must have been in a fog," said Gladys.

She was home before seven and by eight had graded a stack of papers. Recalling then that next week she would have to help judge the debates, she gathered up the books checked out last week, those dealing with World War I and subsequent history, and carried them in to the kitchen table. Consulting an index, she turned to a passage concerning the League of Nations and settled down to read. She was busily making notes when there was the sound of footsteps on the stairs. Toby appeared, grinning under a headdress of tattered turkey feathers; beside him, Frankenstein's monster in rumpled corduroys and a bright green sweater. "Boo!" said George.

They pranced in, pleased as punch with themselves, and flopped down at the kitchen table. They had just come from chorus and orchestra practice, rehearsing for the spring concert.

"Got a beer, Teach? We're dry as Kansas."

George had to take off his mask to drink, but Toby kept the headdress on, the last remnant of his Indian suit resurrected from a toy box in his stepfather's garage. "You should have seen us tonight!" he said.

"We were great," said George. "Poor ol' Miss Maxie! We sneaked in when her back was turned—"

"And when she turned around, George was sitting there at the piano with that green face."

"Miss Maxie let out a yelp, and then she turned around the other way and Tobe had put on his feathers—" They broke up in laughter. "You'd a-loved it! Wish you'd been there."

"Glad I wasn't," Allen said, laughing. "Did she give you hell? She should have."

"Nah, she kept her dignity and just waited. We took pity on her and took the stuff off."

"Sweet kids, aren't you?"

She had found some potato chips in the cupboard and they finished those off, along with nibbles of cheese and sweet pickles. Nothing was said about last night. She might indeed have dreamed it—though sitting across the table from Toby, she couldn't help feeling just a little self-conscious. Unobtrusively under the chatter, she picked up the rubber mask and slipped it on.

"You've aged," said George and went on talking.

Safely hidden behind the Frankenstein face, she felt more secure. "Listen," she said, interrupting, "you know that debate they're having next week? I've got to be one of the judges. They seem to be cramming every extra activity into the last month of school. Tell me everything you know about the League of Nations."

"It flopped," said George. "What else do you want to know?"

"I want to know why. What are those kids likely to say about why?"

"Well, for one thing," said Toby, "they're going to come down hard on the Treaty of Versailles."

"June 1919, Hall of Mirrors." She referred to the open book. "Tell me about it."

"Well," he began, and taking off his feathers, he told what he remembered from his history class. George put in a word here and there. And she made notes and asked questions till she figured she knew all she had to. They seemed to enjoy having their roles switched, teaching the teacher.

"Hey, was that ten o'clock?" Toby said. "I got to get home. How many bells was that?"

"Four bits," said George. "It's only nine-thirty."

"Anyway, I got to go. Murdstone's decree."

"Guess I'd better go too. Got to practice. Thanks for the beer, Teach."

"Thanks for your help," she said. "Don't forget your feathers. And here's your face, George."

"Keep it in case of ghoulies."

"The only ghoulies around here are the two of you. Here, take it. 'Night, you-all."

"'Night. Thanks."

She stood for a moment taking in the fresh night air. She felt relieved; everything seemed back to normal. Turning back to the kitchen, she cleaned up the table and set the glasses in the sink. Funny, she thought, as she sprinkled soap powder and turned on the water, that none of them had mentioned last night. But they were busy with their high jinks at rehearsal, that and the League of Nations. Anyway, last night was last night, and maybe she had made it all up in her head.

But there had been fog. Verna said so. And Mae Dell saw the moon. "So there!" she said aloud and turned, startled, to find Frankenstein's monster at her door.

Caught between fright and laughter, she stopped with a tea towel in her hand and stared. The Frankenstein face, but no bright green sweater.

"I thought if it's not too late—"

He stood outside the screen door, and for a moment there wasn't another word out of either of them. Then he took the mask off. It was Toby's face, all right, but this was not the same boy who, moments ago, had sat at her table. He was not quite the same, but she recognized him. She knew him at once. She had been looking for him all spring, in the night, through the alleys and into the park, all over town, drawing closer and closer, never knowing that this was the one—not the other, but this one—nor that he would stand at her door with his heart in his mouth and a crooked green face in his hand. It hit her like a ton of bricks. "Come in!" she said.

Twelve

She drifted through the following day, twice re-moved. Somehow or other she got through her classes, but with only the faintest idea of what she had taught, and no idea what she had said to the Ladies at lunch at the Show-Me Cafe. Voices seemed to come from a great distance. And the only face she saw was Toby's. The rest were asterisks.

Somewhere along in the afternoon the dean summoned her to his office. His pink-and-white head shone like a peony bud, and he conveyed welcome news. Her contract had been renewed. All the teachers were reelected for the coming year. The formal documents would be ready for signing within a week or two.

"I'm greatly pleased," he said, "that we'll have you on our staff again. I feel you're making a real contribution."

She believed that she had thanked him.

She muddled blissfully through the rest of the afternoon and hurried home.

There had been others before him to whom she had been wildly attracted, though the attraction hadn't often taken her very close. She had imagined love (almost, but hadn't, made it once), but she had never loved, in the active voice—of that she was certain. That she did so now could be questioned. But that she was

In Love, head over heels in some glorious concept, there could be no doubt. Nothing like this had appeared before on her landscape, and she advanced toward it unswervingly, like a confident walker in the night who, sure of his ground, walks into a pond and promptly, without so much as a flap of the arms, sinks like a stone. It was a strange, astonishing element, as new to Toby as to her, which they explored with curiosity and delight.

There was a ritual closely followed: the screen door left unlatched after dinner, the lights off except for the reading lamp, a record playing, and books open on the couch. Then the quiet sound of Toby letting himself in, coming through the dark kitchen, and with a grin of satisfaction settling into the threadbare refuge of the big armchair. First they would go through the secular day, what each of them had done or said that might entertain the other. Then she would read to him, poetry, most often. He listened, leaning back, watching her, and then, settling deeper, "Talk to me," he would say.

And she would begin, like Scheherazade spinning her lovely lies. She told him stories of what he would do some day, work as a reporter, or write the definitive book on Joyce. She would write books too, fiction, and poetry, and live in New York and come to visit sometimes, cross-country. And she would read poetry while Toby sat in the big chair and ate fresh strawberries dipped in sugar.

By that time they'd have gone through "Clair de Lune" and "La Mer." And with scarcely a break in the words she would have wandered over and changed the music. Toby would rise from the depths of the chair and they would begin to dance, in this way daring to touch at last, then sink to the couch, still with the light on, holding on for dear life. They never had enough of marveling at each other, nor that each had chosen the other.

She knew that he was too young and she too old. She was a teacher, he was a student, and this was perilous business. She could be fired for this and land in her mother's lap like a cannon-ball. But not one part of this got through to her better judgment. "For love," as Burton could have warned her, "is fire, ice, hot, cold, itch, fever, frenzy, pleurisy, what not?" It is also bats in the belfry and hot fudge in the veins.

She went forth by day in a perfect dither, carrying with her the night before. She overflowed with good will toward everything in sight. She quite astonished Maxine one day, coming at her with a flying tackle meant as a girlish hug. (How could she ever have been envious of Maxine?) As for the Ladies, she found them paragons. The very power of her ravished gaze was enough to rejuvenate them. And such was the measure of her bliss that she could pour it out to all takers and never miss a drop. She was a fountain of in-dulgence, handing out pardons and benisons on all sides, so full of benevolence and indiscriminate praise and giggles that Verna was moved to inquire one day if she was running a fever.

"You look flushed. You feelin' all right?"

"Never felt better in my life."

"You better slow down. School's not over yet."

She knew her behavior was less than seemly. She knew she was walking on her hands. But for the life of her, she could do nothing about it and wouldn't have if she could. It was incredible, this affair. She had come down in the orchards of Tantalus and she could eat.

She gorged herself. Her rooms were stocked like a pantry with the viands of romance—flowers, poetry, music, lucent syrups and spiced dainties. Scarcely Porphyro for his Madeline set such a heap as she, nor lavished them on a lover with so prodigal a hand.

She talked (all those glittering prophesies!). They listened to "Nights in the Gardens of Spain." They played Glenn Miller and Benny Goodman and they danced. She no longer read poetry of her own; she was writing none. Possessed by the experience, she had no time to explore and interpret. In the thick of it, she could not see but only revel in it. And so they read other poetry, and they kissed and danced and ate fresh strawberries, thoroughly bedazzled by themselves.

"Toby?"

"Hm?"

"It's late."

"I know."

They had fallen asleep, propped up against the velvet cushions.

"It's after eleven."

"Kee-rist," he said, "why is it always after eleven!" He tightened his hold on her and within a moment was asleep again.

Down the street the steeple clock chimed the half hour. The elm branches stretching across the sidewalk scratched discreetly at the window. She leaned against him, feeling the rhythm of his breathing. He was clean-smelling and smooth and firm like soap fresh out of the wrapper. She loved him.

Why was it Toby, she wondered, why him and not George? She loved George too. But that was in another way. There was something about this one. . . . George had a purpose, he had somewhere he was going. But Toby was lost somewhere between a past he hadn't loved and a future he did not trust. Neither country was his. He was homeless. This narrow present was all his refuge. And so he had turned to her because she made it for him, and so it was that she loved him best, because of his homelessness and his need. She reached up and smoothed the dark stubble-cut head. "Toby?"

"Hm? Did I go to sleep again?"

"Only for a minute. Go home now, it's eleven-thirty."

"I don't want to go."

"I don't want you to go, but you've got to."

He yawned and slowly untangled himself. "Always got to go blattin' off."

In the dark kitchen they clung to each other, dead for sleep. The steeple clock chimed another quarter hour. Abruptly Toby pulled himself loose. "Nothin' for it," he said and went home to climb through the window again.

They didn't see very much of George; he was hard at work, practicing for the spring concert. He had been called back to Kansas City for a second audition, which meant he was among the finalists for the scholarship. On nights when the orchestra and chorus rehearsed together, Toby would come to her afterward. But George went straight home to work on his audition piece.

It wasn't until the night of the college concert that the three of them went out again together—across town to Sutt's Corner. They were out to celebrate. The orchestra and chorus, under the guidance of Mr. Delanier and Miss Boatwright, had outdone themselves. George played a Chopin prelude, and after much applause, came back with a short piece by Satie.

"You were wonderful," Allen said. "They loved you."

"It was easy," he said, "homegrown audience, predisposed." A grin spread across his face. "It's not going to be this easy next week."

That's when he would go to Kansas City; they had requested he play Mozart's *Sonata Pathetique*.

But they rejoiced anyway. The scholarship now seemed in hand.

It was fun being together again, keyed up and celebrating. But she and Toby could not keep their eyes from meeting, nor control the secretive smiles. And she was glad when, after a couple of beers, George said he'd better get home; tomorrow was Saturday and he had to work at the store.

"But I'm only going to work half a day. I've got to practice at least six hours. And more on Sunday."

They bid him good-bye at the bus stop and went on together to her dim-lit room to settle into their usual places and turn on the phonograph and talk until it was time to dance.

In an affair of "love" (not the long Victorian engagement but a mutual obsession of some intensity), it is usually understood by both parties that this is no lasting condition. It will run its course. And the length is neither spoken of nor considered. Such an affair can last for a number of months, rarely as long as a year, before it becomes something else. But rapture of the most irrational sort, when the world and all its atoms compact into a single form, so that nothing exists that is not contained within that form, that face, that voice, can scarcely sustain itself for long. The affair you remember is the one that lasted three days. Or a week, perhaps even a month. The fine, lovely flash in the pan; the compressed affair, all the astonishment, the delight, and the anguish fused by a sudden explosion, with no time for thinning out or diminishing before it goes almost as it came, in a burst.

Hers lasted for nearly three weeks.

Somewhere along, she became aware, mostly when Toby was not around, of some vague lack. It was not sex she wanted. Brought up as they were to restraint, respectability, and fear, the game was to flirt all around it but carefully hold back. It was the romance of the thing that mattered. But something was missing. She felt the need of something beyond the circumscribed pattern of their meetings. The ritual had been enough at first. But there was a restlessness in her now, the vaguest murmur of something that said *move*: the need to stretch after a long time in one position. She wanted to bust loose, out of this room, this apartment—but with him. She imagined them driving together in an open car on a sunny afternoon, as the Maxes did, and dancing on terraces at the country club.

What touched it off, no doubt, was Maxine's announcement party. The account of it appeared in the paper, written up in detail. It had, in fact, taken up the entire society column that day. According to the writer, no more lavish affair had graced the country club since the Chrysanthemum Balls before the crash. The decor, the floral arrangements, the lovely gowns, the elegance of the gentlemen, and the joyful spirits, the orchestra that played until two in the morning. Lovely, all of it, lovely, lovely. Allen read it a number of times.

She was not envious of Maxine, but envious of what Maxine could do—wear evening clothes and go to dinner, have lunch with her lover, dance until two and drink champagne (she supposed, though the paper didn't come right out and say so). Maxine lived in a world where such things were sanctioned. Besides, in a few weeks she would no longer be part of the school. The rest of them would be. And in their world, one did not ride around with a lover in the middle of the day. Even if one had a car.

Restrictions notwithstanding, the wistful visions danced in her head, the glitter and glamour of a world where affairs of the heart were conducted with style and *éclat*. They were beyond her reach. She knew this well enough and never for a moment persuaded herself that they weren't. But neither did she concede that some approximation of such pleasures was not available to her. Casting about for some way to extend, to vary the pattern, keep it fresh and diverting, she came up with the notion of an intimate dinner party.

Just the two of them. A real dinner, not potato chips and cheese, but an elegant dinner for two, with candlelight and background music (that part was easy) and hors d'oeuvres, and wine. And just for the hell of it they could dress up.

The idea struck her all of a heap on a Sunday afternoon, when Toby was home and writing a paper and George was practicing and Monday was eons away. Letting no grass grow, she got herself dressed, sashayed off to the Bonne Terre Hotel, and after leafing through the women's magazines at the newsstand, bought two of them and hurried home. She studied them thoroughly and spent the rest of the afternoon agonizing over a menu and how to get the kitchen table through the door into the living room.

The dinner party occupied her for the next three days. But at last, guided by the magazines and memories of intimate dinners in the movies (with William Powell or Charles Boyer), she had it planned to the last detail. And on Wednesday night, before Toby was about to leave, she issued her invitation.

"Saturday night," she said, "about seven."

"Oh nuts! Murdstone has invited somebody for dinner that night and I have to be there."

"Can't you get out of it?"

"Not without a row. I'll come over later, soon as I can get away."

"But I have it all planned. Isn't there some way you could weasel out?"

"There must be."

"I wish you could."

"Let me work on it."

It was Friday noon before she saw him again. The halls were clearing for the lunch hour. She had started toward the lounge when George hailed her from down the hall. "Hiya, Teach, want to go eat? I didn't eat lunch at home, so I could come early."

"Sorry, I—"

"Hey, Tobe!" Toby was coming up the stairs from the lockers. "Want to go eat with us?"

"Sure," Toby said.

"I can't," Allen said. "Wish I could, but we're taking Maxine to lunch."

"Do you have to go? Let the rest of 'em take her."

"No, I have to go. I'm one of the bunch."

"We're a bunch too. Come with us, you'll have more fun."

"I know that. But not this time. I've got to go now."

"Hey, wait, Teach."

"I'm already late."

"Look, I've practiced till I'm blue in the face. Want to go to the movies tomorrow night? I'll be done with my audition and need to blow off some steam"

"Well, I—"

"They're showing *Rebecca* at the Osage."

"Oh boy! I'd love to see it, but—" She glanced at Toby—there was a look in his eyes that gave him dead away—and hastily back to George. "But I can't. I'm tied up tomorrow night."

"Tomorrow's Saturday," George said. "You don't have to go out with the biddies on Saturday night!"

"It's not the biddies," she protested, laughing. "And keep your voice down."

Slowly George took off his glasses. "Hear that, Tobe? There's another man in her life."

"Sure there is," she said. "Cary Grant."

"All right, abandon us. See if we care. We'll get over it, won't we, Tobe?"

"Oh, go on away! You are not abandoned. I just happen to have something else cooking for a change."

"Cooking! You hear that, Tobe? For who or whom?"

"Cary Grant."

Again the quick glance at Toby, who had said nothing. "George dear, I can't and that's that. Really."

"Oh. Okay. Well, better luck next time. You want to go, Tobe?"

Toby hesitated only a second. "Jeez," he said, "I can't go either. My folks got something planned."

"You mean I've got to spend Saturday night by myself? And after my audition, you don't want to help me celebrate?"

"They'd be mad as hell if I don't stay home."

"Poor George," said Allen. "Why can't we all go Sunday night?"

"I got a paper to do."

"Do it tomorrow night."

"I don't want to write a paper after I've been to Kansas City."

"I'm really sorry, George."

"Oh well, what the hell. I'll find somebody else to go to the movies. You guys have fun with your folks—and Cary Grant." He grinned and socked Toby on the arm. "Let's go eat."

She lingered a moment, watching them lope off up the hall. He would come to her dinner party! Covering her excitement, she put on a sober face and went in to join the Ladies. They were waiting for her. Verna was in a swivet.

Thirteen

$\mathcal{S}$he had said about seven. She was ready by six, the salad in the refrigerator, slices of baked ham covered with brown sugar and waiting in the oven, and she, bathed and sneezing in a cloud of Houbigant, was all dressed up in her brand-new dress, a red checkered affair with a long skirt and straps that crossed over her bare back. She looked nice, she thought. Maybe a bit skinny for a low-cut dress. But fetching. The straps helped.

In the living room the kitchen table, maneuvered through the door earlier in the day, was covered with a white cloth, with candles in clear glass holders (bought at the dime store along with two wineglasses), and two gardenias afloat in a cereal bowl. She surveyed it happily, breathing in the heavy, distinctive perfume of the flowers.

Seven o'clock came but no Toby. She was already nervous, and by 7:30 she began to be jumpy. Maybe he had not been able to get away and wasn't coming at all. But no. That look on his face yesterday noon—he would be here. Ten minutes later she lit the candles. Then she blew them out. Using a kitchen chair as a barre, she did some leg extensions and a few *pliés*. At the bathroom mirror she combed her hair again and touched up her lipstick. Any minute now she was going to be sick. By the time the screen door opened, after eight, she was furious with him.

"Hi," he said.

"Well! I thought maybe you'd changed your mind."

"Am I late?"

"You know damn well you are."

"I'm sorry. I had to stick around long enough to be polite. Anyway, I thought I ought to wait till it got dark, sort of."

He stood there, hesitant, in his good suit, with a starched white shirt and a tie. Straight and sturdy and dark, glossy from soap and water and a touch of the razor. There was a luster about him, like a polished apple. She wanted to bite into him. "Come on in," she said, forgiving him everything.

"Oh—here," he said as they went into the living room, "I thought I'd better return this." It was her copy of A *Portrait of the Artist*, borrowed weeks before. "Figured it was about time."

"Oh, that. I meant you to keep it. You like it so much."

"Nah, it's your book. I wouldn't feel right about it."

"But I'm giving it to you. Don't you understand?"

"But I—"

"I'll get another copy."

He laid the book on the table. "No, you keep it. Thanks anyway."

"But I thought—" she said, and stopped.

Toby sank into the big chair. "Looks nice," he said of the room.

She hesitated, with a wistful glance at the book. "Thank you." But then she smiled. "Want to light the candles?" (Give them something to do, the magazine said, make them feel at ease.) He stood up, fumbling in his pockets. "There are matches on the table," she said.

"Oh. I didn't see."

She drew the blinds partway and set the music going. Then she came to him and lifted her face. "Kiss me. Like you mean it." She took his arms and put them around her and for a moment he held her. "Would you like some wine?"

"Yes, thanks."

They talked across the room, saying nothing of consequence, in short sentences with gaps between them. Toby drank his wine at a gulp. She noticed and pretended not to. After a bit she rose and refilled his glass. This time he timed his drinking to hers. After two glasses she went to the kitchen and lit the oven.

Always before, when she'd scrambled eggs after the movies, or late afternoons when they walked her home from school, the boys would be all over the kitchen, astraddle the chairs, in her way at the icebox door, rattling potato chips out of the sack, washing their hands at the sink. This time she had to invite him in.

"You can toss the salad," she said. "Better take off your coat."

"How do I do this?" he said.

"Just pick it up with the spoon and fork and sort of throw it around." She poured more wine and Toby loosened up a little as he harried the lettuce.

"Kee-rist," he said, dropping the salt shaker. "Ol' butterfingers."

"Bad luck. Throw some over your shoulder."

"Which one?" His hand struck the salad spoon, knocking it to the floor. "Oh, for godsake! Where's a mop—anything?"

"Don't worry. It's good for the linoleum. Did you get oil on your shirt?"

"I don't think so. I better get out of here before I mess up the whole place."

"Have some more wine."

"I wouldn't dare." He poured himself another, drank it off, and filled both glasses again.

"You can take them in to the table, if you want to. We're almost ready."

"Do you trust me to get there with them?"

"Frankly, no."

"Then we better drink 'em here."

They lifted their glasses, said *mud in your eye*, and laughed. It was beginning to be all right. They made a parade, bearing food to the table. Toby put on his jacket.

But seated at table they were awkward again. Eating made them self-conscious. They made small talk, hewed, hacked, and carved out of wooden silence. Mostly they kept their eyes on their plates, horribly aware of the sound of their chewing. They had ice cream for dessert, with chocolate sauce. Toby gulped it in silence and looked up guiltily, seeing that she had not finished.

"I'll clear the dishes," she said. "Won't take a minute."

"Should I help?"

"You relax, make yourself comfortable."

When she came back he was sitting primly in the big chair. She put Debussy on the phonograph and curled up on the sofa.

"Come over here with me," she said. She made him take off the jacket again and plumped up the cushions for him. "I found a wonderful poem for you."

It was a lyric by Elinor Wylie, gently sad, full of lovely words. Toby listened with his eyes closed. After a long pause he said, "That's nice."

"I love it." She wriggled in against him. "Clair de Lune" filled the silence, which grew longer and longer. He wasn't talking and she was running out of things to say. He sat stiff and straight, one arm dutifully around her.

There was something she had done wrong. It ought to have worked. The room was pretty, the candles gave a soft light, the music was soft and soothing in the background. But it wasn't any *fun*. She said, on a sudden inspiration, "Let's have some coffee!" and, remembering the article (give them something to do), "You make it while I get the cups."

"I don't know how."

"Oh, you can make coffee, can't you?"

"I can't even drink it."

She laughed. "Then we just won't bother."

"You have some if you want it."

"I don't like it that well, myself." She turned the record and they sat silent again, listening to "La Mer."

Toby stared across the room, one of his solemn spells, as if there were something he disapproved of. "Who did you say the artist was?"

"The composer? You know, it's Debussy. We've played it hundreds of times."

"The picture," he said with a lift of his chin toward the opposite wall.

"Oh, that. That's Renoir."

He went on staring without comment. She thought of telling him something about Renoir, but she had been over that before, with him and George. And tonight he had not said, "Talk to me."

"I want to dance!" she said, jumping up. She stopped Debussy in his groove and replaced it with Benny Goodman.

When they had danced in silence through "Moonglow," she put on another record, and Bing Crosby's cozy voice oozed into the room.

Soft lights and sweet music
And you in my arms—
Soft lights and sweet melody
Will bring you closer to me . . .

With scarcely room enough to turn, they danced close together, her head tucked under his chin like a violin. One of the candles burned out. The other flickered, and the music went on, smooth and seductive. They danced in place, barely moving.

Chopin and pale moonlight . . .
Reveal all your charms.
So give me velvet light and sweet music . . .

The other candle went out, leaving the room lit only by the glow from the kitchen. They had stopped dancing. They stood wrapped in each other, letting the needle grind on.

Suddenly then, Toby let go. He turned to the record player, took the needle off and slammed the lid. "I hate that music!"

She looked up with a startled smile.

"All those sappy love songs," he said.

"I thought you liked them."

"I want to hear a buzz saw—a jackhammer."

"We can't dance very well to a jackhammer."

"Why do we have to dance all the time?"

"Why not?"

"I'm sick of it, that's why."

She looked at him, uncomprehending, and he turned away. "I'm sorry," he said and picked up his jacket.

"Toby? What's wrong?"

"I don't know."

"I have a right to know, haven't I?"

"It's a goddam hothouse," he said, flinging the jacket down.

"Well, if that's how you feel about it—!"

"We're swimmin' around in pancake syrup."

"You're mixing your metaphors."

"Screw metaphors!"

"What's *wrong* with you, Toby?" They faced each other in the dim room, angry for the first time.

"The whole thing is a goddam mess."

"What thing?"

"The whole world," he said, "and we sit around reading poetry."

"What's wrong with that?"

"I don't know. But it is."

"Would it help if we didn't?"

No answer. Then with a sweep of his arm, "All these goddam pillows and candles and stuff—I've had 'Clair de Lune' up to here! And that stinking flower!"

"Well, why didn't you say so? I thought you liked it."

"I do like it. Or maybe I don't. Hell, I don't know what I like anymore. I just want to blow up the bridge."

"Then go off and be Hemingway if you want to."

"I'd rather build a bridge—anything but sit around all the time and listen to sappy music."

"Then why do you come here?"

"I almost didn't tonight!"

She turned her back, stung.

"No, I didn't mean that," he said. "I mean I wanted to come, but I got talking to the man from Washington who Murdstone invited over for dinner. He works in some government agency."

"You were talking to him all that time?"

"Well, not all the time. But just to listen to him—"

"What were you talking about?"

"Washington. And Germany and what's going on over there that we never hear about. I never knew the Germans were building planes in Russia and Italy before the war! Fighters and bombers. They couldn't build 'em at home because of the treaty, so they by God built 'em in those other countries and let on they were civilian planes. And now Mr. Holloway says there are rumors around Washington that the Nazis are planning to invade Russia and Roosevelt knows it. Good God, they're already in Greece. And blitzing Great Britain and sinking merchant vessels with their goddam U-boats! The war's bustin' out all over the place. And we're going to get sucked into it—George and me and Spike, all us kids. And I want to know as much about it as they'll tell me. So I just kept asking questions and Mr. Holloway kept on answering and we talked all through dinner—"

"You had *dinner*?"

"I didn't eat very much. But he was so interesting and he was talking to *me*, not to Murdstone all the time. Jeez, I could have listened to that man all night. But I promised you I'd be here, and I wanted to come, but we just kept talking and Oh hell, I'm sorry!"

She looked up at him for a long moment and turned her back again. "I'm sorry too," she said. "For everything."

"It was my fault."

"I shouldn't have planned all this. I just thought it would be fun."

"It was nice."

"No, it wasn't. I wish I'd never thought of it. You could have talked to the man all night, like you wanted to."

"But I wanted to come here too."

"Then why did you say all those hateful things?"

"Because—hell, I don't know why. I don't hate it, not all the time. Only tonight, it seemed like there were more important things—no, I don't mean that. But it seemed like . . . I'm *sorry*, Allen."

"Maybe you'd better just go."

"I don't want to go."

"Maybe your man's still there. If you're more interested in him than me—"

"Don't talk like that."

"From what you said—"

"I don't care what I said, I like it here. You're skinny and bossy and you don't know nuthin' but poetry and I still want to be where you are. I do and I don't. I'm all mixed up," he said, near tears. "Allen?" He turned her around and pulled her up hard against him. "I want to stay. Please?"

His hands were on her bare back, and he was kissing her, not in the old way, but rough and greedy and over and over.

"Toby—"

His mouth was on her throat, her shoulders. His heart pounded against her like hooves on a hard road. This was not soft and cozy as they'd always been. This was real. It was dangerous. And she liked it.

"Toby—" she said, breathless. Whatever was happening, she had asked for it—with the dim light and the wine and the naked dress, and what if Toby—

But Toby had let go of her. He turned away, clutching the back of the big chair, and drew a long shaky breath. "Yeah," he said in a dry whisper, "I better go." He picked up his jacket and started toward the kitchen.

"Toby?" A whisper.

He paused in the doorway without turning.

"I'm sorry."

"You don't have to be."

"I only meant—"

"It's okay."

"Next time . . . you'll come back?" she said, fearful.

He beat the doorjamb once, gently, with his fist. "Yeah," he said.

She heard him go through the kitchen, heard the screen door open and quietly close, and the soft sound of his footsteps hurrying down the stairs.

Fourteen

O h, it's lovely! Look at this!"
        Maxine lifted a luncheon cloth from the
tissue. "And napkins to match! They're beautiful." Sliding a perfect fingernail under the flap, she opened the small envelope and
drew out a card. "And this is from . . . Verna! *Thank* you, Verna.
My goodness, all these lovely things!"

She sat in Mrs. Dean Frawley's living room, surrounded by
boxes and tissue paper, all the faculty women, and the wives of
the faculty men. Turning her blue-violet gaze upon them, she
gave them a helpless smile. "You've been so nice, really. I don't
know how to thank you."

"You don't have to," said Verna. "The pleasure's ours."

"Oh, but it's mine! And I do thank you all so much. You're all
so generous. It's been wonderful working with you this year. I'm
going to miss every single one of you."

"The married ones too?" said Gladys.

"All of you," said Maxine. "I've loved my work, and all you
lovely people." She smiled, blinking a tear.

"Aw, don't cry!" Verna said in disgust.

"Oh no!" cried Mrs. Frawley. "Let's not *cry* about it, dear. We
can't have our little girl crying, can we? Come along now, you

have more presents to open. And *then*," she said with a wink at the others, "we have a surprise! Haven't we, girls?"

The girls agreed they certainly did have. They had worked on the bridal shower for days; conspiracies in the faculty lounge, and much whispering and rushing about. All this going on in the last three weeks of school, in the midst of finals and term papers, with the main events bearing down upon them—commencement and, of course, Maxine's wedding.

"Monograms!" said Maxine, opening another package. "How pretty! Mae Dell, you didn't! I'll bet you did—you're so artistic—and with your own hands too."

"They'd have been better maybe if I'd had them done at the Singer place. But I thought you'd like the personal touch."

"They're perfect. I love them. So will Max. I don't know how you found the time."

Against the wall, between a window and the baby grand, Dr. Ansel's mother sat alone on a rose velvet love seat. She looked left out. She always did. Perhaps because she preferred it that way. But in case she didn't, Allen moved over to sit beside her and ask how she was.

"I can't complain," Mrs. Ansel said in her small childlike voice.

She was a stout little woman, straight up and down, with no perceptible waistline except where the belt went around. She wore a navy blue dress with a crocheted collar, and navy blue shoes. The straps across the instep cut into the flesh. The feet were puffy. (A heart condition, Dr. Ansel said.)

Allen said, "I suppose you're going to the wedding?"

"I expect we will. Clarence wants to go."

"It's going to be a beautiful wedding, from all I've heard about it." Mrs. Ansel didn't reply. "I like your collar," Allen said, trying again. "Is it hand crocheted?"

"Yes ma'am."

"It's pretty work. Did you do it yourself?"

"Yes ma'am, I did."

"It's lovely."

"Thank you." The little woman glanced at her with the merest glimmer of a smile in her small pale eyes and turned to watch Maxine open another package.

At the window the curtains parted in a breath of wind. It carried the scent of damp earth and fresh-cut grass. Under the orchestration of voices, the predictable inflections and antiphonals, she heard the wind browsing in the shrubs beneath the window. She shifted against the rose velvet, recrossed her legs, and turned resolutely to join the party. Her body was here under protest, unaccompanied by the mind. Her thoughts were twelve blocks away. And she was frantic with impatience to run for home, obsessed by the notion that Toby was waiting for her.

By all that was reasonable and sane, she should not want him back. And she had no reason to think he would come. He had made no promise, not a real one. But how could he not come, after all those nights? She was important to him. If he hadn't meant it, why did he say it? And if she mattered that much, he must intend to come back. After last night, surely he'd want, as she wanted, to set thing aright between them again. He could at this very minute be waiting on the landing.

"I love that design!" Maxine held up a rectangle of embroidered linen. "Pineapples! Aren't they beautiful—they're so different, so unusual. Let's see . . . oh, from Mrs. Frawley! Thank you, Mrs. Frawley."

"In Hawaii," said Mrs. Frawley, who had traveled, "the pineapple is a symbol of hospitality."

"Isn't that lovely! I'd like to have the pineapple motif all over my house!"

Mrs. Frawley, twinkling with pride, handed Maxine another package. "Two more now, dear, and then the surprise!"

"Oh, good granny!" Allen muttered, unheard under the cackle.

It was her fault. It had begun in the faculty room, while they were planning the party. The faculty men were to join the party in time for refreshments, and the Ladies had decided that Max should be brought in—"in some real clever way"—as a special surprise. After a few lame suggestions, Allen had quipped, "Why don't we put him in a box and gift wrap him?"

"That's it!" Gladys said.

"I was kidding."

Mae Dell squealed. "That's *cute!*"

"I wasn't *serious.*"

"But it's such a cute idea."

"Oh, come on!" Allen turned to Verna, appealing to her better sense. "Tell them it won't work."

But Verna thought it just might, and Allen listened, in some horrification, as in spite of her protests—Max would never do it, who was going to ask him, where would they find a box that would hold him—the Ladies took the idea and ran.

And any minute now, the surprise would come, special delivery, brought in by the faculty men: a cardboard box with a reinforced bottom and a bow on top, and inside—Max, all doubled up with his head on his knees, ready to spring out like a jack-in-the-box. The men were gathering now in the dean's backyard. She could hear them through the window, muted voices and the careful closing of car doors in the drive. What, she wondered, was dear Mr. Frawley making of all this!

Verna, glancing at her watch, vanished into the kitchen and reappeared, beckoning to Mae Dell. The Ladies glanced at one another. The tension was mounting and Maxine still exclaiming with her pleasure.

"Excuse me," Allen said into Mrs. Ansel's ear, "I have to leave early. It's been nice to see you again."

"Yes ma'am."

"I hope we'll see you at the wedding."

She rose and worked her way bit by bit around the edge of the circle. Under cover of the general hubbub she leaned over Mrs. Frawley's shoulder. "I have to leave a little early," she whispered. "Thank you for a lovely party."

"Isn't that cute?" said Mrs. Frawley as Maxine lifted a figurine out of the tissue. She cocked her head enough to turn an ear toward Allen. "What was that, dear?"

"I'm sorry, I have to leave early."

"Now who is that from?" Mrs. Frawley had not taken her eyes off Maxine.

Allen edged away unnoticed, slipped through the double

doorway into the entrance hall, opened the front screen, closed it soundlessly behind her, and fled.

Hair blown back and the damp wind on her face, she ran up the empty street away from the cackle and gabble. She was sorry to run away. They were good women; they were her friends and she was attached to them. They were like blood kin to whom, though she might not have chosen them, she was bound by common ties. And Maxine was very gallant. She would have liked to join in with a whole and willing heart, but the heart wasn't in it. Remorseful and eager, she ran pell-mell toward home. It was close to seven P.M.

She had reached her corner when a figure emerged from the shadows, coming toward her with a familiar loose, loping stride.

"George!" she cried out, running to meet him. He was the next best thing, and where he was, Toby mightn't be far away.

"What are you doing out here? Where've you been?" he said.

"Over at the Frawleys'. Shower for Maxine. Come on up, I've got some beer."

"Sounds good."

"Where've *you* been?" she said, running ahead of him up the steps.

"Orchestra practice. I walked Lulie Moss home after."

No one was waiting on the landing. Though she had left the door unlocked, Toby was not inside.

"There's some potato chips in the cupboard," she said, going into the other room. No Toby there either, though she'd known he wouldn't be. Taking her saddle shoes out of the closet, she said innocently, "Where's your sidekick tonight?"

"Damned if I know," George said from the kitchen. "He was supposed to be at rehearsal, but he wasn't there."

Where was he then? She stopped with one shoe on.

"Shall I get out the beer?"

"Bottom shelf. You know where the glasses are."

Where was he? And how was he? She went back to the kitchen and sat down at the table, sick with worry.

The beer didn't help much. It didn't do much for George either. Neither of them could drum up much fun. They tried, but the laughter was forced and the wisecracks not very wise. And anyway, George was gloomy about yesterday's audition. "I played that damn sonata better than I ever played it in my life, and when I finished they didn't say a word. None of 'em. The not knowin' is the hard part," he said.

"Didn't they even smile?"

"Yeah, one of them did. They thanked me politely and said I would be hearing from them, and Mr. Delanier and I came on home. That was it."

"Well, George, I wouldn't worry about it too much. It's a committee, and you know how committees are—they have to go off and confer, hash it around a while before they commit themselves."

"Yeah, I guess."

"But they might have said something and not kept you dangling like this. That was mean."

George stared gloomily into his beer, and for a moment only the crunch of potato chips broke the silence. She thought Toby should come by and say something too; she was dangling as much as George.

"I wonder where he *is*?" she said. She hadn't meant to say it, it just slipped out.

"Who? Oh. Home studying, maybe. I don't know." He drained his glass and stood up. "Gotta go, Teach. Thanks for the beer."

"George—I'm sorry about last night, I'm sorry I couldn't go to the movies."

"That's okay."

"I don't have to do anything Friday night. If you and Toby want to come over, we could have a sandwich or something and go to the movies after."

He picked up his empty glass and set it down. "I guess I'm the one who's tied up next weekend."

"Oh?"

"Amy Jean Proctor's having a party."

"Oh. Well, that'll be fun."

"I'm going to take Lulie."

"That's nice."

"Little ol' Lulie," he said, grinning.

"She's cute."

"Those white eyebrows. And that funny little lisp. 'What I don't underthtand, Mith Maxthine . . .' But she sure plays the fiddle good."

"You'll have a good time."

"Yeah. Thought I'd better show up at one of those parties. I haven't gone to one for quite a while. And school's almost over. Well, see you in the halls. Oh," he said, turning with his hand on the screen, "I'd better take my bike."

"It's not in my way."

"I better take it though. I been grabbin' the bus too much. Got to start savin' my money."

"Guess you better." She held the screen open while he walked it out. "How did you ever get it up and down these stairs?"

"It wasn't easy."

"Here, let me help you."

"Nah, that's okay. I can make it. See ya, Teach. Thanks."

"Glad you came by. Let me know if you hear anything about the scholarship."

"I will."

She sat down again at the table, the glass between her elbows, a swallow of beer left in it. The bubbles winked and went out. Foam shrank and dried around the edges.

In the Frawleys' living room they would be drinking coffee now out of Haviland cups, nibbling the heart-shaped cakes around the table they had dressed like a bride in white lace. Max and Maxine would behave as they were expected to, royalty for the season and perhaps forever after. But she couldn't hold that against them.

Maybe they'd think she went to the john.

She rose and brushed away the crumbs of potato chips. Putting the light out, she stood a moment at the door, listening. Well, anyway, he would never arrive, Max-in-the-box, with a bow on top!

She hooked the screen, turned back and unhooked it, and went to bed.

Fifteen

*M*onday and Tuesday passed, then Wednesday, and still no sign of Toby, though she stayed at home every night and waited. Sometimes she played records to keep from listening for him. When she could stand it no longer, she turned the music off. In the silence her two rooms echoed like a barn, and the emptiness where the bicycle had stood was a rebuke. Even George didn't come by to report the results of his audition.

In the mornings she hurried to school, eager to get there, where she could catch glimpses of Toby. That's all it was, only glimpses and an occasional quick greeting as they passed in the hall. In the afternoons she stayed late in her classroom, hoping he might come in. So far, no one had come except Dr. Ansel.

On Thursday Ansel came in exultant, waving a long white envelope. Earlier in the afternoon Mr. Frawley had handed around the contracts for the coming year.

"Well, looks like we're going to work again."

"Looks like it," she said.

"I'm sure glad to know."

"Yes, so am I."

"Good teaching jobs don't grow on trees."

"Not in this climate. We're lucky."

"You can say that again." He nodded sagely. "Sure is a relief to get the contract. Ever hear of a board waiting this late?"

"Guess I hadn't thought about it."

"They've been a little slow this year. I wasn't really worried, understand. I figure I stand pretty high with Souder. That's what counts, since he's head of the board. I'm in pretty good with that Medgar woman too, I think."

"It doesn't pay not to be. She's a tough one."

"Ah, she's all right if you know how to handle her."

"She has a mean heart."

"Well, she's got problems, you know. That invalid husband, for one thing."

"Oh?" said Allen, remembering the photograph in Mrs. Medgar's parlor.

"Something wrong with him. Lost his mind, I've heard, something like that. They had a kid, a son, but something happened to him. Drank himself to death, some say. The report I read said he was killed in an automobile accident somewhere up by Chicago. I found it in the files down at the newspaper office."

"I didn't know about all that."

Ansel always knew everything about everybody. "You don't hear much about it. If the old gal ever caught anybody talking about her, she'd probably take 'em to court."

"I heard she used to teach here in town."

"Thirty years, in the grades and then the high school. So she's got her notions about it. Anyway, we've got our contracts. It's a relief to know I can pay the taxes on the place again next year." A worried frown came over his face. "Mother wants me to resign."

"Why?" she said.

"She wants me to get down to the farm as soon as school's out and stay there. She thinks we're going to get into the war, thinks if I'm putting in crops and milking cows, they won't draft me."

"She's right, isn't she? Farmers will surely be exempt. My brother's a farmer and he has a family. They couldn't take him, could they?"

"Well, if things get worse, who knows? But I'm not a farmer. I'm an educator, and I'm not about to quit a good job and give up my chances for advancement. If they let Frawley go this year—"

"You don't really think they will?"

"You never can tell."

"Have you heard anything?"

"Not yet. But I wouldn't be surprised if that's what held them up. They were debating over him. The old man just may get let out this time."

"I'd hate to see that happen."

Ansel grinned. "That's right, you were the holdout, weren't you?"

"I like Mr. Frawley."

"Ah, I like him all right. But we need a younger man."

She made no reply to that, and after a few more comments Ansel excused himself to take his mother to the grocery store.

"By the way," he said, "I'll have the car out. Guess you wouldn't want to take a little spin this evening?"

It was not the first time he had asked her out. He had done so often here of late, flying in the face of faculty ethics. He had been so persistent that at last, two weeks ago (with a fleeting vision of Toby) she had told him she was "going steady." She didn't say engaged, but Ansel took it to mean that and it cooled him a bit; he was very proper. But now and then he still tried.

"How about it?" he said. "A little breather after supper?"

"Thanks, I'm afraid not."

"You sure? Just for a little while, go get a Coke or something?"

"I really can't."

He shook his head. "Too bad you met that guy first."

She was on the verge of saying what guy, but managed to say she hadn't meant it that way. "I've got work to do. Look at this stack of papers!"

"Yeah, okay. Well, don't work too hard."

He went away and she sat for a moment staring out the window at the street. Then, turning her attention to the work, she began to read.

Except for an occasional voice in the hall, the building was quiet. She heard Lordy and Pickering passing a comment, and the occasional slam of the outside door as someone left. Presently from upstairs came the sound of singing. Maxine, rehearsing the chorus again, George at the piano, Toby among the baritones.

The stack of term papers went down slowly. Taking up another, she smoothed it open. "The Seasons as Depicted in Oliver Goldsmith." She made her way through the handwritten sentences, underlining here and there in red, with notations in the margin. The next paper attempted an analysis of Andrew Marvel. She laid it aside and rifled through the others, reading titles. "Love in the Writings of My Faverite Poets." A swayback purple hand, circles over the i's, under the title a broad flourish, and under that an extravagant purple flower. That was one thing Lindsey Homeier could do: he could draw.

Lindsey's "faverite" poets consisted solely of Elizabeth Barrett Browning. She read the first three pages and stopped to count the rest. Lord have mercy, seventeen. But of course, Lindsey's handwriting was large. "Miss Browning"—she circled the "Miss," wrote "Mrs." in the margin—"uses many large words and you can't always understand her but if you read between the lines you can understand her. . . . When she says Thee and Thou she does not mean God as we do in Church. She means the person who was going to be her husband . . ."

From the second floor there came a roar of laughter. She looked up, listening. It went on for fully a minute, followed by abrupt silence and, after another minute or two, more singing.

"She used to lay awake nights" (another red circle and "Gr" in the margin) "and dream about him. That was not because she was a sick woman. She was sick but some might say she was lovesick too."

Bravo, Lindsey.

"Miss Browning's poems are famous for their universilty. Everyone knows what they mean because everyone feels the same way about somebody. When you love somebody you want to write poems."

Skipping through the pages she learned that "Miss Browning's" sweetheart had "adducted her to Italy where they were warm and got married." Then a paragraph about marriage. Lindsey was in favor of it. "Miss Browning had long brown hair but short brown hair is nice too especially when its curly like some peoples that I know." (Oh dear.) "When Miss Browning counts the ways she loves there are a lot of them. I can think of lots more."

She had stopped making corrections. Swept up in Lindsey's purple prose, she read on through the slaunchways declaration with an amused frown on her face. She looked up only as someone went past the door singing "The Hut Sut Song."

George and Toby. George backtracked a couple of steps and looked in. "What are *you* doing here?"

"I work here," she said. "Come in."

"Hey, you didn't find a stray library book, by any chance?"

"In here? No. Have you lost one?"

"I laid it down somewhere."

"Not in here, you haven't been here."

"Thought somebody else might have picked it up."

"Maybe they turned it in."

"I checked. It's not in the library. I better go look in the gym."

"What book was it?" she said, trying to keep them there. Toby had followed George in but was hanging back by the door. He hadn't said a word, hadn't even so much as looked at her.

"A history book—American politics nineteen hundred to nineteen something. I had to do a paper on it."

"You guys been pretty busy?"

"Up to the bustle-bone," George said.

"Maxine's sort of working you overtime."

George looked over at Toby and grinned.

"I heard you up there this afternoon. How'd it go?"

Both George and Toby's grins grew broader. "Oh, it went just fine," George said.

Toby sputtered, trying not to laugh out loud. "What's so funny?" she said. "Have you two been up to no good again?"

"Aw, we didn't do anything. Much."

At that, they exploded, unable to hold it any longer. She was laughing with them, though she didn't know why. "Well, tell me!"

Red in the face, Toby moved into the room now, leaned against the blackboard.

"Come on, you guys."

"Well, it was this song," George said and choked up again. "Ol' Tobe said something lewd in the baritone section."

"How do you know?" said Toby. "You were up there at the piano."

"Your lips were moving, and it wasn't in song."

"You were *thinking* lewd things."

"What did you say?" she said. "Tell me!"

"Well, this new song she wants us to sing"—George let out a whoop—"an iddle, a lay." Pulling himself together he sang solemnly, "'Where the bee sucks, there suck I.'"

"Oh Lord!" said Allen. The line never failed to throw a class into titters. "She doesn't expect you to sing that! In public?"

"She does. She kept tapping her baton and everybody would straighten up and try. And then Toby would look at Spike and Spike'd break up and the girls were all laughing, even if they didn't know why."

"The altos knew," Toby said. "Altos always know."

"And Miss Maxie kept saying, 'E*nunc*iate!' And then she said, 'Clearly, boys and girls. Separate the suck-k-k from the I.'" George cocked his head and looked at Toby. "Then Toby said, 'Miss Maxine, I'm sorry to say it, but this ode has intimations of immorality.' And Miss Maxie said, 'Why, what do you mean? This is Shakespeare!' And ol' Tobe said, 'Well, it sure ain't the Constitution!' And everybody fell on the floor. Whoo-ee!" said George, collapsing in the front row. "Poor ol' Miss Maxie, she thought she was going to have to call out the militia."

"She should have," said Allen, laughing, "You were terrible!"

"Ah, she took it pretty well."

"Yeah," said Toby. "Miss Maxie's okay."

"Too bad about her," George said.

"Sure is. *Orare*, Miss Maxie."

"Why?" said Allen.

"Gettin' hitched to that jerk."

"Max? He's a very nice man."

"He's so nice you can't stand him," George said.

"You don't even know him!"

"We see him around."

"Well, I've met him, and he is not a jerk."

Toby said, "You know how he got that commission, don't you?"

"How?"

"Politics. He knows a congressman."

"I know. He's a friend of theirs. I've heard Maxine say so."

"He sure was friendly to ol' Max."

"How do you know?"

"Murd was talking about it. Max got a reserve commission as a captain in the finance section. That takes an act of Congress."

"Is it against the law?" she said.

"Nah, it's legal, I guess."

"I don't think Max would do anything illegal."

"Not him," George said, "he's too nice."

"What have you kids got against Max?" she said.

"Nothing," he said cheerfully. "Except that he's a jerk."

"It's the breed," said Toby. *"Homo rotarianus kiwanus."*

"Pompous erectus. I bet Miss Maxie has to salute him every time he walks in. I can see her now, in a ruffled apron, standing at attention."

"After a hard day at the bank, when he comes home to his vine-covered mansion," said Toby

"At Three-point-nine Percent Lovers' Lane."

"Is that anywhere close to Sappy Avenue?"

Suddenly Allen didn't feel so jolly. Toby had said to her after the dinner that he was tired of listening to sappy music and poetry. Did he now consider her sappy like Maxine? It had been five long days since the dinner. She tried to read something in his face, but he and George were already off on another tear, moving the Maxes up in the world, from Happiness Hollow, hard by Rapture Road, through Ecstasy Springs, and up to Gloria in Excelsis Heights. "Smothered in honeysuckle vines!"

"'Where the bee suckles . . .'" George sang.

Now the boys sat in the front row, spraddle-legged, loose and easy. Their skin shone, brown from the spring sun. They were bright-eyed and limber. They were her boys again, the way they'd been in the early spring. It was good to laugh with them.

"Whoo-ee," George said again.

And she laughed softly in contentment.

Then suddenly the joke was over. It was gone, like that. Played out. They sat for a moment staring out the window at nothing. The silence grew uncomfortable. A minute ago they were all shuffled together by the laughter. Now they seemed to draw back from one another, as if, without the joke as protection, they were a little afraid.

She shot an anxious glance at Toby. Something else hung in the air, something unsaid, which ought to have been the most natural thing in the world for one of them to say: Let's go to the movies. . . . Let's go have a beer! Then everything would have been right again.

But nobody said it. And they were about to leave. Already, George was unwinding himself from the chair. "I guess I better go look for that book."

Toby stood up.

"Wait," she said, before she could stop herself. If he got away now, she might not see him again for another week, and then there would be only one more week and school would be over. "If you guys aren't too busy tonight, maybe we could—"

"Hello, Miss Liles." Lindsey Homeier walked in.

Addled, innocent Lindsey, bearing a bunch of purple irises in a tall glass vase.

"I brought you some flowers," he said.

"Why, how nice."

"Hi, Lins," said Toby.

The boy's gentle smile swung like a light across the boys and back to Allen. "I hope you like these."

"They're lovely. Thank you very much." She saw George and Toby making their way to the door. "You fellas leaving?"

"Gotta get home," George said. "See y' around, Teach."

"See ya," said Toby. But he didn't look at Allen. He gave Lindsey a friendly jab on the shoulder. "Don't cross the road without red suspenders."

"I won't," Lindsey promised.

She followed them out with her eyes.

"They're my favorite color."

Their footsteps down the stairs and the slam of the outside door.

"I like purple," he said.

"Oh. Yes—they're very pretty."

"I picked then myself, out of our yard. My mother let me bring them in this vase. It's an antique."

"My goodness."

"It's an heirloom. It'd cost quite a bit today, I guess."

"I'm sure it would. Let me see now"—she pulled open a drawer—"I'll just wrap these stems in paper—"

"Oh no, ma'am, I want you to keep it."

"The vase? You don't want to leave it here."

"I mean you should take it home with you."

"I should say not! It's an heirloom—I might break it."

"I could carry it for you."

"I think you'd better take it home. I'll find something to put the flowers in."

"But they look so nice in the vase. Anyway, it'll be mine someday, when I have a house of my own."

"Then I certainly wouldn't want to break it." She lifted the irises out of the water, holding them over the wastebasket to drip.

"But I want you to have it," he said. "I want you to keep it for me."

"I can't do that, Lindsey. What would your mother think?"

"She knows it'd be in good hands. She likes you."

"I'm glad she does. But I won't even be here—I'll be gone all summer."

"You're coming back next year, aren't you?"

"Yes, I am, but—"

"Then you keep it." He beamed with benevolence. "And I'll come over and see it sometimes to be sure it's all right."

Lord help her! How did he know that Toby and George came over? Did everyone? And did he think he could too? Poor Lindsey, who couldn't tell a topic sentence from a manhole cover and didn't know a noun from a horse! She picked up the vase and thrust it firmly into his hands. "You'll have to excuse me, Lindsey, I have a lot of work to do." She marched to the door and stood aside, inviting him out.

"I'd really like to get to know you better," he said, forced to follow. "You're my favorite teacher."

"Thank you, Lindsey. You'll have to excuse me now."

"You're not old-fogey like the others. You're more like one of us."

"Thank you very much for the flowers."

"I bet you're not much older than me."

"Than I, Lindsey!" She gave him a little push and shut the door on his heels.

"Miss Liles?" timidly, through the door.

She leaned on it, red with annoyance.

Again from outside, "I'll see you tomorrow."

For godsake, go away, Lindsey!

There was a shuffle of sneakered feet and, after a moment, silence. She opened the door and peered out. Lindsey was gone.

But so were Toby and George. She'd been so flustered she hadn't even asked George if he'd heard anything about the scholarship.

Gloomily she returned to the desk. "Oh hell!" she said. Lindsey had managed, after all, to leave the vase in her keeping.

"Well, as long as you're here—" She jammed the irises down into the water and picked up the red pencil.

As she did so, there was the sound of footsteps again in the hall. She rose quickly to close the door. But hearing Gladys's voice and Verna's, she started back to the desk, stopped on the way by something Gladys was saying.

"You said anything to Allen?"

Verna's voice in reply: "Haven't seen her. Have you?"

"Only for a minute in the lounge."

"You say anything?"

"I didn't think I should unless she did. If she didn't get it, it would be embarrassing."

"I'd sure like to know whether—"

The voice broke off. Dead silence. Allen tiptoed back to the desk and sat down just in time. The next moment, there was Verna, peering around the edge of the door. "You still here?"

Allen said she was.

Caught, Verna came on in, followed by Gladys. "We were just going by," said Gladys. "I didn't know you ever stayed this late."

"I've got a lot to do. Term papers."

"Where'd you get the flowers?"

"One of the kids brought them."

Gladys's bright little black eyes glittered. "Thought you might have a secret admirer."

"Who's got a secret admirer?" Mae Dell stuck her head through the door. "Oooh, look at the pwitty flowers. Did your secret admirer send them?"

"Let's go," said Verna.

"What's his name?" Did he enclose a card?"

"Only a term paper," said Allen.

"Oh shoot, that's not very romantic."

"Come on," Verna said, "the dime store's going to close before we get there."

"Is it that late?" Mae Dell buried her nose in the irises. "They smell so sweet."

"Come on. I've got to buy some Odorono."

"I just love flowers. Where we going to eat tonight?"

Gladys and Verna glanced at each other. "We'll decide later," Verna said. "Let's go."

But Mae Dell, her face lighting up, burst out with, "Oh, we're going to the Bonne Terre, aren't we? Isn't this the night? Didn't we say as soon as we got our contracts—"

"If you don't hurry up we won't get anywhere."

"I wanted to wear my new suit."

"You look all right. Come on, the dime store'll be closed."

"You-all came dressed up this morning. I didn't know we were supposed to do that. I want to look nice too."

"Well, go on then," said Verna, "but get a move on."

"It won't take me a minute."

"Gladys and I'll meet you in front of the store. 'Night, Allen."

"Isn't Allen coming with us?" Mae Dell paused in the doorway. The other two stopped, a funny look on their faces. "Do come," Mae Dell said. "You haven't gone to eat with us for a long time."

"She's busy," said Verna. "Can't you see all those papers she's got to read? Come on, you girls, let's get out of here and let her get to work."

"I'm sorry you can't come," said Mae Dell. "We'll miss you."

"Thank you," Allen said. "But I do have work to do."

She sat motionless, listening as the lounge door opened and shut and presently opened again and the Ladies went off down the hall. As the front door closed behind them she picked up the red pencil and looked down at Lindsey's paper, still open on the desk.

" 'It's hard to understand what Miss Browning says. But when she says I love her for her smile . . .' "

She stared at the purple page, no longer reading. They didn't want her to go to dinner with them. Not Verna anyway, and not Gladys. Why didn't they want her? They had always been a friendly bunch, asking her along for meals and trips to Kansas City. At least they used to. Until she turned them down so many times they stopped. Maybe that was the trouble. She thought back to the many times in recent weeks when she had made excuses. Maybe she shouldn't have. She should have gone out with them more often instead of going off to Sutt's Corner with the boys. But she doubted that the Ladies knew about that.

What was it then that Gladys didn't think she should say, that might be embarrassing? What did they think she might not have got? Her contract? But she did have it, right here, sealed in a clean white envelope. Maybe that was it—they weren't sure that she would be hired again. And why not? she'd like to know. The thought of Sutt's Corner and other such diversions ran through her head again.

For several minutes she stared across the classroom chairs at nothing. Then she drew a long breath and turned another page of Lindsey's paper. They had all got their contracts today, and the girls were splurging tonight and they didn't want her along.

Not that she wanted to go along. Although she might just as well have. She might as well be with them or in Butte, Montana, for all the good it would do her to stay at home and wait. If Toby meant to come back he would have said so, one way or another. There would have been some sign. Or maybe he was waiting for a sign from her. There would have been one too, if Lindsey Homeier hadn't walked in. Old Lindsey from Porlock. And there went Toby, and George with him, and there went the evening and there went another week, and that left only two weeks before school ended.

"Oh hell!" she wailed under her breath. She set her elbows hard on the desk, reached for the red pencil, and knocked over the heirloom vase. Purple sunbursts spread over Lindsey's paper and Miss Barrett Browning was all wet.

Sixteen

$\mathcal{I}$t was Friday, just after noon. Coming back from lunch, Allen arrived at the building just as Max's car was pulling up to the curb, a convertible with the top down, and Maxine beside him, her honey-brown head close to his shoulder. Max bent his head and kissed her, in public, in the broad light of day. But it was all right; they were about to be married.

"Oh, hi!" said Maxine as Max drove away. She wore a dress the color of her eyes. "You disappeared early from the shower. What happened to you?"

"I had to leave a little early. I'm sorry."

"You missed the surprise. It was such a cute idea—even if it did fall apart."

Allen had already heard about it from the Ladies. The box collapsed with Max's weight. The bottom dropped out and so did Max and it was a bigger surprise than they had expected. "Poor Max," Allen said. "It must have been embarrassing. Was he hurt?"

"Not a bit. And he was such a good sport. The girls felt terrible about it, but it wasn't their fault. It was such a cute idea. I'll bet you had a hand in it, didn't you?"

More than she cared to admit. But Maxine prattled on without waiting for an answer. "You're staying for the wedding, aren't you?"

"I wouldn't miss it."

"I should hope not! But honestly there's only a few weeks left and there's so much to do—I may miss it myself!"

"If you do, I'll stand in for the bride."

"Thanks, you're a pal." Maxine gave her a quick hug. "Oh, and thank you for the darling teapot. We just love it, both of us. You've all been so wonderful."

"It was easy."

Maxine was lit up like a marquee. Her skin glowed, the eyes were sapphires. Being in love could do that—tone up the skin, make the eyes sparkle, all the glands working overtime at the right things, the hormones doing whatever they did. It probably even cured warts.

"Oh gosh," said Maxine with a glance at her watch. "I'm ages late. Thanks again, Allen. See you in church!" The laugh ran up the scale as she ran up the walk in a flurry of blue voile.

"Well, anyway, I'll see you." Allen climbed the stairs slowly. She wasn't sure that being in love had cured much of anything for her. Maybe at first. But whatever it did was all undone now.

Down the hall a gang of girls stood at the gym door, in their midst, Toby and George. The two of them broke away and came up the hall, pleased as punch with themselves, whatever they'd been up to. Slaphappy and carbonated, in their crew-neck jerseys, George with one shoe on, the other one in his hand. She expected some creative explanation, but they simply said Hi and went on. Old Lordy was right behind them, looking abstracted. He merely nodded. Not even a wink out of him or an Oh-you-kid! But down by her door Dr. Ansel was lying in wait. She caught sight of him through a gaggle of kids. Neither she nor Ansel had a class that period and he was often lurking about, ready to take up her time. She was in no mood for Ansel today. Ignoring him, she ducked into the lounge.

"Why, it's Allen!"

Mae Dell, who was facing the door, announced her like the master of ceremonies. The other two heads, close together in the middle of the room, turned toward her, their mouths still open.

"H'llo," said Verna.

"We were just talking about the wedding," said Mae Dell. "Isn't it getting exciting?"

Gladys's smile spread ear to ear but she was, apparently too taken aback by the sudden entrance to say anything witty.

"Come on," said Verna, grabbing her pocketbook, "it's time for the bell."

The lounge door wheezed shut behind them.

Wedding, her hind foot. Allen stood at the big mirror, idly combing her hair. Whatever the secret was, they didn't want her in on it. That little sneaking voice of warning murmured again in her head. What did they know about her—the boys walking her home from school now and then, the three of them together at the movies? Just enough to gossip about behind her back. She guessed she wouldn't worry about it. Killing time, she smoothed her eyebrows, gave her teeth an absentminded examination, pulling her mouth this way and that, smiled prettily, and at last, when Ansel should be sufficiently discouraged, cautiously opened the door. He was gone. With any luck she was safe until four o'clock.

The after-lunch stupor invaded the building. In the safety of her room she listened for a moment to the fussing of a pair of jays in the maples just outside the window, then took out her notes for the two o'clock class. Her seminar on the novel had been the course she enjoyed most. But that had ended in mid-March. Next to that, she liked this class best—Engl. Lit. I—both the course and the students. Lively, bright, attentive kids, all of them (except Lindsey Homeier, who had to sit *some*place). She was teaching *The Tempest*. Appropriate to the end of the school year, when the kids would be released to summer and holiday. "Then to the elements / Be free, and fare thou well . . ." With the book open before her she ran through her notes for Acts IV and V, laughing to herself as she came to Ariel's final song. Where the bee sucks, indeed! After that performance by Toby and George, how was she supposed to get through this with a straight face? It would need some careful handling, especially since several in the class were also in the chorus. She turned to the passage and read through it again.

Lost in the dependable magic, she did not hear him come in. She looked up, startled by a discreet cough. "Oh, hello, Mr. Frawley!"

"Miss Liles," he said in his courteous way, "I wonder if you could come to my office?"

She went with him up the hall, passing the time of day and wondering briefly why he had come on this errand himself. Ordinarily, if he wanted a conference, he sent his secretary. The dean seemed distracted this afternoon, but then he usually did. His duties lay heavily on his shoulders. He was close to seventy, so they said. Maybe Pick and the others were right; maybe he was getting too old.

In the outer office the secretary looked up from the typewriter. "Hi, how are you?"

"Fine, thanks. How are you, Roberta?"

The dean ushered her into his sanctuary, closed the door, and pulled up a chair for her.

She sat easily, swinging her foot, and glanced about at the instruments on the walls, those that had so fascinated Toby. The dean had a passion for weather recorders—barometers, thermometers, humidity gauges, charts of wind patterns and cloud formations. On one wall an artist's rendering of a sailing ship, locked in ice, flanked a large framed map of the Arctic Circle. Beneath it a fine globe stood on a mahogany stand.

The dean sat down, brushed a speck from the polished desk, and picked up a paperweight. It was a particularly beautiful paperweight, a crystal globe holding simulated snow. Nothing else. No miniature house and pine trees, no Santa Claus, only the fine white particles, which sparkled, iridescent, as the weight was turned. He turned it once, watched the snow fall, and set it back.

"I hesitate," he said, and did so. Then making another start, "I'm reluctant to bring up this matter. However . . ." Another pause while he looked out the window. "I'm sure it's of no consequence—that is, no substance. But it's a matter of some concern, I suppose you might say."

The old gentleman was having trouble coming to the point. He spoke in bits and pieces, the sentences tending to lapse, unfinished. His mind was full of words, but like an old scholar among many books, he was obliged at times to stop and search for the one he wanted. She listened, faintly amused but puzzled.

"As I say, I'd rather not have to go into this at all. But I suppose as a formality . . ." He turned to face her. "It was Mrs. Medgar who brought it to my attention."

Allen's foot stopped swinging. Now what was eating that woman who wouldn't believe her name was Allen? "And I suppose as a courtesy to her—Mrs. Medgar seems to think that some reevaluation might be in order."

Reevaluation?

"We have to keep in mind that Mrs. Medgar takes great pride in the development of our college," he went on. "A proprietary interest, you might say. It's due in great part to her zeal that the school was established. The tax referendum. Without her efforts—"

He was interrupted by a peal of thunder. "Ah yes," he said and swiveled around to tap a barometer. "Down a bit from this morning." He checked the thermometer, rose, and went to the window. "Can't see much of the sky with the trees leafed out."

Money! Was that it? Were they—Lord help her!—about to cut the budget and eliminate her job? Since she was the newest faculty member and the youngest—

"I was saying—" The dean sat down and picked up the paperweight, holding it in both hands. He gazed into it as if for a clue to just what he *had* been saying. "Mrs. Medgar . . . as I say, she has been a conscientious guardian of our standing. We all want to maintain our standing, of course. We're a young institution in this city, and in our opening years, especially, we

want to do our best. Mrs. Medgar is right to demand it of us
. . . as we demand it from ourselves." Fidgeting and swiveling
in the hard oak chair. "I could wish, however, that she might
bring a little more . . . moderation, shall we say, to her guard-
ianship. She has brought up such matters once or twice in the
past, in other situations. But this time . . ." He turned toward
the window, letting the sentence hang. "Although I suppose
she is within her rights to question what might appear to her
to be irregular. Perhaps if you had more years in the teaching
field—"

Up from the cellar of her heart came a little warning squeak.
There was something else that Mr. Frawley was finding hard to
say.

"As I say, I feel sure it's of no real substance," he went on. "I
would find that hard to believe. But I can understand how you
might in all innocence—"

She sat very still, her eyes on his face.

"No doubt it seemed harmless enough at the time. But your
lack of experience might have led you to believe—well, I can see
how you might have made a mistake."

And then she was sure.

"Perhaps it is others who are mistaken. I hope so. Outward ap-
pearances are often misleading. But these rumors are of a rather
serious nature, and for Mrs. Medgar's sake . . ."

He faltered and plunged in again. "It seems certain stories
have reached her—I'm sure it's hearsay; I don't believe I have seen
any evidence—that you may have been a little too familiar, as it
were, with some of the student body."

"Oh," she said faintly, opening her mouth for the first time.

She smiled, with a modest dip of the head, but warily, knowing worse was to come.

"And so far as I'm concerned I see no harm in mingling with the students, being entertained in their homes on occasion. I'm sure the parents . . . and an occasional picture show. Chaperoning young people can be a pleasant experience from time to time." Here he straightened himself, placed his arms on the desk in good executive manner, and looked across at her. "However, Mrs. Medgar seems to see these things in a different light. In fact, I gather she puts some credence in the rumor that some of the students . . ." He turned toward the window. "It has been suggested that certain young men . . . have been known"—he turned to her with a face full of consternation—"to visit you at your home in the evening."

By the time he got there she was almost ready for him. She met the dean's gaze with no more than a look of astonishment. Then quickly gathering her wits, she laughed in disbelief. "Oh, for heaven's sake!"

The dean's face remained solemn, although he looked somewhat relieved. "I'm sure we agree this is hardly a laughing matter."

"Oh," she said quickly, "I didn't mean to imply—"

"Though I admit it's rather an excessive claim."

"Oh, but it's true!"

It was the dean's turn for surprise.

"They—a few of them—have been in my home. And I have gone out with them now and then—to the movies or—"

"That was mentioned."

"Maybe I shouldn't have. I just never thought about it. Some of the students from my seminar, we just sort of carried on informally. I'm interested in the theater and poetry, and some of them are very much interested too. We read *The New Yorker*, you know. The movies are hardly the same as the stage, but since it's all we have . . ." She raised her hands in a helpless gesture. The dean nodded. "Of course they walk me home from the movies, sometimes from activities at school. And sometimes—once in a while—I may ask them in for a few minutes. We talk—about their work—this and that—" She was feeling her way along. "About books and art. Several of them have quite an aptitude for literature. And we talk about books and the theater—rather like we did in the seminar!" she said eagerly.

"I see."

"When I was a graduate student we always went to our professors' homes in the evening. That was a little different, maybe. But I just never thought . . . We've had wonderful discussions. We read poetry . . . and listen to music. . . ." She was bumbling along, just as badly as the dean had.

"Yes. Well," he said, moving the paperweight, "I don't know that there's anything wrong in that. I'm sure you meant well. A little overenthusiasm, perhaps. . . . Let's see, you live where?"

She gave him the address. "About five blocks from here."

"I don't recall the house. You have a sleeping room?"

"I have an apartment. A kitchen and living room. It's a sort of penthouse."

"There are other tenants in the building?"

"Several. The owners live somewhere else, south, I believe."

"Are you acquainted with the other tenants?"

"Only to speak to as I see them going in or out. That's not very often. We all go our own way."

"And how do you go in and out, by a central stairway?"

"I have a private entrance. In plain view," she added quickly, "just off the street, in the back. The others go through the front."

"Ah. Has anything ever been said to you by the other tenants, about your visitors?"

"Nothing. Never." Though she marveled suddenly at their respect for her privacy. They could hardly not have known, some of them, that the boys were up and down those stairs day and night. "I don't have that many visitors," she added truthfully.

The dean nodded and sat for a moment, thinking. "Well, so far as I can see. . . . It was necessary, you understand, that I speak to you about it."

"Yes, of course." She drew a long, careful breath and leaned forward, ready to stand up.

But the dean had not yet dismissed her. Tilted back in his chair, he turned again to the window. "It may be a little difficult to convince Mrs. Medgar. I'm afraid she has certain biases. I realize the need for propriety on our part, however. The community demands certain standards of its teachers. Higher than for others, perhaps, but still, I can see the point. As teachers we're in charge of their children for a good part of their lives. We have an obligation to them. We not only have their minds to form, but their moral character as well. Any action on our part, any attitude, can leave its mark."

She kept her gaze steady.

"I often think of something Henry Adams once said: 'A teacher affects eternity.' A broad statement, but you grasp his meaning."

She nodded.

"What we do and what we say have an effect on the students. We influence them more than we know, for better or worse." There was a long pause and he went on, talking as much to himself, it seemed, as to her. "As teachers we can't always allow ourselves certain freedoms that others take for granted. Any lapses of dignity on our part, any thoughtless word or action, can be damaging. In the right circumstances, as damaging as more deliberate offenses . . . drinking, smoking, profanity, the teaching of atheism. Such as that. Although," he said with a wry smile over his shoulder, "I don't suppose smoking is considered a social disgrace these days; still, as teachers, we set an example." He turned back to the window. "We're older, we've had more experience than our students. Let us hope we have gained some wisdom from it. This necessarily sets us apart. By the time they reach college they should have a certain maturity. But we cannot expect them to behave strictly at an adult level, any more than we would wish to behave at theirs. And we have to remind ourselves that most of them at college level are still very young, very impressionable." He paused. "More so than they may seem, perhaps."

The dean swung around then, with a genial look on his face. "I'm not suggesting that any of us is in that particular danger. I hardly think that any of us would knowingly contribute to the delinquency of minors. As for these . . . rumors, I felt all along that they were overblown, a matter of hasty judgment. Even, I might say, a touch of resentment because of your youth. None of us likes to admit . . ." The thought trailed away. "And I feel certain," he went on, "that you would do nothing to jeopardize the reputation of our college."

"I would certainly not want to," she murmured.

"Nor your own."

"Nor that."

She looked up timidly but with a faint hopeful smile. He had delivered his sermon; it was time for the benediction.

"But I must add," he said, "that there is a serious implication here."

Her smile vanished.

"There is the matter of your continuation. Your employment here," he said in reply to her puzzled look. "You have your contract for next year. I believe I mentioned that the board reelected you unanimously."

She murmured something in appreciation.

"Mrs. Medgar did bring up the matter of your credentials, your lack of credits in education. But you'll take more hours through the summer and you have an excellent record, otherwise. We have no problem there. But then later this other matter came up. It was only yesterday that Mrs. Medgar came to me with these . . . rumors. I'll do what I can to reassure the good lady."

"Thank you," she said.

"However," he ran a hand over his bald head, "I must tell you frankly that Mrs. Medgar is asking for a reevaluation. She wants a thorough explanation. In short," he said, summoning his courage, "she has requested that you appear before the school board and clear yourself of these allegations."

She had turned to salt. She stared for a moment, then looked down at her clenched hands. "I see." Then, briskly, she raised her head. "Well, if that's what is necessary—"

With his arms on the desk, the dean studied her thoughtfully. "I just don't believe it is," he said and leaned back in the chair. "I see no real need to call in the board or involve them in any way. I see no reason to carry it that far. A hearing, in itself, could put a black mark on your record."

"Yes," she said, knowing just how black.

"Leave a shadow that could be damaging in the future, make it difficult to advance. A suspicion of guilt . . ." He again contemplated the snowfall in the crystal globe. "In my experience, it is ill-advised to let these things get out of hand. It causes exaggeration, distortion. I, for one, do not care for witch hunts, and I shouldn't like to see you let go on mere suspicion."

"Thank you," she said in a whisper.

"Mrs. Medgar hasn't spoken to anyone else about this, and I've asked her not to. It's all confidential so far. I don't see that it needs to go any further. After I've met with her again, now that I've talked with you . . . and perhaps if you were to meet with her yourself—"

She hesitated. "If that would help—"

"—she would be satisfied. But let me speak to her first. Maybe that will be sufficient. Meanwhile," he said, standing up, "it might be well, these last few days, to be especially careful."

"Indeed," she said.

"Maybe a little added precaution—"

"By all means."

"I'll speak to Mrs. Medgar as soon as possible."

"Thank you, Mr. Frawley. I appreciate your concern." She went on in a low voice, "I'm sorry to have done anything that could be misconstrued. I'm sorry to cause you worry. You've been very kind."

"Well . . ." he said, with his distracted smile, and opened the door for her.

All the way down the hall the dean's words, and all their implications, drummed in her head. She was about to lose her job and with it any chance of another. She would be cast out, in disgrace and in debt—because for a time it had slipped her mind that she was no longer a schoolgirl. Unthinking, she had gambled it all. And all that stood between her and ruin was this pink, troubled, trusting old man who would not believe what she'd done was true.

Seventeen

Reaching the safety of her room, she closed the door quietly, put her back against it, said *Oh God*, and slid down to her heels.

Moral character, lapses of dignity, the delinquency of minors—was it *that bad*? She knew it wasn't altogether right, but was it so altogether wrong? Except for Toby—"Oh God!" she said again. The only comfort was that they had not made love. They came close but they hadn't done it. But they might have if Toby hadn't left when he did. Maybe he knew better than she did when wrong was wrong.

She sat with her head on her knees, too wretched to cry. But that was one thing, at least, that they couldn't know. No one could know except her and Toby, because Toby would not have talked, not even to George. It was not his way.

She pulled herself up and went across to the desk. But those other rumors, the part Mrs. Medgar knew about (where had she got her information?)—those were the public sins and they alone could ruin her. Being seen at the movies, eating sugar buns on the curb in front of the bakery—all that could look very bad. And was she seen at Sutt's Corner with them? That would be much worse. And then George and Toby coming up the stairs to her door in the late afternoons and the evenings! She was a *teacher*—all such things were forbidden to her. No wonder she was facing a firing squad!

But she had explained it all. She thought back, reconstructing the dialogue in the office, what she had said, the expressions on Mr. Frawley's face. She had explained all that. He believed her. And it was true. No harm had been done, none that she could think of. They had done exactly what she said—gone to the movies together, talked about books and listened to music and held their own seminars. It was no more than graduate students did as a matter of course. Mr. Frawley understood.

What they did in addition was harmless enough. For the most part. Sutt's Corner—well, that was a mistake, even if she wasn't the one who led them there. The boys knew where it was long before they knew her. And they had had a beer or two before she knew them. Anyway, who could have seen them there? Nobody, except railroad men and stockyard workers and a few sociable ladies of the evening. No one who knew or gave a damn. And though it was always only the three of them, who knew that for sure? As for those informal "seminars," Maggie had been there for the first two and there could have been other girls as well. How did Mrs. Medgar know whether there were or weren't? The only thing Mrs. Medgar knew was that Miss Liles had been seen at the movies and students sometimes came to her house in the evening.

And all that had been explained. Well enough too. Mr. Frawley believed it, he could explain to Mrs. Medgar, and things would be all right. She might have to go on the carpet first and let

Mrs. Medgar pick her liver. But she could do it if she had to. With Mr. Frawley behind her, the whole affair would blow over. And she would still have a job. She pulled her chair up to the desk and opened the book to Act IV.

But what if it didn't?

She looked up, staring across the empty chairs. What if it did not blow over? Suppose Mrs. Medgar would not give in? Mrs. Medgar was a bitter woman. And what if—she put her hand to her mouth in horror—what if, in spite of Mr. Frawley, she had to appear before the board? *Tell us, Miss Liles, is there any truth to the rumors . . . we have it on good authority . . . a saloon down near the stockyards at odd hours. . . . Do you realize, Miss Liles . . . the moral character of students . . . ethical code . . . the privacy of your rooms . . . young men . . . would you give us their names, please . . . their names, Miss Liles—*

What would she do? Grovel for mercy or stand there barefaced and lie?

She would lie through her teeth. She had to. She had obligations, loans to repay, a living to make. She had Toby and George to protect. The truth at this point was a luxury she could not afford.

She realized tardily that the class bell had rung, and rose and opened the door. Maybe she wouldn't have to lie. Maybe Mr. Frawley would take care of it and Mrs. Medgar would be outmaneuvered. She sat down at the desk, erect and teacherly, and began hastily to review her notes.

The students came in promptly, settled themselves with a light scraping of chairs. She bent over the notes, making a few additions. In the stillness of her kitchen one recent evening she had thought of some rather perceptive things to say about Caliban, a question or two that would set off a good discussion. She waited until the room was quiet and looked up.

"Well now," she said, "after these several weeks with *The Tempest*, I think it's clear to all of us that this is one of the world's great fairy tales. It has all the standard ingredients—love and virtue, which triumph, of course; and wickedness, which is punished; and we can assume that everybody who deserves to lives happily ever after. So far, this follows the formula. It's the same formula that applies to old melodramas, where the villain is thoroughly evil and the hero is thoroughly good and neither one is true to real life.

"But how much truth do we want it in a fairy tale or a melodrama? Not much, I'd say. It's that suspension of reality, of truth to real life, that allows us to live for a while in an ideal world where storms are safely ordered, and in the end everything comes right. So it is in *The Tempest*. But Shakespeare doesn't stick strictly to the formula. Throughout the play he gives us overtones of reality, of humanity and growth of character, which make the play more complicated than your run-of-the-mill fairy tale, and more satisfying. Now, along this line of fantasy and reality and good and evil, I'd like us to take another look at a couple of the symbols—Ariel and Caliban. Let's begin with Caliban and to refresh ourselves, let's turn back to Act Three."

There was a rustle of pages. Lindsey, in the front row—he was always in the front row—smiled tenderly.

She looked down and quickly up again. "Now about halfway through the scene, you remember—" She glanced at the book, but the train of thought had come uncoupled. Flustered, she picked up her notes, laid them down, and turned a page of the text. "Let's start at the beginning of Scene . . . Three. Would you read to yourselves, please, the whole scene, before we start the discussion." She added lamely, for no reason, "Pay particular attention to the choice of words."

The heads went down.

It was not at all what she intended. Caliban wasn't even in that scene. Somehow she would have to wrench it around to make a point about him. Where the hell was he? She scanned the page for a clue. Old Gonzales, Alonso, Prospero . . . What if Mrs. Medgar did not give in?

She pulled the book closer and tried again. Again the mind went its own way. Her thoughts darted from Medgar to Mr. Frawley to Toby and George and back. Visions of the board, mitred and robed, rose between her and the page—*Tell us, Miss Liles . . . can you explain*—and mobs of outraged parents behind them. She stared hard at the page. It was no use. The horrors of inquisition beat kettles in her head.

But what could they know? she asked herself again. How could they pass sentence of guilt with so little to go on? Rumors. A movie or two, the boys on her stairs. *It was not what you think it was, not that at all. If I could explain . . . No, it would not happen again. . . . I am sorry, I never intended—*

They would boil her in oil.

For she was guilty as charged. And who had she thought she was that she could get away with all that? All over town under cover of darkness, careless as blown trash, dancing in the moonlight and drinking beer, prowling through churches, up and down the streets with a hoot and a holler and then the night of the fog and she and Toby and any way you sliced it, it was Immoral Conduct. *Had she thought nobody would know?*

"Miss Liles?" A small voice from the front row.

They were waiting for her, patient and courteous.

"I finished that whole scene."

Eighteen smooth attentive faces turned upon her, waiting.

"Are we supposed to keep on reading?"

"No . . ." she said, and looked down before she turned to stone.

The fact was, she realized, all of them knew. Knew some part of the story. And the other fact was that she had been glad they knew. For Toby and George were good to look at, and bright and coveted, and hers. She had been proud of that. Her illegal, undersize catch. And there was in those faces—all except one—something she recognized. She had seen it before, elsewhere and close up and not too long ago: a haughtiness, sweetly unconscious, and a cool, young pity. The look that children turn on their elders, that says, *You are not one of us.*

Head down over the open book, she searched in frenzy for a clue to Caliban. Her face was hot with shame. She was Lindsey Homeier in reverse, and everybody knew—most of all, Toby and George.

Eighteen

*O*ver and over in the next days, the whole spring flashed before her, not the spring she had thought it was, but as the others would see it—Mrs. Medgar and the school board and Mr. Frawley, and as the children saw it. She looked at herself through all those eyes, and the sight appalled her.

And how would her mother see it?

She knew very well how Mother would see it, and she would be right. Little Allen was guilty of misconduct and there was no getting around it. It would be a few days yet before error would be analyzed and absolution handed out right and left. As it was, she could see no way to forgive herself, and no way either, for anyone else to forgive her.

It was an ordeal for her, appearing at school each morning. As she stood before her classes, sober and correct, every face seemed to accuse her. As for the teachers, they might as well have known to the letter what had gone on in the dean's office. It was deduction from hints and symptoms studiously observed. A particular talent of the academic breed. And inevitably, she must have given herself away. Chastened as she was, it was difficult not to show it and impossible for the others, especially the Ladies, to ignore it. In the lounge, when she was present, the chatter was conspicuously idle. Busier was what went on behind her back. It was not malicious; they were kindly women. But they were curious. Whatever was happening with Allen, and *something* was happening, had them mightily intrigued. And it gave Gladys something to comment on in her own brand of wit. Allen was always appearing in the lounge in the wake of the punch line, catching Mae Dell in spasms and Gladys still sizzling between her teeth. Both of which expressions of merriment stopped abruptly as she walked in.

"Oh, *there* you are!" Mae Dell was likely to say, and Verna as likely as not to grab her purse and herd the pair of them out. "Come on, Allen's not ready yet and we've got to stop by the bank." Or some such excuse to get them away before she asked to join them.

She wouldn't have asked, not for the world (even pariahs have their pride), for the Ladies were not merely curious, they were afraid. Guilt by association was something they could not risk. They were taking no chances, and she couldn't blame them. One can't be too careful around one who hasn't been careful at all. No wonder they avoided her; she was repellent. Corruption gives off an odor.

Lordy passed her in the hall now with no more than *Good morning*. Even Dr. Ansel seemed distant. He hadn't asked her out once last week. No wonder. If the rest of them had wind of her disgrace, think what Ansel must know! Nevertheless, he had come in a time or two to air his views on proposed munitions plants and what Roosevelt was up to. But that was a pretext, she suspected. Curiosity getting the better of him, he probably came in the interests of research.

In a way it was a comfort that more and more was being said about the war. It was in the air, you heard it in the halls—rumors and predictions. Although such talk alarmed her, she took some solace from the thought that in their concern with the larger issue, they might forget about her.

She went about her business all week as inconspicuously as was possible for a girl who might have been wearing a scarlet letter. Mornings, she crept to school; during off hours, as often as not, she hid in the library. No more free and easy banter with the students in the hall, no slipping out for a Coke between classes. Now she came early and, like the other teachers, stayed late. And crept home nights to stay there.

Her shame was an occupation. The only other, the only distraction, was work. She made out questions for final exams next week and plans for next year's classes, persuading herself that Mr. Frawley must surely prevail and she would be back at work.

Joblessness haunted her. Visions of breadlines flitted through her head. She had never stood in a breadline, nor sold pencils on a street, nor lived in a Hooverville. She came of farm country, where they lived well enough. Even so, it was not always easy. The great drought dried up the fields and burned the gardens and orchards; the cattle, those not sold at a loss, shriveled and some of them died. On Sundays the preacher stood up in his shirtsleeves (his trousers darned where they had worn through at the buttocks) and prayed for endurance of faith through this plague which the Lord had put upon us as upon Egypt, and for the repentance of sins for which it was punishment. He had given up praying for rain. Through the open windows dust had blown in and settled in the pews. Women brushed it off with their handkerchiefs before sitting down.

Those were the years when the banks failed, more than five thousand of them (Ansel reminded her), and fifteen million people were unemployed. In cities a grown man would shovel the snow off your driveway and the sidewalk for a dime. A woman would clean your house for a quarter, if anyone had the quarter. Farmers went broke and left the land. Men left their families and went looking for jobs in St. Louis and Kansas City. And half the boys in town shipped out on freight trains, looking for work, any kind, anywhere. Girls sewed up the runs in their rayon stockings until the toes and heels wore through. A stray bobby pin was considered a find, and luxury most extravagant was a candy bar for a nickel.

Those times were not long ago and she had not forgotten, even though she had been better off than most: Her mother taught school—she had a salary! Because of that, her daughter could go to college, and because of that, she had a job.

What would she do if she lost it?

Soberly she considered the alternatives. She could type; with luck she could get a job in an office. Or she could clerk at Woolworth's. She could go back to the farm, maiden aunt to her brother's children, and help with the butchering and the canning. Or go home to her mother in the country town, turn inward and hide from the world.

In view of those grim prospects, any notion she had had about quitting her job quickly faded. She could not watch the dream go without a pang of regret—that long dream of cities and excitement, theaters and galleries and dance studios, and people rushing through the streets on marvelous, mysterious business. Hadn't she thought about it through those long fall nights, thought seriously, and planned how she would get there?

Others had done it—gone to New York, gone to Paris. She knew a girl who had bicycled through Europe. Why couldn't she do the same, just pick up and go, on a shoestring and a bike? But Europe was at war now. England, Italy, Spain, all in turmoil. Paris fallen to the Nazis. No more seeking your fortune there, or anywhere else in these times. She hadn't a shoestring anyway, and she fell off bikes.

She looked over her shoulder wistfully as the vision receded. But recede it did. The best she could do now was behave herself and hang on to the bird in hand. If indeed it hadn't already flown.

With that possibility in mind, she had written to her mother, a cheerful dissembling letter suggesting that because of other ambitions, wayward though they might appear, she just possibly might resign. She would get a job with a magazine or a newspaper, start at the bottom, work her way up, and so on. Never so much as a hint that resignation might not be voluntary.

She went so far as to draft a letter to Mr. Frawley, giving him all the reasons she gave her mother: she felt the need to broaden her horizons; she had thought about it for a long time and felt she should leave before she got in a rut. It made a good story.

And she might as well say she was swimming to China, for all the faith he would have in it. For Mr. Frawley knew better. And to resign at this point would be a clear admission of guilt. She tore up the letter.

But to her mother she kept up the pretense.

Mother's first response was amused disbelief, a "There, there" letter: Mother understood; restlessness, just like her father's, a touch of spring fever; it would pass. This was followed the next day by another letter, expressing bafflement, then by dire warning, and at last resignation: "great investment in you . . . faith and hope."

Oh, Mother knew how to play it. Gave you what you wanted, and if you took it, made you feel guilty as hell. But in the next letter, two days later, the plain facts: "Why in the name of reason are you being so foolish? Aren't you mature enough by this time to know . . . For heaven's sake, daughter, use your common sense!"

That one stung. Truth usually did. She had been foolish. To leave now would only make it worse. If she had any common sense, she wouldn't. And furthermore, she wasn't sure she wanted to. She had been happy here in more ways than one.

She studied the university catalog, weighed and considered and chose courses she must take in order to go on teaching. Somehow she must squeeze history into the schedule and find time to study Greek drama.

Each morning she would read the news from last night's paper, left on her desk these mornings by Dr. Ansel. There was word now of munitions plants proposed for southern Missouri. The president said the international situation was on an hour-to-hour basis. She was horrified by the bombing of London, bewildered by Harry Hopkins. Dutifully she memorized the names of fallen countries and the number of bombers built or about to be built in American factories.

Alone in her rooms, at the kitchen table, she struggled to atone for her sins and achieve salvation. She studied, read, graded, wrote, and listened for a step on the landing.

She tried not to listen. But it was a habit not easily broken, even though no one would come. Not Toby. And not George. For George knew. No one had had to tell him. He knew, though he made no accusation. Only his distance reproached her. He had gone back to his own kind, and Toby with him, resuming the old easy camaraderie of best friends. But not with her. It was in their eyes too, that she had seen that look, the gentle reproach of the young. She had erred, and all of them were sorry.

And yet, she protested, Toby was guilty too. She hadn't forced him to come up her stairs that night. Why should he be absolved and back in grace and she alone be the outcast? It was one of the questions that harried her through the long, still nights.

Sleep was skittish. No ritual seemed to help, no rhymed words nor the counting of sheep nor the black mass of the Lord's Prayer said backward. No matter how she coaxed it, it came when it pleased or not at all, and halfheartedly at that. She turned and turned in the darkness, enduring the snaps and nibbles of remorse. Until one night, as the clock struck two, she had had enough and she put on her clothes and ran.

It was a reflex, involuntary. She couldn't have said why she did it, only that she had to escape. And she ran down the alley like one running to freedom. Between the high hedges, the fencerows of mulberry and bridal wreath and the lilac bushes, past the bins by the carriage-house doors, and on to the house with the empty fountain, where she stopped to breathe. The cool air washed her skin. It smelled of green growing things and moist earth. She walked on slowly, taking deep breaths. Here the scent of viburnum lay across the path, made heavier by the dampness. It followed her for a long way and she turned and went back, counting the number of steps of its reach, the point where you first could detect the fragrance and where you no longer could. She played at this for several minutes, absorbed in the counting, the precise demarcations, then went on to where the willow drooped over the fence. She waded into it, into the long, thin hanging branches that made a soft clicking as she moved. Out and in and stopping a moment, letting them close around her, a familiar whispering element.

She drifted, aimless and careless, with little thought to how far she was going, conscious only of her joy to be in the open, received again in the hospitalities of the night. Leaves brushed her face.

She began to sing under her breath. She sang, because it rose unbidden,

Au clair de la lune. Mon ami Pierrot . . .

and, singing, came to her own corner, where the tree stood at the entrance to the alley, its branches touching her windows. She stopped in its shadows and looked up at the thick, dark leaves. Here she was safe. How many times had they sheltered here from the fine rain, measured the trunk with their arms, and scratched against it like horses! She laid her hand on the rough bark. *Tell me tell me tell me elm*. Where did it go? And what was she doing here, alone and absurd in the middle of the night, playing her solitary games? The time was gone and maybe should never have come, not for her. She was not a child. Yet she had behaved as one, all seemliness forgotten, all rank and position, decorum, and consequence. She, a grown woman, prancing about in the dark singing nonsense songs, fishing up busted parasols. . . . How *could* she? she asked herself once again. And what was she doing here, alone in the night, trying to bring it all back?

For that's what she was doing, and no use pretending she wasn't. And it wasn't Toby alone she wanted, she wanted George too, and the fun and laughter and James Joyce under the streetlamp, and the three of them singing together as they had in those fine spring nights before the night of the fog and the moonlight, when the laughter stopped and the spring and everything they had made it was over.

She stood for a long time under the elm tree, thinking back. Well, it was over, all of it, and perhaps it was just as well. Gone and good riddance. And for this she could thank her own iniquities. She had turned greedy. It wasn't enough that she should invade two lives—one of them she must possess. That was the first sin. The second was that they had been false to George. And there was another. She could see it now, clearly, out here on the dark field alone, all the players gone home, except her. Somewhere in the heat of the game, when she was too fevered to notice, the boys had suddenly grown up. And it wasn't the times alone that had done it, or the war she did not understand. It was she who had led them out of childhood before they were ready to go. That was the third sin, and that one undid her.

High in the tree a robin whistled, answered by another somewhere in the alley. She looked up through the branches, still dark against a dark sky. But it was no longer night. Morning had come. Heaving a sigh, part regret, part relief, she climbed the stairs and went in, locking the door behind her.

Nineteen

She awoke with the sun at the window and the clock ticking toward 9:15. Saturday morning. She turned over on her stomach and pulled the pillow over her head, making it dark again. A long day ahead and no place to go. Nothing to do but grade more papers and worry.

She was trying grimly to go back to sleep, when an assertive knock at the kitchen door brought her upright. Toby. No, not on Saturday, not at this hour. Then who—? Bounding out of bed, she grabbed her robe, ran through the kitchen, and stopped at the door in panic.

Mother! She had come!

Another knock, louder. She unlocked the door, opened it cautiously, only a crack, and peered out.

"Open up, lady, it's the FBI!"

She flung the door open with such relief that for a moment she was speechless. Dalton stood there, her own dear old hayfoot-strawfoot funny old brother, solid and beaming in a blue work shirt and a new straw farm hat. Squealing welcome, she hugged him, pulled him inside, hugged him again, and pelted him with questions: How were the kids, had he had breakfast, how was Gwennie, why hadn't she come too, and how come he was here *this* weekend? "You didn't come to take me home today, did you? School's not out for another week!" She stopped with the coffeepot in her hand. "Did Mother send you to check up on me?"

But Mother had had nothing to do with it. He had come down to take a neighbor boy to Camp Crowder. "Forrest Nail's boy. You remember—Clyde? He's been drafted. His dad was going to take him down there, but their car's not running very good, so I offered. And I thought as long as I was this close—well, here I am."

They sat at the kitchen table over coffee and eggs and oranges. Dalton had been up since five and was ready for another breakfast. He was feeding ten head of cattle now, besides the horses. Milking two cows. He had already sowed oats and planted corn. "It's near a foot high now."

"Dalton," she said, "you don't think they'll take you, will they?"

"Take me? Who?"

"The draft. They won't draft farmers, will they?"

"Well, I don't know," he said thoughtfully. "Those of us with a farm and a family might be exempt. But you can't be sure."

Allen asked, as she asked anyone she encountered, if he thought the country might yet get involved in the war. Really.

"At this point, hard to tell. I hope not, but—" He shrugged and looked out the window, and for a moment neither of them spoke. She was thinking that if he were drafted, maybe she should, after all, go back to the farm and help out. If she couldn't stay here.

Toying with her fork, she said casually, "I'm surprised Mother didn't come with you."

Dalton said with a wink, "Didn't tell her I was coming."

"She'll find out."

"I'll tell her, next time I see her."

"I guess she's told you I may quit my job."

He laughed. "Yeah, she's flaring her nostrils about that. What's it all about anyway?"

Allen spelled it out again, and he listened, nodding as if he understood. There were the usual questions and objections, and her usual rebuttals, and after a while he said, "Well, it makes sense to me. Risky, but if that's what you want to do—"

"If I could afford to. But the money—I still owe you some, and I won't be able to pay you back right away."

"Don't worry about that. I don't."

"Well, I do."

"You've already paid me back more than half."

"But if you *should* get drafted, how would Gwennie manage?"

"We've thought about that. But with Gwennie's kid brother and her dad, she could manage right well. We've all talked it over. So if it should happen that they call me up," he said, pushing crumbs around on his plate, "I'd feel like I ought to go. I'd rather not, God knows. But if I have to—" He pushed back his chair and stood up. "Hey, let's worry about that when the time comes, and it ain't come yet. What d'ya say we go out and do something? Let's have some fun. I haven't had a day off in a coon's age. Want to go to the carnival?"

"Where?"

"Up north a little ways. I saw it as I drove in."

"That would be Jackroad. Well—"

"It ought to be open by now. It's nearly noon. Grab your hat and let's go!"

It had been a while now since she had had any fun, and she hardly knew how to go about it. But it was a sunny, maypole kind of day, and it was good to be driving through town with her brother, who used to tease her and boss her around and take care of her. Kept her from falling out of the hayloft or drowning herself in the horse tank. Defended her at school if the big kids teased her. She was glad he had come, and without Mother. And mightily relieved that she had brought up the job-quitting business and got that over with. She sat beside him with a heart lighter than it had been for some weeks.

It was a shabby little carnival, set up in a field against a backdrop of mine tailings. Already, this early in the season, it looked road-worn and weary. But the Ferris wheel and the dipper and the merry-go-round whirled and swung and clattered bravely. The mechanical music blared and the carnies bawled from their canvas booths. Come win a Kewpie doll, come see Mother Nature's awesome mistakes. The poor freaks were painted larger than life on the walls of the sideshow tent.

Dalton said, "Not The Greatest Show on Earth, is it?"

But it didn't matter. They strolled among the booths, pitched pennies, ate cotton candy. They were on holiday, and after a long spell under a rock, Allen took it in, blinking: The racket, the aimless busyness, the dolls and feathers and balloons, all the tinseled junk, the stimulating carnival stink of burning grease and sugar. More than an hour had passed and she hadn't thought once of Toby or Mrs. Medgars.

At the Kewpie-doll booth they threw twenty cents' worth of baseballs and Allen knocked down three of the five tenpins. "You got a mean arm on you there," Dalton said and paid for another five balls. They still didn't win, but Allen bought a long pink feather for Nanette, and a yellow balloon.

They skipped the freak show in favor of the "Dodgem" cars, and after that took two small boys for a ride on the merry-go-round. One was named Raymond and the other one Hosey, as well as they could make out. They lived near the stockyards and wished they had a pony. Their sister had brought them to the carnival; she was somewhere around.

"Well, you'd better go find her," Dalton said as he lifted them down. "You wouldn't want to get lost." They ran off, waving over their shoulders.

Around two o'clock they followed their noses to a hamburger stand. Behind the bare-board counter a red-haired woman was slapping raw meat onto a griddle. A gent with a straw katie raked over one ear stood with an elbow on the counter. Although they came up too late to hear what he said, they caught the gist of it and the leer on his face.

The woman flipped a hamburger onto a bun, laid it on a napkin, and shoved it across the counter. "Just what condition were you referring to, mister?" She faced him, reared back, her hands on her hips, letting him stare at the bulge under her apron. "Ketchup and mustard over there. That'll be fifty cents, please."

"What are you tryin' to pull on me, woman? It says up here fifteen."

"Woulda been, if you'd kept your mouth shut. Take it or leave it. Yes, folks, what'll it be?"

The man muttered, "Fuckin' bitch," and left it.

"We'll take it," said Dalton.

"You don't have to. I'll make you another'n."

"This one will do just fine. We'll need another one for my sister. And two bottles of red sody pop. Put your money away, kid, I'm paying for this."

By the time they argued it out, another woman and a young boy had come into the booth. After a few murmured words, the red-haired woman untied her apron and dropped down in a chair, fanning herself with the bunched apron. She took a chunk of ice out of a tub where pop bottles were cooling and rubbed it over her face and throat. Her hair, piled high in an untidy heap, was the color of marigolds. Damp tendrils straggled down the back of her neck. She had the kind of fragile white skin that ages early, with fine wrinkles like the surface of scalded milk.

"You better get goin'," the second woman said.

"Soon as I catch my breath."

"Where you think he went to?"

"I don't know, but I'll find him. Then I'll kill him."

Allen made a great business of slathering mustard on the bun. Dalton had trouble with the ketchup bottle. They hung around as long as they thought they could. But no more was said between the women, and they moved off reluctantly.

"Shucks," Dalton said.

They circled casually, trying not to be obvious as they watched the red-haired woman leave the stand and vanish behind the freak-show tent.

When they had finished their lunch, across the street in the shade of an ash tree, Dalton said they must ride the Ferris wheel now. "And then I've got to get going. It's a long haul home."

Crossing the grounds, they happened on Raymond and Hosey again. "Hi," Dalton said. "Find your sister?"

The boys nodded and pointed to the Ferris wheel, where a blonde girl and a boy in a little carnival hat were climbing into a swing.

"You guys want to have a ride?"

They shook their heads and the older one said, "Sis took us. We were scared."

"You were? What were you afraid of?"

"Fallin' down."

"There's a straight answer," Allen said.

By the time they bought their tickets, another ride had begun. They watched the great wheel circle four times, bearing the swings high in the air and down again with their squealing cargo. "Remember how crazy you used to be about these things?" Dalton said. "You'd ride it a dozen times if I'd take you. Got away once and rode it by yourself. Remember that? You weren't any bigger than Hosey, little bitty thing up there, waving at us. Scared your mother half to death."

She remembered. It had been a whee of a ride. And she climbed aboard now with a familiar pit-of-the-stomach thrill. But the ride hadn't started before the palms of her hands were damp. She had never before been scared on a Ferris wheel. They didn't jerk you around and leave your head behind you as other rides did. Just the same, her hands were sweaty and her mouth was

195

dry and the attendant had fastened her in with the lockbar and slammed the gate shut.

"Hang on," Dalton yelled, "here we go!"

Slow at first and easy as a porch swing, then faster and faster, the seat tilting with the curves, till they reached the top and plunged down, picking up more speed. Up again and over and down. Allen shut her eyes tight, daring to look only when the pace slackened and the wheel came to a full stop. They were sitting at the very top, she and Dalton, the seat rocking gently. "Why are we stopping?" she said in a tight voice.

"To let people off. Look at that view, would you! You can see for miles around." Allen gripped the lockbar and stared at her hands.

"Clear from here to Tipperary! Look down there at the kids, wavin' like crazy."

Dalton wasn't even holding on. He was waving at the kids, looking up and down, all around, with a big smile on his face. Because his heart was pure, because he was honest and truthful and hadn't done a lot of dumb things and because— She took one look down and shut her eyes tight. The ground was ten miles below. The gears were stuck. They were trapped up here till the bolts rusted out and the swing fell down. The wheel was never going to turn again and she had sinned or she might have if Toby hadn't left her and what she had done was bad enough and she was going to be fired and what was she going to do?

Down below, the gate crashed and the music picked up. "If they draft me," Dalton shouted, "I'm going to fly airplanes!"

After a while then, it was over. Allen climbed out, her legs like string.

"You look plumb pale. You weren't scared, were you?"

"Spitless."

"You never used to be."

"A lot of things scare me that didn't used to."

"Like what?'

She lifted a shoulder. "This and that."

"Well, come on, I'll buy you some ice cream. That'll settle your butterflies. Then I got to get goin'."

Allen was brought up short, after they were on their way back to town, when Dalton said quietly, "You're in some kind of trouble, aren't you?"

She gave him a quick glance and quickly looked away. "Why would you say that?"

"Well, when there's a storm coming, the cattle can get kinda nervous. I figure it's about the same with people. If they feel it coming."

"I don't know about any storm," she lied, "and I'm not a cattle."

"No-o, but—"

"Why should you think I'm in trouble?"

"Because you never have been. If you had, I'd have got wind of it. Sooner or later everybody runs into trouble of some kind, and you've gone a long time without it. You're about due for some. And all this flimflam about running off to New York or the moon or Lord knows where . . . Why, only a month ago you were writing home what a swell time you were having, how much you liked your job."

"I do like it."

"Then why do you want to quit? Right now, with everything so unsettled, it seems to me—I don't want to pry into your private affairs, but something's eatin' you. And if you're in trouble, maybe I can help." He gave her a glance that went straight through her. "You aren't knocked up, are you?"

"No!" By the grace of God and Toby's forbearance, that much was the truth. "Nothing like that."

"Well, I'm mighty glad to hear it."

He had pulled up to the curb by her house. She opened the door, ready to get out. But Dalton hadn't finished. "Are you thinking they might let you go?"

"You mean fire me?"

"That's what I mean."

"Oh," she said in a small voice. "They could."

"Why?'

"Because . . . maybe because I'm popular with the kids."

"How popular?"

"Well, they like me. Most of them. More than some of the other teachers."

"Do the other teachers resent it? Professional jealousy?"

"Maybe. I don't know. People can twist things."

"What did you give 'em to twist?"

She didn't answer, and he let that one go by.

"Well, when you're young and kind of a live wire, that can be a problem for some folks. They may get it in for you. And folks like to gossip. You haven't been called on the carpet, have you?"

She drew another long breath. "Sort of."

"What do you mean, sort of?"

"In the dean's office. He said—he said maybe I should be a little more careful. About associating with the students. I did go to the movies with some of them. A time or two."

"Isn't that what they call chaperoning? No harm in that."

"I didn't see any."

"Hm. Well, I don't see how they could fire you for something like that and maybe a little gossip. If there's nothing to it."

She was tempted to spill it out, how she ran around in the night, all over town, and stole forks and drank beer and went crazy over a schoolkid. "They might," she said faintly.

He sat for a moment, thoughtful, looking out at the street. "See here," he said, turning to face her, "if they've got a reason to fire you, or if they can make one up, if you're really afraid, I say beat 'em to it. Go in tomorrow and hand in your resignation."

"But—"

"Take off for New York if that's what you want. Or the Amazon! Maybe now's the time, even if it is a bad time. Maybe you ought to just cut and run."

She cried out forlornly, *"Mother won't let me!"*

"For the love of little green apples!" He slapped the steering wheel. "Are you going to let her run your whole life? She's done it up to now. But you're a grown woman. Take charge, be your own boss!"

"I don't know how!" she wailed in misery.

"Oh, now, now," he said, "calm down. We'll work it out."

"You got a handkerchief?"

"Here."

She blew her nose on the red bandanna. "I'm sorry."

"I didn't mean to come down on you so hard. I just thought—well, I still think—listen, how much money do you have saved up?"

"Forty-five dollars," she said, wailing again, "and eighty-five cents."

"Whoa!"

"And I'm still in debt."

"Maybe not as much as you think. Come on, kid, don't cry. Your nose is all red. You're going to be okay, really you are. But you got to stick to your guns. Don't give in because of Mother. She wanted me to be a lawyer, y'know. But it wasn't what I wanted. She can be got around. Just keep that in mind." A slow grin spread across his face. "Do you remember the time when—no, you wouldn't, you weren't born yet. And of course you can't remember much about Dad. You were so young when he went."

"Not much. Except what you've told me."

"Dad and I were good friends. And when he left home that time . . . Did she ever tell you about that?"

"Last summer."

"Tell you why he left?"

"Said they'd had a few problems. Didn't say what."

"Of course she didn't. Because most of those little problems were . . . her."

"I thought so."

"You know how Mother is. Bossy. Her way is always right, and come hell or high water, she's going to have it. I caught onto that by the time I was seven. So he stood it as long as he could and took off. He had himself one last great big beautiful fling."

"What did he do?"

Dalton was smiling to himself, remembering. "What he did best."

"*What was that?*"

"Gambling." He turned to her, grinning. "Our father was one hell of a poker player."

She opened her mouth, shut it, and opened it again. "Dad was a gambler?"

"That's how he got the farm."

Her mouth fell open again.

"In a poker game in St. Louis. Won it from a banker who had foreclosed. Fair and square."

But a gambler was the same as a drunkard. A lowlife, a disgrace. Insofar as they thought of it at all, that's what they had been taught to think. But her own father! She stared for a moment and began to grin. Then she laughed. "Did Mother know?"

"He never told her. She knew he had gambled some before they were married, but she thought she had him cured. Maybe she had, more or less."

"How did you know all this?"

"I didn't, for, a long time. All I knew was he could play poker. He taught me how."

"He did? Did Mother know?"

"She never found out," he said gleefully. "Dad kept a pack of cards in the barn. We'd sneak out there sometimes and play in the hayloft. Played for straws. I got right good at it too. I was lucky though. I never caught the fever. But Dad had it in his blood. Feel kinda sorry for him, looking back. He must have loved her a lot to carry around all that frustration."

But he had never told Dalton about winning the farm. "I found that out from Uncle Woodrow. When I was about seventeen he sent for me to come down. And I was to come by myself. He didn't want Mother along or you. He made that plain. Mother never got along with his brothers, you know."

So Dalton had gone down to Ste. Genevieve alone, and he came back rich. "When Dad left home that time, he and Woodrow went up to St. Louis and got in a big poker game. Dad won six hundred dollars." It had stayed in a bank in Ste. Genevieve till long after Dad died and Uncle Woodrow himself was dying. "That's when he gave me the letter, when he was about to die. Dad had left a letter with him for me. He wanted me to have charge of the money, he said. But when the time came, you were to have your half. And that's what you thought you were borrowing from me. It wasn't a loan. The three hundred dollars is rightfully yours."

She looked at him in astonishment. Three hundred dollars was a fortune.

"I've dipped into my half when I needed it bad. But I've always paid it back, sooner or later. And I've never touched your half. Just left it there to draw interest—till you were going back to get your master's. I thought you needed it then."

"But why didn't you tell me?"

He laughed. "Because if you'd known it was yours, you might have spent it all by this time. I know how hard it is to save money, 'specially when you never had it to save. This way, when you thought you were paying it back, you were paying yourself. So it's there now, the hundred bucks plus interest you've paid me back so far, and another hundred and fifty where that came from. You've got a stake now, kid. And if you want to take it and run, I say do it. Remember, you're a gambler's daughter."

"Dalton," she said at last, "you always did look after me."

There was one more question. "Does Mother know where this money came from?"

"His letter said I was to tell her. And I did. She'll never tell you where it came from. But she knows."

Twenty

*A*nd so Father had had the last word!

For all those years of good behavior he had paid her back. And there wasn't a thing Mother could do about it. It was tainted money, but good usage could take off the tarnish. She might even have admired the way he did it. With a wink and a grin, as befitted the winner, and probably a pat on the fanny. Better than a kick in the butt.

Mother in the backyard that night last summer: *I loved him and I wanted him back.* And he came. And maybe it wasn't his love that brought him back, but hers. How seductive being loved could be.

And how seductive it was now to take her share of the money and do what she wanted to do. Or wanted once. Go in and resign, Dalton said. Well, maybe she should. Get out before they fired her, no matter what Mother would say. After all, she hadn't meant to stay here forever, not with all there was to see and do out there. She resolved to go in and write the letter tonight. She rose from the landing, where she had sat for the last half hour, and opened the kitchen door.

But what if she resigned?

She stopped in the doorway and thought about it. What if she did it—and they had made up their minds to keep her? Don't count on it. Go in and resign. Her mind tossed it back and forth, around and around until in the end, she decided to trust Mr. Frawley. There was still the chance that he could save her.

It was the last week of school, and still she'd had no word from the dean. She took it as ill omen. By this time, surely, he would have talked to Mrs. Medgar; if he had convinced and pacified her, he would surely have said so. On the other hand, perhaps it had slipped his mind. He was old and forgetful, and this time of year there were many responsibilities. Maybe it was only that; he had more important things to worry about than her transgressions. But it wasn't likely. She might yet be called to account before the board, and she went to school each morning cold with dread.

Maxine's wedding provided some distraction. In the lounge the Ladies were much preoccupied with what they should wear and when to present the gift. They had gone together to buy it. Although they had asked her to come in on it, Allen obligingly declined. They didn't really want her to and, anyway, she preferred to choose on her own. She wasn't sure what the Ladies had bought. From the chatter, it was some sort of cut glass something, rather large. "Something that will *show*," Mae Dell said. Verna thought it should have been a pressure cooker.

Allen's gift came from an antique shop, a slender crystal vase that had caught her fancy. A small thing, it would hold one rose, maybe two daffodils, and it cost too much. But she liked it and hoped Maxine wouldn't consider it secondhand.

She had bought a new dress to wear to the wedding, pale green like new poplar leaves, and a new ribbon to put on last year's hat, a little straw thing that sat on the back of her head, with the ribbon down the back. The slippers were two summers old. They would have to do.

Reluctantly she began to pack her belongings. On the Sunday after the wedding Dalton would come for her. A week later he would deliver her to summer school. She thought, with a sinking heart, of John Dewey and Theory of Education. Meanwhile, there were reports to make out. She did all this faithfully, and faithfully each night listened to the news reports and studied the evening paper. The British were dying and losing in Crete, their cruisers destroyed, Nazi troops dropping out of the sky in parachutes. The Germans were sinking merchant ships faster than England and the United States could build them. In a Fireside Chat the president said we would step up our efforts, the Axis powers were trying to strangle us. "We will not hesitate," he said, "to use our armed forces . . ." She felt in some odd way that her ignorance had helped to bring it all about, that the war would not end unless she acknowledged and understood it.

She recalled tales of the World War, heard in her childhood: frozen trenches, mud and rats, starvation and poison gas. And shell shock that sent men home with their minds half gone and their bodies a mass of twitching nerves. Like the man in Grigsby, just a boy, they said, who sat in the porch swing all one summer, his mother beside him, or one of his sisters. She remembered him. "The crazy man," she called him. "No, dear, he isn't crazy. He was hurt in the war. You don't have to be afraid of him." She imagined Toby and George wounded on the field, dragging their shattered bodies through the bloodstained snow. But it was too painful to dwell on for long.

Leaving her books, she stepped out onto the landing, where the damp air cooled her face. The branches stirred lazily. Far across town the long muted warning of a train whistle. Silence again. The night spread wide around her, filled with its wonders.

But no more of that, no more at all. The time had passed. Sighing, she went in to study war again and redeem herself.

It was in further atonement that she surprised the wits out of Dr. Ansel and agreed to go out with him. On Wednesday afternoon he had come in to ask if he might escort her to baccalaureate services that Friday night. "Your steady won't object to a little thing like that, would he?"

"My who? Oh, him," she said, recalling the excuse she had made months ago. "Well, maybe he wouldn't."

"We'll be well chaperoned. Could I call for you then, Friday?"

Dr. Ansel could be more tiresome than not; he was pompous and stuffy, and there was the blotch. But he had *asked*. No matter how much he knew about her fall, he was willing to be seen with her. He stood by the desk, his anxious pale blue eyes looking down at her. And spurred by a curious jumble of feelings, she smiled and said, "Thank you. That would be very nice."

The Holder of the Third Degree stared in astonishment. "Gee, swell," he said, "swell!" so taken aback that he could only repeat himself. "That's swell. I'll see you then Friday night."

"What time?"

"It starts at eight. About seven-thirty, shall I come for you then? Or seven-fifteen, so we'll have plenty of time? It's up at the high school, you know, way uptown. And we have to get into our gowns and all that."

"Seven-fifteen will be fine," she said. "Or make it seven. I like to be early." The sooner they got there, the fewer people would see them come in together.

"Good! Seven o'clock sharp. See you then!" And turning back from the door, "Mother'll be with us, you know."

She hadn't known, but she might have.

"I hope you won't mind. She doesn't get out much unless I take her and I'd hate to leave her home on baccalaureate night."

"Of course not."

"She gets a big kick out of seeing me in my gown and hood. She's really proud of that. We'll take her right home afterward."

Me too, she thought.

"I hope you won't mind."

"Not at all."

"That's swell. Thanks ever so much. You're a swell sport."

She wasn't a swell sport. Neither Toby nor George had come by all week, and now classes were over, and she was left to spend the last week grading finals, entering grades and cleaning out her room. She still hadn't heard anything from Dean Frawley, and it weighed on her heavily. So why not go with Ansel, and pretend everything was all right, and she was a member of the faculty in good standing?

So Dr. Ansel, in the polished blue Essex, called for her promptly at seven o'clock on Friday night, and they drove to the high-school building, his mother in the backseat with his cap and gown on her lap. They arrived a few minutes after seven.

The graduates had beaten her there. Ganged up at the side door, they were clowning about in their ceremonial garb and parted like the Red Sea for Dr. Ansel's triumphant entry, his mother on one arm, Allen firmly held on the other.

Nor were they in advance of the Ladies. Backstage, Verna and Gladys and Mae Dell were already getting into their robes. "Well, hel-lo!" said Gladys, her smile spreading.

Verna looked around, assuming the practical. "Get a ride?"

But Dr. Ansel wasn't letting it go at that. Making clear that she had been brought, he hovered around with a proprietary air that gave her the collywobbles. There was no way she could shake him. Wherever she turned, there he was, adjusting her hood, helping with hooks and tassels and this and that that she didn't need help with. He was in wonderful spirit, strutting in the vestments of Higher Education, which he and he alone of this company was privileged to wear. When they filed into the auditorium, he was immediately behind her.

The faculty sat on the platform, behind the speaker's lectern; sat and rose and sat again, through the invocation, the choral selection (which, to her relief, had nothing to do with Shakespeare's bee), and the introduction of the speaker, the local Congregational minister.

In the rows down front Toby sat with his mortarboard cocked back on his head. George, his cap pulled to the bridge of his nose, kept biting the tassel. The girl next to him was going to die of laughter any minute.

Allen fixed her eyes on the speaker's back. Beside her, Dr. Ansel sat erect in his dignity, turning his head now and then as if to assure himself that she was there. She pretended not to notice.

Old Ansel, with his mother, his blotch, and Harold Bell Wright. But Ansel was Doctor-of-Philosophy Ansel, and she had allowed him to bring her here. She sat beside him and she sat bravely, shored up by the visible proof of his ripeness: that gown and that hood that separated the man from the boys.

Twenty-one

Afterward, Dr. Ansel drove his mother straight home. Allen had been rather glad to have her along; that made it less like a "date." And she had every intention of going straight home, herself. But Ansel, having seen his mother into the house, came bounding back with other intentions.

"Want to go for a little ride," he said, releasing the brake, "get a breath of air?"

"I've got an awful lot to do," she said, but she hesitated. After all, Dr. Ansel wasn't afraid to be seen with her. Unlike the others, he had not turned the cold shoulder and crossed to the other side of the road. "Well, maybe, just for a little while." She had to make some small show of gratitude.

But she did not have to stop for a Coke at the Breeze Inn, otherwise known as the Grease Pit. "I really don't want a thing," she said.

"Chocolate malt? A banana split? They make swell splits out here."

"Oh, please, no. I don't think I could get around one of those," she said, who could polish off two at a sitting.

"Root beer?"

"Not a thing, really." A mean trick to play on Ansel's sweet tooth. But she had been seen with him once tonight. That was enough.

"Okay, we'll drive around awhile. Maybe you'll change your mind."

He drove slowly through the dark streets, most of them as familiar to her as her own two rooms. Presently, turning west, he said, "Guess you haven't had a chance to see much of this town, not having a car and all."

She leaned against the door, looking out, and said nothing.

"Lots of interesting spots around here. Interesting region. Ever been out to Chisdale Park?"

"It's rather late," she said.

"It's not far—just at the edge of town. Nice out there. It's a big park, sixty acres or so, I'd say. More, if you count the country club. That's more or less part of it. One runs right into the other. Beautiful spot. Old Chisdale was a millionaire, you know. Mining and land. He built one of those big houses not far from you, by the way. The land for the park was deeded to the city in 1890 and the adjoining acreage sometime later, after the war. That's the country club now. They've got a swell clubhouse, a real mansion from the looks of it. Guess we'll get to see it on Saturday at Miss Boatwright's reception. You're staying for the wedding, aren't you?"

"I plan to."

"I sure hope so. We'll have a good time at the reception."

They had come to the high bridge across the ravine. "This is the main entrance," he said. "The drive winds around clear across the park, but a lot of little roads leading off. Country club's over there to the right. You can't see the clubhouse from here, but that's the golf course all around it. Ever play golf?"

"I've—been on a golf course."

"Always thought it would be an interesting sport. You'll have to teach me how to play."

"I don't know much about it."

"I'll bet you do, I'll bet you're good at it. Dang! I wish it weren't so near the end of school. I bet you play tennis too. There are some nice tennis courts out here, right up that way."

And beyond the courts, the long hill sloping down to the creek where the fog sometimes rose over your head.

"I never learned to play tennis," he said. "Always meant to in college, but never could find the time. Now over on this side there's a lake, spring-fed. In summer they rope a part of it off where people can swim. Right over there, see? Lean over this way—see that long building? That's the bathhouse. You like to swim?"

"Wherever there's water."

"Same way with me. Learned in the creek down at the farm. My mother tried to keep me out, afraid I'd drown. But I sneaked in every chance I got. Don't have much time to swim nowadays. Now up here a little ways—up this drive, I think—there's a large playground. Swings and teeter-totters, slides, everything for the kids. I don't see it though. Must've been up that other direction."

She could have led him to it, blindfolded.

"Well, anyway, it's out here somewhere. And a bandstand and picnic area. This is a nice stand of trees along here."

Tiresome old Ansel, rattling off facts and figures, pointing out places she knew better than he did and wanted to forget. She sat in her corner of the seat and looked out the window.

"The majority of trees out here are oak, lot of scrub oak and hickory. Ash and sycamore down by the creek, and some willows."

He prattled on as they meandered through the maze of byways, through groves and hollows she knew by heart.

But soon, when they had left the park, driving along a road unfamiliar to her, she found that she was listening to his tales of feuds and hauntings, barn-raising and hell-raising in that hilly countryside, and high drama enacted here long ago in rude accents still touched with Elizabethan. He really did know a great deal.

"But I'm talking too much," he said. "You probably find it pretty dull."

"No," she said, meaning it, "not dull at all."

"I get wound up on local lore and forget when to stop."

"I like it."

"I didn't mean to monopolize the conversation. You haven't hardly got a word in edgewise. Let's talk about you for a while."

"Oh, that's not very interesting."

"I bet it is."

"What time is it? I should be getting home."

"But there are still so many places to see around here. Let's run out to Bunkin's Mill—I bet you've never been out there."

"That's a long way, isn't it?"

"Nah, mile or two."

It was more like five or six. If it had been any closer, within walking distance, she and Toby and George would have been there. But he entertained her with a story of old Bunkin's daughter, how she stood off her brothers with a forty-four when they tried to take over the mill. "That was after the old man died, around 1897. He got in some trouble with the half-breed his daughter married, some Osage wandered over from Oklahoma or left over from the days when they inhabited this neck of the woods. Rumor was that the gal used that forty-four on the husband not long after. He wasn't around when she took over the mill and ran the brothers off. It's a recreation place now, swimming pool and a dance pavilion. Right up this road here."

They turned off on a dark lane winding among the trees and across a narrow bridge. Beyond it the mill stood, tall and featureless in the darkness.

"You ought to see it when there's a full moon," Ansel said. "It's really picturesque. Mother and I came out here one night last summer. We spend most of the summer here in town, you know. Sometimes spend a few weeks with some kinfolks down close to the farm, but we're here most of the time. It was one of those real hot nights in July. We were just driving around, trying to get a breath of air. This place was all lit up around the pavilion. We could see people dancing and swimming. It's real swanky out here, so I've heard. There's the old mill part over there. Listen, you can hear the water."

He stopped the car and she sat back in her corner, expecting him to reach for her. But he left the motor running and after a moment drove on. The road was dark; it crossed a creek by a spillway, took sharp turns this way and that. She had no idea where she was until they were coming up Center Street, with the Grease Pit dead ahead, all its bare bulbs blazing.

"How about it," said Ansel, "you ready for something to drink now?"

There were cars (ceded for the evening by cautious fathers, in honor of graduation) nosed up to the Pit all around. The place would be swarming with kids. Toby and George might be there. "Thank you, no!" she said. "I couldn't. Really, I ought to get home."

"Well, if you think you have to."

He drove past the Grease Pit slowly, on past the bakery, re-marking on the aroma, and so at last to her corner.

"That was fun," she said, hopping out of the car before he could come around to help her. "It was fascinating, all that about the landmarks around here and the old settlers. You really know your local history. You should write about it."

"I've thought about it," he said, following her up the steps. "I'd like to write a novel about the region, something on the order of Harold Bell Wright."

"Something like that." She paused at the door and turned. "Thank you very much, Dr. Ansel. See you Monday."

"I sure hope we can do this again."

"Not another baccalaureate address!"

"I mean ride around like this. And talk. Gosh, it's too bad you're not going to be here this summer. Mother and I are going to be here most of the time."

"I've got summer school on my shoulders," she said. "Have to finish my education credits."

"Guess you'll be seeing a lot of your fiancé up there."

"Who? Oh."

"Your steady, your whatever you call him. What's his name anyway?"

"Max," she blurted. It was the first grown-up name that popped into her head.

"Max! Don't you gals marry anything but Maxes?"

"I didn't say I was going to marry him."

"I thought you were engaged."

"We—broke it off."

"Oh. Well. Golly, I'm sorry. I didn't mean to . . . Say, maybe if you're not going to be busy with him all summer—"

"Oh, I'll be busy!" she said, opening the screen door.

"It doesn't take long to drive up there."

"I've got an awful schedule." She reached inside for the light switch. "Education courses—you know how they are."

"But I guess you'll be back in the fall. You are coming back, aren't you?"

She took her hand off the switch, leaving the kitchen dark. One more step and she would have been home free. Ansel knew all about it. Give him a rumor and he would research it. She was regional history to him. "They—gave me a contract," she said.

"I—uh—heard they were trying to make some trouble for you."

"Who was?"

"That Medgar woman. Some gossip she picked up."

"She never did approve of me."

"Why not?" he said, with one foot across the doorsill.

"Oh, she thinks I'm too young. And she doesn't like my name."

"That's not enough to fire you for. I don't know just what it's all about. . . ." He waited for her to say. "Guess you know what it is."

"Sort of."

"You sure are tops with the students. Everybody knows that."

"They're nice kids."

"They sure think you're nice—especially the boys! Can't say I blame t'em." He hesitated and, when she said nothing, went off at another angle. "I like it when students want to know more than we have time to teach them in class. They're worth a little extra attention. I reckon you've found that too."

"Sometimes."

"It doesn't take much to start people thinking the wrong thing."

"No."

"I bet Mrs. Medgar imagines all kinds of things going on up here, you with your own apartment. Wild parties and all that."

"She'd like to think so."

"Stories get started. You know how it is. I certainly don't believe it."

"I should hope not."

"I don't know about the rest of them—Pickering and them. Lord's okay. He says if you want to go wild that's your business, long as it doesn't rub off on him. But Pickering and them . . . Some folks like to talk. You know how it is. Especially about someone as young and cute as you are."

"Oh, come on!" she said crossly.

"Well, you are cute. All of them think so whether they say so or not. Some of them just want to believe everything they hear."

"Seems like it. Well, good night again."

"I tell them it's not so. I do, I tell them. You've got more sense than that. And I can vouch for it. We've had too many good conversations for me not to know you're pretty smart. I tell them that too."

She turned to him slowly. "Thank you, Dr. Ansel."

"You don't have to call me Doctor."

"It's good of you to speak up for me. Not everyone would."

"I do. You know I'll do it, anytime."

"I appreciate it. Thank you," she said, humbled. "Thank you very much." She held out her hand. "Well, good night."

"Say, I sure did enjoy this evening."

"So did I," she said, pulling her hand away. "See you in the morning."

"Maybe we can do this again before you leave."

But he was faced with the door gently closing.

Twenty-two

*I*t had not been a bad evening, not bad at all. He had acquitted himself very nicely. And he had not laid a hand on her. She was grateful for that. She would not have wanted to have to rebuff Dr. Ansel. After all, he alone, of all her colleagues, had the courage to defend her. She wanted with all her heart to like him.

She worked at it all the following Monday, as she wrote out her class reports and began cleaning out her room for the summer. She willed herself to see him as distinguished and urbane, even, in a way, handsome. His hair, now that she gave it a second thought, was quite dark and glossy. It even curled a little at the edges. Or would have if he hadn't tried to paste it down with so much hair oil. She was nice to him, very nice. The nicer she was, the easier it became, until by the end of the day, after he had been in and out of her room half a dozen times, she had begun quite to enjoy it. It was like a game one learns to play well, that gets into the blood. She went home that night, if not altogether happy, at least for the first time in many days modestly pleased with herself.

She was therefore not precisely displeased, though certainly taken aback, when that evening a little after eight Dr. Ansel appeared at her door.

"I was just passing," he said, "and saw your light."

"Oh!" she said brightly. And they stood, he outside the screen, she inside, looking at each other.

"Would you mind if I came in?"

She lifted the hook. He stepped inside, smelling of lotion and Sen-Sen. He carried a white box under his arm. "I don't want to bother you if you're busy."

"I was just finishing supper."

"Go right ahead, don't let me interrupt."

"No, I'm through." She seemed to have taken root in the linoleum.

"Could I help you wash dishes? I help Mother sometimes."

"Oh, thanks, I'll just leave them. Again," she added, with a glance at the many left undone before. "Come on in. The place is a wreck." Shoes and books lay scattered on the floor. She had left the ironing board up with a skirt draped over the end.

Dr. Ansel looked hesitant. "I should have asked—maybe I shouldn't be here like this."

"It's all right. If you don't mind the clutter. I wasn't expecting anyone."

"I was just going by. Oh—here," he handed her the package, "I thought you might like these."

"Why, thank you! My goodness," she said, opening the box, "how nice!" Chocolates. The ritual offering. "They look delicious. Thank you very much." She held out the box. "Won't you?"

"Thanks." He lifted a candy from its paper cup and ate it in one bite.

"Will you sit for a minute?" she said.

He sat down on the sofa, she across the room in the big chair, and they waited. It was easier at school, with a desk between them.

"You've got a nice place here," he said.

"It's nicer when I clean it up. I've been pretty busy."

"Yes, it's a busy time of year." Another pause. "You've got a Victrola," he told her.

"Yes," she said, jumping up. "Want to hear some music?"

"That'd be just fine. Is it all right to play it this time of night?"

"Of course. Why not?"

"Your landlord won't object?"

"He doesn't live here. And I don't think the other tenants can hear a thing. This is a penthouse, nothing under it but attic. And the apartments downstairs. But they're too far away. What would you like to hear?"

"I don't care. Anything. I don't know too much about music. Got anything by that guy—you know, the one that wrote, 'I— must—go'?"

"Rachmaninoff, 'Prelude in C Sharp Minor.'"

"I like that one all right. You have that one?"

"I don't happen to have that, but here's another one of his. It's called 'The Isle of the Dead.'"

She had once seen a photograph of an island said to be the one Rachmaninoff had in mind; a small, steep rockbound island, gloomy with cypress. It was thrilling, and she bought the record because of that. The music, she found, was disappointing. But if she kept the picture in mind, it helped.

Dr. Ansel listened with a conscientious frown, his gaze studiously abstract, wandering from the phonograph to the candy box, up the wall to the Renoir dancer, and down again to the box.

She held it out. "Help yourself." She left the box on the table beside him.

Absently, he ate one piece and then another, his attention still on the music. Finally he shook his head. "I don't know, I'm afraid this kind of music is beyond me."

"It isn't one of my favorites. Let's play something else."

She would not play Debussy for Ansel, nor Gershwin. No, not "Nights in the Gardens of Spain," either. But she would let him have Tchaikovsky. She drew a record out of the jacket and set the needle on the First Concerto.

Dr. Ansel said he liked this one better. "This is mighty nice," he said, leaning back against the cushions. "You really know how to live, don't you? Books, classical music, flowers—"

His glance slid quickly past the withered tulips left in a vase, and up to the Renoir. "And pictures—that looks like real art. Boy, you know how to do it!" He smiled at her across the room and something a little sly crept into the smile. "There's only one thing missing right now," he said. To her astonishment, he drew a brown bottle from an inner pocket. "Good books and good music and good conversation need a little whiskey to go with them."

"Oh brother!" she said, laughing. "I'm in enough trouble without that! What would Mrs. Medgar say?"

"What's she got to do with it?"

"I'd never keep my job!"

"How's she going to know? She's not looking in the window." But he glanced over his shoulder to make sure. "Look, we're free, white, and over twenty-one. If we want to have a civilized drink together, that's our business. That's how I look at it."

"Yes, but—"

"Who's going to know? A civilized drink among friends. It's just like up at the university. The faculty get together and relax, have a few highballs. You know they do. Had one offer me a drink once. I bet you did too. I figure any graduate student did. It's nice. Really brings out the conversation."

"Yes," she said uncertainly.

"Why don't you get us a couple of glasses? Or tell me where they are."

"I'll get them." She took down the little tray she sometimes used on Sunday mornings when she had breakfast in bed. She covered it with a paper napkin, washed out two glasses, filled them with ice, and carried them in.

"Now that's what I call swank!" Dr. Ansel jumped to his feet, swallowing a mouthful of candy. "You really know how to do things. I hope you like bourbon," he said, pouring. "I could have got something else."

"Bourbon's fine. Just a little for me—that's enough."

But he poured the glasses half full and sat down again, looking pleased with himself. "Well, what is it they say? Here's to your health."

"Thank you."

He took a long pull at the drink and leaned back. "This is swell. Good literature and good company and whiskey." He smiled, raised his glass to her, and drank again.

Ill at ease, she sat holding the glass. Mrs. Medgar might not be at the window, but things had a way of being found out. Still, this was not quite the same; this was not a schoolkid across the room from her. It was a Ph.D., the most distinguished member of the faculty—who at this moment had opened a book from her table and was reading aloud from Walt Whitman. He read dramatically, as if from a platform, and rather too loud. But he read well and she said so.

It pleased him. "I read aloud to my classes a lot," he said. "I think it helps them get the meaning."

He then read a passage from Sandburg and from there, by way of the prairie poets and this one and that, got off on the frontier movement and its effect on American letters. Leaning back on the cushions, his legs stretched comfortably, he talked of the nineteenth century and the forces, political and geographic, that had shaped its writing. He was in familiar territory, and as he talked his assurance grew. Gone was the studious self-importance he wore around school like a barrel. Without it he wasn't so clumsy.

"The Frontier was the purifying agent," he said. "It settled out the dross as it moved west."

"The dross?"

"European influence. You might say it was like a big threshing machine." He laughed and drained his glass. "It separated the wheat from the chaff. Cleansing, defining. American writing wasn't thoroughly American until there was an America, and there was no real America until we went inland, away from Europe."

"How about Cooper? Wouldn't you consider him thoroughly American?"

"Well, yes, certainly," he said, rising to fill his glass again.

"The European dross sure wasn't purified out of him. Look at old Leatherstocking—right out of French Romanticism, except for the rawhide. And those Indians!"

"Well, I have to admit many of the early writers found the Noble Savage hard to resist. Even Cooper went a little overboard."

"I'll say he did!"

"But bear in mind, Cooper had a great deal more."

"Yes—anarchy."

"But also a sense of social order. That's the thing we have to remember. He might deplore the need of social order, but he knew it had to be. He had the Romantic viewpoint of uncorrupted values."

"The ones he saw fading. Like Faulkner," she added for the hell of it.

"Like *who*? Get outta here! How can you compare James Fenimore Cooper with a distortionist like that!"

"Easy," she said, and they were off on a fine argument, each in hot defense of his own man, until at last she retired from the field because Ansel had out-talked her.

Flushed with conviction, he had left Cooper as well as Faulkner well behind and was into American literature in general and its progress across the country. " 'Thou Mother with thy equal brood,' " he declaimed, " 'Thou varied chain of different States, yet one identity only . . .' " Names of people and movements began to tumble out, and ideas that had not occurred to her before. Nothing seemed to have escaped him, not Jefferson and the physiocrats, nor the Letters of Crevecoeur, nor obscure lady novelists known only to candidates for the Third Degree.

She had never heard him so impassioned. Ansel tonight was a far cry from the lunch-hour defender of Harold Bell Wright. He made sense, even though in the outflow of verbiage she wasn't always sure she was getting the point. She listened in surprise as he rushed headlong across the continent, stumbling over words as his tongue tried to keep pace with his thoughts. He was all over the map, jumping from the East to the North and West, from the Bay Psalm Book to the Veritists and West again to fetch up Ramona and plunk her down in Tocqueville along with Uncle Tom. It was a torrent of words poured out pell-mell, one over the other, his speech slurring in his haste to overtake his vision: America as he loved it through its literature, America in the beginning— infinite, abundant, and sublime.

"There's never been anything like the exuberance, the— the *en-nergy* of the American mind. I don't care if you talk about Cotton Mather or—Bret Harte—it doesn't make any difference. . . . Those writers in the South, what they've come to now, but at first . . . It doesn't make any difference. . . . Ol' Cotton Mather and ol' Increase . . ." He stumbled and stopped, a look of confusion on his face. "I lost the point I was going to make."

"You've made some good ones already."

"What I was going to say—" He gave his head a little shake. "It doesn't matter. By God, Miss Liles—" Smiling, he hunched forward, his hands dangling between his knees. "I never can talk like this to anybody else. I didn't mean to m'nopolize the conversation."

"You were wonderful."

"Was I?"

"You must have read everything in the Expansionist period."

"Not all of it."

"The Colonial period too, and remembered it. I wish I had retained as much. I'm not sure I agree with everything—"

"You don't have to agree."

"—but you make a very good case."

"I don't know. . . ." He sighed heavily and leaned back. "It's funny: Miss Boatwright, Miss Maxine Boatwright . . . doesn't know beans about literature," he said, with a try at nonchalance. "I took her out once, before she got engaged. Try and talk to *her* about anything." He drank from the empty glass.

The bottle was dry and it was more than apparent that the whiskey, as well as the vision, had overtaken Dr. Ansel.

"I like you, Miss Liles . . . Allen. Thass a funny name for a girl. I really like you. You knew that, didn't you?"

"You need some coffee," she said, rising.

"All those times we talked after school—you knew I didn't come in just to talk about James Fenimore William Faulkner." He laughed, catching himself as he tipped sideways. "Where you goin'?"

"I'm going to make coffee."

"Aw, don't go." He stood up and caught her by the arm, lurched sideways, and fell backward onto the couch, pulling her with him. In the struggle that followed, books and pillows hit the floor. One of her shoes came off. She was pinned against the back of the couch, dodging his mouth, when a sharp rap from the kitchen drew him up short.

"Wha's that?" Dr. Ansel struggled to his feet. "Somebody's knockin'." He gave a terrified glance around the room and bolted for the first door in sight.

There was no one on the landing. And no one in the alley below, though she ran halfway down to listen for a footfall or a snicker under the steps. No one. And up in her room, only Dr. Ansel, drunk as a goat and hiding in her closet.

"It's safe," she said, opening the closet door. "You can come out."

The dresses parted. "Did they hear me? Did they know I was here?"

"Nobody was there. It was only the ice tray—it slid off in the sink. That's all you heard."

"I thought somebody knocked. Maybe the landlord?"

"It wasn't the landlord. It wasn't anybody. Come on out."

He hesitated. Then, with a glance left and right, he threshed his way through a snarl of hangers, one foot in the laundry bag. "Whew! That was a close one!" He popped a chocolate into his mouth and collapsed onto the couch. "You're not expecting anybody, are you?"

"No," she said, picking up books.

"Nobody's liable to drop in on you?"

"Nobody's going to drop in."

"That's good. You don't care if I stay a little longer, do you? We were having a good time—boy, I don't very often—it was a good conversation, wasn't it?"

She had gone to the kitchen. Without bothering to measure, she ran water into the pot and poured in coffee. She wasn't sure he could find his way home or even stay on his feet. She turned the burner up high.

In the other room Dr. Ansel was mumbling on about conversation and people who didn't know beans. He broke off with a chuckle. "Allen? Where'd you go to? Come on back . . . Allen? Tha's a funny name for a girl. You know what my name is? Clarence. Dr. Clarence Ansel, Ph.D." He laughed drunkenly, mumbled something else to himself, and fell silent. After a moment, a wistful murmur: "You said I was wonderful. Am I wonderful, Allen?"

She was setting out cups and the sugar bowl. Dr. Ansel liked his coffee sweet, three spoonfuls at the Show-Me Cafe. Dead quiet in the other room. Lord help her if he passed out. She was afraid to look. She stood by the coffeepot, urging it on.

"What you doin'?"

She turned quickly. He stood in the doorway, his hair sticking up on the sides, his glasses missing, a dribble of chocolate at the corner of his mouth. He was all rumpled and bleary and askew. "What you doin' in here?"

"Making coffee."

"I don't want any coffee. What you tryin' to do, sober me up? Come back in here."

"You'd better go home, Dr. Ansel."

"I don't want to go home. Aw, Miss Liles—" He swayed a little, holding to the doorjamb. "Why don't you be nice to me? Give me a break."

"Now please—"

"We been good friends. Come on in here."

"You've got to go home!"

"Be nice," he said, lurching toward her. "Come 'ere."

"Dr. Ansel—" She picked up the coffee pot like a weapon. "Go home. Please!"

"Aw, what's the matter?"

"You're drunk."

"I can't help it." The smeared chin suddenly trembled. "I didn't mean to be—I mean, I never—" The pale eyes without the spectacles peered across the table, trying to focus on her. "We were having a good time and I—aw, *shit!* Something always goes wrong—I mean every time I try to—oh, God *damn!*"

And slumped against the icebox door, Dr. Ansel just came apart. He stood there all rumpled and chocolate-covered and poured out his burden of woe. The whole story of skimped pleasures and shattered hopes, clumsiness, frustration, and failure. A jumbled, untidy inventory. It gushed out from a bottomless well, pumped up by his strenuous sobbing.

Hypnotized, she listened to the blunders and humiliation, the small triumphs, honors so bitterly won, and the girls who had failed him. And always, over and over, the mother, the constant, incomparable mother. Who had scrimped and mended and fried country ham on coal-oil stoves in dark rented kitchens. Who had broken her health and paid the taxes and given him her life. The loving, beloved, pluperfect mother, whom he would risk death to escape.

"A bullet'll get me, I know it will. A bomb—I'll get killed, it'll kill her too. But I'm going—she's not going to stop me. If they call me and want me to go, I'm going to go. If we get mixed up in the war—she says we will—I'm going to enlist. I don't care if it kills her. It'll kill me too. I don't care. With my luck . . . I never could win anything. I couldn't do . . . anything right."

He wept without shame against the icebox door, the tyrannized child, weeping with fear and remorse.

She turned away to spare him her watching. "Let me pour you some coffee," she said gently. "You'll feel better."

Gradually the weeping subsided.

"Here, can you drink this now?"

"No, thanks."

"I put sugar in it."

"I don't think I could." He blew his nose. "Maybe," he said, a little calmer, "they might send me to officers' training school."

"They just might, with your qualifications. You'd make a good officer."

"But I haven't got the pull he's got, that fellow that's marrying Miss Boatwright. Maybe, though—I've got a doctorate—that ought to count for something—" He broke off abruptly, a horrified look spreading across his face.

"What is it?" She glanced quickly over her shoulder. "There's nobody there."

Dr. Ansel's cheeks puffed out. "Bathroom," he mumbled.

She had barely time to shove him through the door.

She stood on the landing in the cool spring dampness until the sounds from the bathroom stopped. Chocolate, whiskey, frustration, and failure. Dr. Ansel had sickened for a long time. When he came out, white-faced and sobered, she went back into the kitchen.

"Can I get you anything?" she said.

"No, thank you. I got to go home."

"Maybe if you drink some milk . . . Can you get it down?"

He drank. For a moment she thought the milk was coming up too. Then he belched mightily and looked happier, like a burped baby. "I'm sorry."

"It's all right. Button your pants."

"Oh!" He turned his back.

She went off to the living room and found his glasses. When she came back he was buttoned and buckled, the shirt tucked in. "I'm sorry," he said without looking at her. "I didn't mean to—I don't know—I always louse up."

"It's all right, don't worry about it. Here, put your glasses on. Go home now and get some sleep."

"Yeah."

"Everything will be all right. Nobody's going to find out."

He wavered, walked to the door, and said without turning, "But I do know something about American literature."

"Yes, you do, you know a great deal."

"The nineteenth century, and the sources."

"You were wonderful."

He hesitated, about to say something more. "Sorry," he said then in a low voice, and went out.

Twenty-three

*F*inally, on Wednesday the dean sent Roberta to fetch her. "Have you got a minute, Allen? Himself would like to see you."

More than two weeks had gone by since he first called her in. She went up the hall with Roberta as if to an execution. Things had been bad enough before, but now, added to her other crimes, was Dr. Ansel. If Toby and George had been seen going up and down her stairs, he could have been seen—the scrupulous Dr. Ansel, Ph.D., reeling out of her alley, stinking to heaven. She would be accused of corrupting him too.

"They say it'll hold for the next several days," said Roberta. "Be wonderful if it stays this nice for the wedding. Everybody will be so gussied up. What are you wearing?"

"New dress."

"Chiffon, like the rest of 'em?"

"Pique. Sort of plain."

"I bought a summer suit. I hate it already. All I could find I could fit into. I've got to shed some of these pounds. I always put 'em on during the winter. Sit at a desk too much. Go on in, he's waiting for you."

Mr. Frawley sat at his desk, peering intently through a magnifying glass. It was trained on a large gray moth, spread-winged on the blotter. "He's been flying around in here—have a seat, Miss Liles. The light must have roused him. Very interesting markings. Care to have a look?"

She rose and bent over the glass. Chocolate brown upper wings, light brown below, traces of pink, dark eyespots. "Pretty. What kind is it?"

"I'm not too expert on lepidoptera. But I would guess perhaps a spotted sphinx. He's a beauty, isn't he?" He touched a wing gently with the tip of a pencil. The moth quivered and rose, flopping off the desk like a hen too heavy to fly. "Ah, there he goes." They watched it rise to the top of a bookshelf and stick there. "Interesting insect," he said, putting the magnifying glass in a drawer. "Well, now."

The respite was over, and for the second time in five minutes, dread bit into her like the snap of a steel trap.

The dean folded his arms on the desk and looked across at her. "I'm sorry—" he said, and at that moment the moth fluttered down from the shelf, brushing the top of his bald head. "Mercy me!" he said, fanning it away. "Restless creature. If I could catch him—" The moth flitted across the desk, the dean chasing it with light slaps of his cupped hand. "Don't want to squash him. . . . There! If he'll sit still—no, missed him again."

She watched dumbly, without moving. He was sorry. Mr. Frawley had lost. And he was sorry.

"Ah, maybe this time. He's on your hair. If you could just—no, there he goes, on the barometer. Maybe he'll stay up there now for a while and stop bothering."

Nothing he said now could matter.

"Well, as I was starting to say, I'm sorry I couldn't get back to you sooner. I had hoped to see Mrs. Medgar right after we talked. But something happened—she had to be out of town—and it wasn't until last Thursday that I was finally able to meet with her. We had quite a long talk." He picked up the crystal paperweight and turned it so that the snow would fall. "I told her about our meeting and my opinion of the matter after talking with you. She wanted to think it over for a few days."

"Yes," Allen said faintly.

"We met again yesterday afternoon. And I believe"—he set the paperweight down carefully and looked up—"that Mrs. Medgar is satisfied with your explanation."

She hung for a moment longer.

"She accepts my judgment. And you will be with us again next year."

Still she hung. The rope had not yet been cut.

"We're not going to call in the board or carry it any further. So the matter is closed. No more need be said about it."

Then she let her breath out slowly and her feet touch ground. "Thank you," she murmured, half afraid to say it, afraid to believe.

But the dean, looking pleased, tipped back in his chair and swiveled toward the window, looking out at the sunny afternoon as he went on talking. Though her posture was attentive, she picked up only bits of what he was saying. She was afraid to let go of the dread. But the voice was comforting, reassuring, and she began cautiously to believe that this might indeed be acquittal.

"And so we can look forward," he said, turning to face her, "to having you with us another year. As many years, I'm sure, as you choose to stay here. Though you'll want to move on, in time. You'll grow in the profession."

"I shall try."

"It's a worthy profession, and a good life, if one addresses one-self to it . . . with devotion." He was talking to the window again, in his fashion. "You work at it, as one does, say, at a marriage . . . not only for personal satisfaction, but for the ideal of what a school should be, what education means. A dry word, education. There's much more to it than meets the ear. I'm sure you're aware of that," he said over his shoulder. "You seem to comprehend it better than some. I'm glad I could say that to Mrs. Medgar."

She smiled.

"My only regret is"—he turned to face her—"that I'll not have the privilege of working with you again."

"Oh?" she said.

"Some weeks ago—maybe you'll say nothing about it, it won't be announced officially for a few days yet. Early in the spring I offered my resignation."

She stared blankly for a moment before the words struck. "You're *resigning*?"

"It seems I am, at last."

So they had done it, Pickering and his gang. "But Mr. Frawley!"

"There comes a time," he said, "to step down."

"Surely the board won't let you!"

He smiled. "They very kindly protested."

"I should think they would! After all you've done—" She paused, openmouthed. "What'll we do without you?"

The dean turned pink, looked pleased and embarrassed. "Oh, you'll do very well."

"I shan't."

The old man smiled again. "You'll get along nicely, you'll see."

"But it won't be the same," she said, knowing how little would stay the same if Pick had his way about things. "Things will change. And it's a fine school the way it is. If it weren't for you—"

"Well, you mustn't give me too much credit for it. I've done what I could, but we've built it together, all of us, teachers and regents and the students together, and the townspeople. We're here because the people of the community wanted us. We have a special responsibility to them in all we do. Even to stepping down when the time comes."

"Maybe it hasn't come yet."

"I think I have served my purpose," he said. "It's time for someone new." He looked up cheerfully. "And time for me to go fishing."

"Like the president," she said, attempting a laugh. "I can't quite see that you'd be happy—"

"Oh, I'm quite a good fisherman. And I'd like to travel some, if the situation permits. Though I'm afraid"—he paused and picked up the crystal globe—"it doesn't look encouraging. Maybe another year. Maybe we have that long."

"No more than that?" she said.

"And less, I fear."

"But surely if we send supplies to Britain—"

"I'm afraid that won't be enough, things as they are. And all of Western Europe fallen, North Africa . . ."

She said, fearful of asking, "Do you think the United States will be—? Will our boys be sent overseas? Into battle?"

There was a pause as the snow fell. "Yes," he said and set the round globe down.

For a moment neither of them spoke.

"But," he said, "we'll face it as well as we can, if it comes to that. Meanwhile, we have our work to do."

"But you're leaving."

"I'll find plenty to do, never fear. There's so much to read, new books and old ones again. My education may just be beginning."

"We'll miss you, sir."

"Well, thank you. And I'll miss all of you, teachers and students, the environment. I've been at it a long time. But we'll adjust, all of us. We have a new man coming in, young man from Springfield, from the college over there. Nice family, two children. And well qualified. More experience than I've got in administration. I'm a teacher, primarily."

"Can't you stay on and just teach, without the other responsibilities?"

"I think not," he said slowly, his arms on the desk.

She knew, of course. He was no longer wanted. They had pushed him out. And the school as Mr. Frawley envisioned it would take another direction. The old man seemed to droop as he looked out the window. She tried to think of something to say, some way to restore him to his rightful place. "There must be something we can do!"

He tilted back, facing the window again. He seemed not to have heard her. And then he said something she had not expected to hear. He said, "I never wanted to teach." Quite simply, as if it had just slipped out. "Nor to be part of the educational system. It was not what I would have chosen." He said, "There was something else. . . ."

She waited for the rest of the sentence. She could see him as nothing except what he was, for he was so excellently that. What was it that held him so contemplative as he gazed out at the sun-spattered leaves? What had he wanted to do? Be a writer? Paint a mural? Go to sea, like Conrad? She glanced up at the sailing ship locked in ice, and around the wall at the gleaming instruments of weather. What *was* it he wanted to do—her gaze swept back to the Arctic map—see the top of the world?

"We fall into conditions," he said, "one way or another. And it was all right. It's only that 'there was a road not taken'—" He glanced at her over his shoulder. "Robert Frost, is it? Yes. And I suppose we never stop wondering what lay down the other road."

He said it serenely, as casually, almost, as if he were remarking on the weather. But there was a touch of wistfulness in his tone, and regret.

Her compassion for him, already brimming, spilled over. Oh, she knew! And she found herself, with her own longings imposed on his, weeping for Mr. Frawley that he had not danced in Spain.

"Goodness gracious!" The old man swiveled around, half rose, flustered and looking contrite, as if it were all his fault. "My goodness, now! You've been working too hard, Miss Liles. The end of school, so much to do. A stressful time."

"I'm sorry," she said, tears rolling down her face. "I don't know why I should do this." The tension had been enormous, but it was more than that. She dabbed at her eyes with a soggy Kleenex and fumbled in her pocket for another. The dean came around the desk with the wastebasket, like an old deacon with the collection plate. She dropped the wet tissues and looked up expectantly. "I guess it was what you said about something else. Something you'd rather have done?"

But the old man had allowed himself one lapse, and he turned aside from it now. "Yes," he said, putting the basket back in place. "There's always something else we think we want to do, at some stage in our lives. But we get over it, we outgrow it. And after a while we realize that where we are is where we are meant to be."

"With no regrets?" she said, reluctant to give up Spain.

"Oh no," he said cheerfully, "there are regrets." He batted at the moth, which had come down from somewhere to flit around them again. "Can't help a few regrets now and then. They're natural. But we have to keep in mind that early ambitions are sometimes deceiving, and make the best of what comes. Although you never forget the other, quite. Goodness me," he said as the moth grazed his ear, "he's getting to be a nuisance. I wish he'd find his way out." The moth landed on the desk. Cupping his hand, the dean brushed it toward the window. The creature hit the floor, rose, and fluttered to the windowsill. "Ah!" said the dean. He pulled open a drawer, took out a swatter and, advancing on the moth, cautiously raised his hand. Then with a quick flick he flipped the moth out the window. "There now," he said with satisfaction, "he landed in the vines. He'll be all right now. For such time as he has. Some of them live no more than a day. Well, Miss Liles," he said as he put the swatter away, "I'm very happy that you're going to be here another year."

"So am I. And I thank you for your help. Without it—"

"I was glad to do what I could. I wouldn't want you to have any mark on your record that could be troublesome."

"I'm very grateful, sir."

"You've been a conscientious member of our staff, an asset to us, I should say. I wouldn't want to see your career destroyed by misstep or misunderstanding. You bring a freshness and enthusiasm to your work. Maybe a little too much at times, but that will temper. You're young yet, with time and experience you'll develop in judgment. I've observed you through the year, the way you conduct your classes, the ideas you bring out in the students. You have a good sense of the direction our school has been going, the way I felt was right for us. There are a few who would like to change it."

And they would, if they had their way.

"What they want to offer is what I call training, not enlightenment. I believe in the classical education. History and the arts, all the richness and moral truth of great literature and philosophy. They may not seem relevant to times such as these. In a time of war there will be a need for the practical skills. But I think such training will be available and very quickly. It's the classical values that will fall by the wayside unless we prevent it. It is this that we must hold out to the young. Whether they accept it or not, we must hold it out."

She listened, sitting very still.

"Of course, we're limited, a small college such as ours. But we can point the way. We can place the emphasis where it belongs. Now that I'm leaving, I have to trust to those of you who believe in the classic values, as I do. You are among them, I think. From all I can tell, you lean more than others toward the same goals I have striven for. I'm glad you'll be here to defend them."

"For your sake—" she said.

"I have great faith in you, Miss Liles. It pleases me to leave you as . . . earnest, so to speak, to carry on what we believe in."

It was a moment before the full import of his speech took hold. "Thank you," she said then and felt the mantle settle on her shoulders.

Twenty-four

She walked out of the office in a daze. Not an hour ago she had gone up this hall on the way to execution. Now here she was—acquitted, her head, addled though it was, still on her shoulders and filled with the old dean's praise.

Could it be that the ordeal was over? She did not have to face Mrs. Medgar, she did not have to go before the board, and she had not lost her job. It was more than she could take in.

She stood at her desk in wonderment, gazing at the room. It was hers again. These chairs would be filled again with her students. She would guide them again through the beauty and complexities of grammar and poetry. (And she wouldn't let them come near her after hours.) On winter afternoons she would conduct her seminars. One on the Greeks, for Mr. Frawley. (Although, she would have to work hard learning about them this summer, if she were to know enough to impart anything to anyone.) She would try to be worthy of Mr. Frawley, and of her professors at the university, three or four of the best, whom she thought of now: scholarly and persuasive, able to communicate with wit and wisdom and without pedantry. She would have to work very hard.

The warm, early June air drifted in through the open windows, carrying a hint of roses. It was lovely outside. Leaves, light, sparrows in the street—everything danced. The ordeal was over. She had weathered it, thanks to Mr. Frawley and thanks to him in triumph.

Beginning to believe it, she wanted to exult a little, throw her hat in the air, jump over the moon. At the very least she wanted to tell somebody. Her first thought was her mother. She would write to her immediately. No, the letter wouldn't get there before she did. She would go down to the Bonne Terre to a telephone booth and call her! But what would she say? That she had not lost her job after all? She had never told Mother that she *might* lose it. If she called home now, exulting, it would sound mighty suspicious. Dalton? But what if Mother were at the farm, as she so often was? That would raise too many questions. No, all she could say was that she had made up her mind to stay on. And that could wait till she got home.

But she wanted to share the news now, and how could she, without admitting that there had indeed been trouble. She hadn't admitted that to anyone but Dalton. Except, in a way, to Ansel. Poor Dr. Ansel. She had not thought of him all day. Old Ansel, crying and slobbering in her kitchen, with his pants undone and candy all over his chin. How could he stand himself? He probably couldn't.

Who was there to tell? The Ladies, of course, but that would mean admission, and be damned if she would. What they didn't know they didn't need to know. Anyway, in the mysterious ways of such words, the word was probably out already that she had not been fired.

She laughed and, heeding the clutter on her desk, sat down to finish her work. She had been ridding out for the summer when Roberta came to fetch her and had left the desk piled high with papers, odds and ends accumulated through the year. As she sorted through them, one of the odds and ends slipped off onto the floor. She picked it up, glancing at it as she dropped it into the wastebasket. *Rules for Teachers. 1872.* Something Ansel had come across in the course of his research and had brought in to show her. They had laughed over it one afternoon after school. Amused, she pulled it out of the basket and read it again.

Teachers each day will fill lamps, clean chimneys. Each teacher will bring a bucket of water and a scuttle of coal for the day's session. . . . Men teachers may take one evening each week for courting purposes, or two evenings if they go to church regularly. . . . Women teachers who marry or engage in unseemly conduct will be dismissed. . . . Any teacher who smokes, uses liquor in any form, frequents pool halls, or gets shaved in a barber shop will give good reason to suspect his worth, intention, integrity and honesty. . . .

She laughed and dropped the list back into the basket. Things had changed a little since 1872.

A few moments went by and a few more scraps into the basket before she paused again and looked up. But had they changed that much? She did not have to bring a scuttle of coal, and she hadn't been shaved in a barbershop. But conduct unseemly was unseemly, no matter what the year, and conduct immoral, immoral. Hers had been both. Mrs. Medgar knew. Toby and George knew. Mr. Frawley refused to know. And yet, she had not been dismissed. Not only that—she had been rewarded. She had accepted the dean's praise and his faith, though she was guilty of the rumored sins and a few unrumored, and she had not confessed. She was guilty of duplicity, of concealment amounting to a lie!

Still, she reasoned, trying to quiet her conscience, there had been punishment. Though she was spared the wrath of Mrs. Medgar and saved from the Inquisition, she had not been spared the tortures of remorse. It had cauterized her. And perhaps it had taught her something, something painfully learned from the students. Wasn't it enough that they had seen her descent from the pedestal where their respect had placed her? She had betrayed their respect. And wasn't it enough that in that descent she had lost the two she loved most? She had paid for her transgressions. She would go on paying for a long time yet. So perhaps repentance, even in silence, was enough, and she could be worthy of Mr. Frawley's trust.

She sat for a long time thinking. Then she sighed deeply. She had better be worthy of that trust. Without it, she would be on the streets selling *The Book of Knowledge*!

With one drawer emptied, she pulled out another and dumped the contents on the desk. But in spite of her guilt, the urge to rejoice caught her up again and she thought again of Ansel. She had scarcely seen him since that night in her apartment. No wonder; he was probably too embarrassed to live and probably still hung over. Silly old Phud. She couldn't help feeling sorry for him.

She was going through outdated lesson plans, carefully removing paper clips, when the bell rang for four o'clock. But the kids were already gone. She scooped the paper clips into a box and went on sorting odd pieces of paper.

Presently she heard Mae Dell and Gladys coming up the hall and the lounge door swing open. A moment later there was a polite cough in her doorway, and Verna, with a glance over her shoulder, stepped quickly into the room.

"Oh, hi, Verna, come on in."

"Haven't got but a minute." Verna glanced over her shoulder again and said, almost in a whisper, "I just wanted to say I'm glad you're coming back next fall."

So the news was out. "Thank you, Verna."

"Just thought I'd tell you."

"That's nice of you. Thank you very much."

Verna smiled and, looking embarrassed, sidled to the door and went out.

The lounge door swung open and shut another time or two, and after a bit the Ladies went off down the hall. She could hear Mae Dell asking why they had to go to the Show-Me again and Verna explaining that it was quicker.

As the voices faded, Allen turned back to her work. It was good of Verna to welcome her back, but they hadn't asked her to go out to supper with them. It was all right though. For all their avoidance of her in the last few weeks, she couldn't hold it against them. They were only protecting themselves. They had to; even less than the men could they afford a hint of suspicion. It was unfair.

She worked on for another twenty minutes. Then, with the desk cleared, she took her handbag out of the bottom drawer and pushed back her chair. But she lingered, watching the light break on the maple leaves outside the windows. There had been a time the other night when a different Ansel appeared. A man of some brilliance, who knew what he knew and loved it greatly. She had liked that man. That one did a great deal to redeem the other. Though not without a struggle. She rose with a shake of her head. Too bad it had to be so hard.

Turning to the blackboard, she erased the last chalk marks and stacked the erasers. She wiped her hands on a Kleenex and picked up her bag. But again she hesitated, and after a moment she set the bag down and went across to the windows. Though the sun was still high, the sky was beginning to turn gold over the red brick house. It would be a pretty night—clear, with a first-quarter moon. She turned quickly and picked up the bag. Then she set it down again. Well, both of them had suffered humiliation. And she too, knew something about mothers and the hammerlock they put on you in the name of love. She hesitated a moment longer, then went out and up the stairs to the second floor.

He was still at his desk, working. "Hello," she said from the doorway.

He looked up, startled, and jumped to his feet, upsetting the chair. "Goddammit!" he said, setting it straight, and he turned to her, white-faced and defenseless.

"May I come in?"

"Yeah—sure—come on in."

"I didn't know if you'd still be here."

"I'm still here." Too paralyzed to move, even to look away.

"It's kind of late. What are you working on, final reports?"

"Yeah, reports."

"Tiresome, isn't it? Well, don't let me interrupt. I just wanted to tell you—"

"You're not interrupting."

"—that I had a talk with Mr. Frawley this afternoon."

The look on his face turned to horror. "You didn't say anything about—"

"Of course not!" she said, smiling. "I didn't say much at all. He did all the talking."

"About me?"

"No, silly, about me. That business we were talking about last Friday night, remember? That stuff Mrs. Medgar had told him?"

Dr. Ansel sat down limp. "Oh, yeah, that." Remembering his manners, he stood up again.

"Well, it's all cleared up, the rumors, everything. Mr. Frawley talked to her and explained. He thought she might make me go before the board and explain to them, but he changed her mind about that. Everything's okay. I've still got a job. They're not going to fire me."

"Ah, that's good!"

"I thought you might like to know. You were so nice about it, speaking up. I thought maybe—"

"I'm glad it's cleared up. I mean it, I'm really glad!"

"So am I. Pretty, isn't it, the light outside? I was just wondering. . . ." She paused, looking at him thoughtfully. He stood there rigid, but no longer quite so miserable. Clean-shaven, vested and buttoned, he looked in fairly good shape. She swallowed and said, "I was thinking, that as long as both of us are going, we might as well go to the wedding together."

His mouth opened slowly.

"If you wouldn't mind coming by for me," she said.

Staring, he said in a flat voice, "You—want me to take you?"

"If you wouldn't mind."

"I wouldn't mind." He came around the desk, catching his toe on the chair leg. "Heck, no, I'll be glad to!"

"And it's fine with me if you bring your mother."

"Yeah, I'll have to."

"About three-thirty—would that be all right?"

"Three-thirty, that's swell. Thanks a lot!" He was shaking her hand. "Thanks a whole lot. I'll be there, Johnny-on-the-spot. Golly," he said, pumping up and down, "I didn't think you'd ever speak to me again after—" He stopped, letting her hand drop as he turned away from her. "Oh *God*," he said. It came up from the depths.

"Don't worry about it. You had too much to drink, that's all. And I shouldn't have let you eat candy. They don't mix, you know." She said it playfully, but he kept his back to her, shaking his head. "Except for that, you were fine—reading poetry and talking. You were just fine."

"Allen—" He turned with a face full of humility and hurt. "I don't know what to say."

"You don't have to say anything."

"I was blubbering, feeling sorry for myself."

"We all do sometimes. You're no worse than the rest of us. Look, I've got to run. See you tonight."

"Yes," he said humbly, "thank you."

"I'll be ready at three-thirty."

"I'll be there."

It was a good feeling, restoring a man's self-respect, some measure of it. It would help her. She wouldn't mind so much being seen with him. She wasn't wild about it, but he was so miserable, poor thing. And he was not a bad fellow. Maybe she could forget the embarrassing side and concentrate on the other. She ran down the steps, determined to try.

"*Hey. Teach!*"

She stopped like a reined-up pony and turned around. Toby and George were coming up from the front door.

"We were looking for you!" They came up the hallway at a trot, grinning all over.

"We were over at your house," said George. "Where you been?"

"Upstairs," she said in a shaky voice.

"You still workin'?" said Toby.

"Just getting ready to go home."

"We'll go with you!"

He said it so merrily. They were all lit up, high spirits spilling over around them.

"Well," she said and hesitated. She was a *teacher*—moral responsibility—dignity—"I'm awfully busy."

The boys glanced at each other. "We've got to talk to you," George said.

"What about?"

Another glance between them. "Well, the other night," he began, "at baccalaureate—"

Toby broke in. "When you leavin' town?"

"Sunday."

"Sunday!" Both of them said it.

"Jeez," said Toby, "that's right around the corner."

"Can't you hang around?" George said.

"I'm afraid not. Summer school."

"Do you *have* to go to summer school?"

"Have to."

"That's crummy."

"I don't want to go!" She hadn't meant it to sound quite so woeful and she added hastily, "But I'll like it fine, once I get into it. I'm looking forward to it, really. I have lots of friends up there and, well, it should be fun." She smiled. "Got to run now. See ya."

But George had stepped in front of her, blocking the way. Pronouncing slowly, he said, "You aren't going to be with the Phud again tonight, are you?" He said it in disbelief, as if the very thought were preposterous.

"We saw you with him at baccalaurate. Are you going out with him, like on dates? Gee *whiz*, Teach, he's not one of us—I mean, you shouldn't be—why do you let yourself in for that! Listen, we been awful busy. Term papers and all finals and that. And farewell parties—but—" He glanced desperately at Toby, who stood tongue-tied and wistful, of no help at all. "But jeezy, there wasn't time for much *fun*. Like we used to have. It was—oh, what the hell, Teach, we miss you!"

"It ain't the same without you," Toby said.

The prettiest sounds she had ever heard.

"I got the scholarship." George said.

Restraint forgotten, she gave a cry of delight and opened her arms to him, exultant. But before he could enter, she had drawn them back, clasping her hands together. "I knew you'd get it!"

"The letter came yesterday. I could hardly wait to tell you. We were saving it for tonight."

"So we could celebrate," said Toby.

They had come back! After all this time, after she had thought it all out, faced up to her foolishness, and stopped wanting them, here they were, sassy and serious and funny, just as they used to be. After she thought spring was over!

"Come on!" they said.

They had missed her and forgiven her.

But she had walked out of the dean's office older and soberer and saved. She must go home now and press her black gown. Yet there they stood, in her way, expectant, young and alive, on the side of joy. Her decent, her rightful kin. Who cared that they were only schoolboys! She had been happier with them than with anyone else in her life. Oh, hell and damn, why did they have to come back now!

She drew in her breath and held it till her voice should be steady. "I'm afraid I can't this time. Sorry." And smiling, she walked away.

Twenty-five

The mortuary hush was broken by the swish of footsteps up and down the carpeted aisles and the low groan of the organ behind the tapers and banked lilies. Dim and stuffy, the church was lit with the jewel hues of the stained glass. The afternoon sun, shining through saints, cast a blue pall over heads and shoulders, streaks of amber and the crimson stain of the Blood over the pews. A feeble breeze came through the open lower half of the windows. Maxine's wedding day had arrived clear and serene and hotter than a pistol.

From time to time expectancy rose to a murmur as the ushers went up and down, delivering guests to their proper places. The academic community—college, high school, faculty wives, and Dr. Ansel's mother—sat as a group among the friends of the bride. Allowing for air apace between them, as much as they thought permissible, they took up several rows on the west side of the church.

Allen sat in the middle of the pew, behind Mr. Lord, Gladys on one side, Verna and Mae Dell on the other. They had let her in among them again. Wearing her new hat like a halo, she sat resigned and acceptant, with a feeling of beatification, as if through penance and sacrifice she had come close to sainthood. Or as close as she was likely to get. At any rate, she was chastened and she had given up Toby and George. Though she had strayed, she was back now among the flock. And didn't the Lord rejoice more in the one than in the ninety and nine? Well, maybe. Anyway, here she was.

She glanced along the row: Dr. Ansel on the other side of Mae Dell; beyond Gladys, the Pickerings, and nearest the window, the dean and Mrs. Frawley. Up and down, the alternation of flowered chiffon and Palm Beach suits. The earnest, professional faces, the accumulation there of study, hard work, penury, forbearance, and dedication. A genus to which she belonged.

The ushers in their white jackets and satin-striped trousers still passed back and forth. One of them she recognized as Maxine's brother, looking like an altar boy grown too tall for his surplice. He had come down the aisle with a lady on his arm who, as she saw now, was Mrs. Medgar, wearing a dress of gray chiffon and a bouquet of a hat. A very beautiful hat it was, though long out of date. As the usher handed her in, she looked up to thank him and she smiled. Her cheek was touched lightly with rouge. The boy strode back up, young and tall and intent on his courteous task.

Glancing again at Mrs. Medgar across the aisle and one row up, Allen mused on that unexpected smile and the fluttery gray dress let out to accommodate a body no longer slender and young; the absurd girlishness of the face, its severity painted over. Out of a small round rouge box, she imagined, on an ivory tray with the brush and comb and the ivory hair-receiver. And nearby, in an ivory frame, a man with large, dark eyes. All that was left of her youth, hidden in a small back room. Joy lost, hope dead, love reduced to the tyranny of a hidden voice.

But she mustn't romanticize, she reminded herself, nor let a little sympathy put her off guard. Life had not been kind to Mrs. Medgar, and on any who had not suffered as she had the lady would have her revenge. Though she had lost this round to Mr. Frawley, she would not lose another.

Nevertheless, Allen could not keep her eyes off the hat, nor her thoughts from that tinted smile. Last week Mrs. Medgar had buried her husband. (Called out of town, Mr. Frawley had said. It was Dr. Ansel who told her why. Ansel the omniscient, who had it from a seamstress who knew a lady who lived next door to Mrs. Medgar. The seamstress was a friend of his mother's.)

The organ prelude throbbed to a close. There was a quiet stir among the congregation, and a few heads turned toward the door. But the organist faced them front again, and a soprano in blue ruffles began to sing.

The birthday of my life is come, my love is come to me.

Gladys put an elbow in Allen's ribs. "Shall we sing 'Happy Birthday'?" But there was no sizzle through the back teeth and Gladys sat quietly through the rest of the song and through "I Love You Truly."

A doleful song, when you thought about it. Life with its sorrows, life with its tears, and sung like a dirge every time. Women always cried. Men squirmed. In the row ahead Mrs. Lord touched a handkerchief to her eyes, and Allen herself felt a spasm of sentiment. Weddings were like that. Even Gladys was sneaking a handkerchief to her nose. (Old sizzling Gladys—had she really, as Dr. Ansel said, been married once to some rotter with a few other wives? Or something of the sort. And were all her giggles and dumb little jokes a cover for a broken heart? If so, she was very brave about it. And whatever it was, she wept now about something.) Life with its tears indeed! *Gone is the sorrow.* . . . Like hell it is. Look at it all around. What a jumble life is, she thought in sudden exasperation, how treacherous and splendid and ridiculous all at once—as it was now, all this blest expensive pageantry, the air thick with women's sorrows, lost youth and love gone by, and the church got up like a funeral on a hot June afternoon.

A laugh or maybe a sob or both caught her in the middle, and she felt another nudge in the ribs. "You're chugging," Gladys whispered.

The soprano finished. During the brief organ interlude the bishop appeared in the full dignity of his white and gold. There was a suspenseful pause. Then, with a blast that shook the windows, the opening bars of the processional resounded through the church. Every female head snapped to attention as the first bridesmaid stalked down the aisle, studiously keeping time. Three others followed and behind them, sweating like a pig, the maid of honor in blue dotted Swiss. Then, summoned by Wagner, the bride appeared, smiling, rose begirt, a cumulus on her father's arm, trailing a drift of heirloom lace and delicate sweet scent. Maxine did not sweat. As the groom stepped forth to join her at the altar, a shaft of golden light through the stained glass fell across their shoulders.

"Dearly beloved, we are gathered here . . ."

Up and down the row the handkerchiefs were busy. Only Verna and Dr. Ansel's mother sat unmoved, holding their pocketbooks. Allen leaned sideways to see around Mr. Lord and wondered if Mrs. Medgar had wept all her tears long ago.

". . . and this woman in holy matrimony, which is an honorable estate, instituted of God . . ."

Wedged between Gladys and Verna, with Lordy directly ahead, she could see very little. But the bishop had a fine, resonant voice that carried throughout the church.

". . . not to be entered into inadvisedly, but reverently, discreetly, soberly, and in the fear of God. Into this holy estate these two persons present come now to be joined. If any man can show just cause why they may not lawfully be joined together, let him speak now, or hereafter forever hold his peace."

The bishop paused for a breath, long enough for Allen to think of Jane Eyre and the madwoman's brother, half hoping that a voice would rise from the back of the church and interrupt this marriage. For a reason she could not put her finger on, it had begun to disturb her. The opening blast of the "Wedding March" had shaken loose some premonition of doom and disappointment.

But there would be none of that in this honorable marriage. Not unless Max . . . but what could possibly happen to Max? He would come safely home. And Maxine would be an honorable wife, happy and secure in the place she had chosen.

The heat was stifling. The to-and-fro of handkerchiefs made a nervous flutter all over the church. How could they stand it up there at the altar with candles all around them? How could they breathe? It was hard enough back here. The smell of wax and hothouse flowers was suffocating. She glanced longingly at the open window, many bodies away. Green grass and a strip of deep green shade. Maxine should have been married out there. The poor thing, trapped in ninety-eight yards of lace, and all those candles burning!

"Max Philip," the voice was an admonition, "wilt thou have this woman . . . love her, comfort her, and keep her . . . so long as ye both shall live?"

"I will!"

"Maxine Olivia, wilt thou have this man to thy wedded husband, comfort him, honor, and keep him in sickness and in health, and, forsaking all others, keep thee only unto him, so long as ye both shall live?"

"I will."

"Who giveth this woman to be married . . . ?"

Allen listened with a shudder. Did she know—Maxine, with her head full of dinner dances and pineapples on doilies—did she know what she was getting into? She had walked smiling down the aisle to be delivered into bondage, never to be her own woman again, but the property of another and, for all the honor and comfort, beholden to his laws. Did she *know* what she was doing?

The voices rose and fell, stating, repeating. "I, Max Philip . . . I, Maxine Olivia . . . so long as we both shall live . . . Till death do us part." *Till death* . . .

There had been a time when she thought she might like to be married, someday, far in the future. But now as she listened, amid all the trappings of the wedding, it didn't seem thrilling at all.

The more she heard of the terms of wedlock, the more threatening they sounded. Thou wilt, or else! Thou wilt keep and cherish, forsake all others, honor, obey and bring a scuttle of coal, and thou wilt unto death. Her ear itched. The hat was too tight and her hair was sweating. In front of her, streaks of sweat ran down Lordy's neck into his collar. The poor man was dying of the heat. They were all dying, all around her, upright and proper, all in a row.

She looked out again at the cool, deep shade, the stir of leaves in a little wind, and pools of sunlight quivering like water. Out there the day was alive and breathing. If it weren't for all the bodies in between, she could be out in a flash. And wouldn't that be a fine old ruckus—Miss Liles, conductor of seminars, out the window and gone, with a kick of her heels and the back of her hand to Thou wilt unto death!

She could see herself now, clambering over all those knees, nipping over the sill, to the horrification of everyone around. It tickled her. She held her mouth tight to keep from laughing. She wouldn't dare try anything like that. She would get stuck in the window. But it made her feel better just to think about it. There had been enough here of death and forever.

But now that the thought of escape had come, it would not go away. It hung on, teasing and wheedling, a voluptuous little thought, tempting as sin, that grew louder by the minute—as if some dissembling evil spirit were luring her with sweet sounds and delicious aromas away from safety and warmth. It was whispering slyly of adventures, new, bold, and possible, of all the serious heights she had imagined all her life. Telling her she did

not belong in this place, that there within reach was all outdoors
and a whole wide world full of roads not taken, and how would
she know where they led if she didn't go forth and look! There
would be hell to pay if she did, and remorse such as she hadn't
known yet—fire and brimstone and blizzard and itch—and the
road could end at the town dump. And yet, could she *not* go?

She looked hard at Lordy's perspiring neck.

Up at the altar some business of the ceremony was going on in
silence. A tingle crept down her spine like a spider trapped under
her clothes. Then the bishop's authoritative voice:

"Repeat after me: 'With this ring I thee wed . . . '"

"With this ring I thee wed . . ."

"In the name of the Father—"

In the name of the Father, how was she going to get out of it
now? She came to with a start. She had hoped and repented, even
prayed a little, and promised all sorts of repayment in her heart, if
only they would allow her to stay, and now that they had allowed
it, she didn't want to stay here at all. Her father had delivered her
freedom from beyond the grave

". . . abide in thy peace, and continue in thy favor, unto their
life's end . . . through Jesus Christ our Lord."

But Lord, she had been chosen! And she had consented, forsaking all others, for academe.

"Let us pray. 'Our Father, who art in heaven, Hallowed be thy
Name. Thy kingdom come. Thy will be done, On earth as it is in
heaven. Give us this day—"

Oh, more than our daily bread, Lord! She was praying too, in
her own words and with all her might, praying on past the power

and the glory (did it have to be forever!) and on through the last incantations. She didn't want this job. She would be desperate without it, but she most desperately did not want it. She had told her mother more truth than she thought. Against all reason, with no compass and no place to go, with most of the world in turmoil, she wanted out.

And if the truth were known, she had no right to be *in*. By all that was just, they should have sent her packing. But they hadn't. And here she was now, caught by her own duplicity and trapped in the middle of the row, with the knot tied and the ring in her nose and Mr. Frawley between her and the window. Life everlasting. Amen.

The triumphant boom of Mendelssohn set the final seal.

Solemnity at the breaking point, the congregation rose noisily as the wedding party, in joyous disorderly retreat, charged up the aisle. Allen sat in a sodden heap, tears dripping into her lap. Her sins had turned on her in the mockingest way. Life would always turn on you, maybe. As it had on her mother. And on Gladys and Mrs. Medgar. She wept for them all. She wept for Dr. Ansel.

"Get up, Allen, people are trying to get out! I'm so hot I could die."

They squeezed her into the aisle, Gladys on one side, Mae Dell on the other, close behind Dr. Ansel. Her face was on a level with his shoulder blades, where perspiration had left a dark stain. She could smell the damp mustiness of his coat. The line moved slowly, held up by kisses and congratulations outside on the steps. He smelled of mothballs. Down in among the warm bodies she wept again in despair. And was still at it when they all moved out onto the lawn.

"Why, look at you!" somebody said. "Your face is all wet."

"Can't you dry up?" said Verna. "What is the matter with you?"

"Oh, she's just crying because she isn't the bride."

But she was the bride. That was the trouble. Inasmuch as she had consented, advisedly, soberly, in the fear of Mother and Mrs. Medgar, she was joined in this union. And it wasn't for another year, maybe three, maybe five, it was till death did them part. That's how it went, one year leading to another, until it became a habit too comfortable to break. Security was pernicious. Once you had it, you might never let go, not for the world and all the gardens in Spain. That's how it went and how it would go with her unless she escaped it now. But she *couldn't* escape. And it wasn't her mother who stopped her now, it was Dean Frawley, that gentle, well-meaning old man.

"Here, honey, here's a clean hanky." Mae Dell put a moist arm around her. "I always carry two to weddings. Now stop teasing, you-all. Weddings just do this to us, don't they, Allie? I cried myself. It was a beautiful wedding. Wasn't it?" she said, looking up at Dr. Ansel, who had joined them. "Just beautiful, wasn't it? I bet you cried too. Come on now, one weensie tear?"

"It was very impressive," he said. "You ladies need a ride to the country club?"

"Oh, can we go with you?"

"You got room for all of us?" said Verna.

"Plenty of room. Miss Liles can sit in the front with me and

Mother. She doesn't take up much room. Where is she? Oh, there you are," he said, plucking her from behind Gladys.

Mr. Frawley came up at that moment, mopping his head. "If any of you ladies would like to ride with—"

"They're going with me," Ansel said firmly.

"I'll go and see if anyone else . . ." He wandered off in Mr. Hudgin's direction.

Releasing herself from Ansel's grip, Allen moved over to Verna for protection and blew her nose.

"Where'd you get that hat?" Verna said, laughing. "You look about ten years old."

"It's cute," Mae Dell said. "Oh, isn't it exciting—we're going to the country club!" And lowering her voice, "I bet they serve champagne. Do you think we ought to drink it? Oh, look!" she went on, voice rising again. "They're taking pictures!"

The Ladies stood on tiptoe to see, their faces flushed with the heat and the glow of somebody else's happiness. They were part of it, they had been allowed to share, and they were going to the country club! She watched them for a moment with an unaccustomed ache. They had grown dear to her.

She turned away, and turning saw through a momentary gap in the crowd two figures at the far end of the street. They had stopped at the corner to watch, straddling their bikes. They saw her and waved.

A man stepping back from the crowd paused in front of her and took off his jacket. He was a large man with a good-natured red perspiring face.

"Too dang hot," he said, grinning. He moved away, and the street was empty.

At the top of the steps the bride, all baby's breath and meringue, stood with her rose bouquet, the attendants arranged on the steps below. Flashbulbs popped.

All the way up the street, there was only the sunlight filtering through arched branches, and the line of cars parked at the curb.

Laughter broke out on the steps. She looked up as one of the ushers bounded down them and up again. Maxine's brother, up to some prank. She watched him for a moment—the lithe young body, the fresh intelligent face. And she looked away, with a guilty glance at Mr. Frawley's back. She looked all the way up the street again to where the two of them had stood. And she turned back to the churchyard with a sinking heart, knowing what she must do.

Oh, she had learned her lesson. She would be circumspect. Charged by the dean, she would bear faithfully the standard entrusted to her. She would be diligent, study history and the Greeks. She would partake of the small pleasures, little suppers, endure conformity and prudence . . .

Until one night there should come a footstep at her door and a young face appear there, eager, bright with laughter, with the spring moon behind him and the long, gray deadly waste of years stretching ahead of her, and she would run, reckless with joy, into the dappled beckoning night.

Across the yard the dean stood a little apart from the crowd, a deposed old king, his dignity and courtesy unshaken. It would be a good marriage, this that he left her to. He offered her tenure in the life of the mind, the wealth of books, ideas, and learning, the rewards of passing that wealth along to the young. She wanted that. And she wanted—freedom, to touch and taste and explore whatever the world had to offer, wide open to magic and wonder and the come-what-may of night and moonlight, the lovely lunacy. She wanted that too. And she could not have them both. It would be a good marriage. But she would be an unfaithful wife. She was, after all, her father's daughter. And better that the dean know it now than later, when she had betrayed them both.

"I expect there'll be dancing at the country club." The odor of mustiness and perspiration. "Could I have the first dance? I'm not very good, but—"

She looked up into his anxious face, and for a moment she wavered. (Dr. Ansel weeping in her kitchen for the stifling mother.) But he carried the scent of the failed spirit and eternal regret.

"Look, look, she's going to throw her bouquet!" Mae Dell's voice was a shriek.

"I don't want that thing," Verna said, taking a step back. "What would I do with it!"

Dr. Ansel had turned his head. She moved quickly, sidling around behind the Ladies. Then, little by little, she began to make her way toward the street. Halfway there she stopped and looked back. On the far side of the yard they had drawn together, the familiar group. Dr. Ansel and Lordy and Pick, her Ladies in their brave flowered hats. And the old dean, who had not seen the top of the world. Friends and fellows, whose ways she knew: cantankerous, tedious, well-meaning; flawed and human and hard beset; with debts and dreams, the same as she, and more common sense. She had only to go back and take her place among them.

And again, in an aggravation of humility and love, she hesitated. She stood for another moment at the edge of the yard, weighing escape against years to come, secure and salaried, and an old man's faith. But she was the gambler's daughter. She had chosen. And all unwitting, they had given her leave to go. Out of their disappointed lives they had given her what she needed. It was hers now to take with her, her currency that would buy her way in the world.

She turned, suddenly rich. *Forgive me, Mr. Frawley!* Guilty, exulting, scared half to death, she slipped away unnoticed amid the rice and the cheering and walked up the street, faster and faster, 'till she came to the corner, where she turned and ran for her life.

Twenty-six

*T*hey came home late through the warm murmurous night, between the hedges, past the great houses like ghosts hidden by the darkness. The moon had gone down. They said very little now, though earlier there had been no end of talk. Since early dusk, when the boys clattered up her stairs to find her, till long after moonset, they had made up for time lost and things left unsaid. (The three weeks were not spoken of. There was no need.)

The town was alive this night. Car lights fanned through the shadows, music from radios and phonographs floated through open windows. On lighted porches people were dancing.

"What is it?" she said. "Is it the wedding—contagious excitement? What's got into them?"

"Nerves!" said Toby.

At one spot, where the music was loud and the rhythm good, they stopped to dance on the sidewalk, and she was handed back and forth from one to the other until a voice broke in with a late news report. ". . . while the British count their losses in Crete, fires from the latest German attack burn uncontrolled in London. The sinking of another British destroyer—" The voice was cut off as someone twisted the dial, and Benny Goodman tootled them on up the street.

They had drunk some beer at Sutt's Corner, eaten hot dogs at the Grease Pit. On the corner by the Osage Theater they bought popcorn and carried it to the Scottish Rite Temple, where they sat on the steps and talked and talked. But the hour grew late, and now as they came down the alley they spoke hardly at all.

They walked through the willow branches in silence, the long twigs whispering around them—once through and back and through again. George said, "What'll I do without you and Toby?"

"What'll I do?"

The other said, "Who am I going to talk to?"

They walked on, hand in hand, and slowly up the steps to the landing. Down the street the chimes had begun to ring. Sixteen notes dropped sleepily through the gentle air, and the clock struck one.

"It's Sunday," Toby said.

They leaned against the railing, looking out over the trees. "Will you come and see me," George said, "at the music school?"

"If I can," she said.

"Do you think I can make it, Teach?"

"I know you'll make it."

Toby said bitterly, "Do you think I'll make it in chemical engineering?"

"No, but you will in other ways."

"Maybe."

"You will," she said, "and George will. And maybe I will too. Somehow."

"Now you can write your books!" they said.

"I have to find a job."

"You can go to New York!"

"Someday. Maybe. Right now . . . I don't know where I'm going."

"Neither do I," said Toby.

They went on staring into the darkness, until the chimes dropped four more notes. George drew a long breath. "I better be gettin' home."

"Me too," said Toby.

They turned to each other, awkward and hesitating. "Well," she said, "have fun this summer."

She could go no further, but only stand and look at them. And as she looked, committing to dear memory those faces, they began to change. Two men stood before her, grave and handsome, and they did not know her. Nor she them.

She touched them, and they came back, two wistful boys, batting tears. And the three of them stood for a moment longer, poised at the edge of that kingdom they had held as children, beyond whose borders they would not again recognize each other.

"Write to us," George said in a husky voice.

"I will. You write to me."

"We will."

For a moment then, it seemed they were holding their breath. "Oh, I'll miss you!" she cried out. And they were all in a clump, hugging one another and laughing and crying at once.

She kissed them and let them go. George went down first. Toby lingered, or perhaps he didn't. But he turned once and looked back, and he went down last.

They vanished quickly in the blackness of the alley, only a glimmer here and there and the fading sound of their footsteps between the hedges, past the great houses blind and asleep, and where beyond that, and how far, and through what perils, none of them knew. She watched them as far as she could see and sent a small prayer after them, that they would find their way in the dark.

That was a long time ago. Much has changed since then. New kinds of darkness threaten. The nights are not always friendly. And there has been a change in the moon. Its light is not its own and it never was. But what of that? Remote and unassailable, it shed enchantment. We looked up and saw pure silver. Now the facts are brought home to us. The moon is dust and dead rock and no longer as it was.

But still it shines.

And sure as spring comes on, it will shine again—through that same garden, somewhere, here or there. And soon.

About the author

About the book

Read on

Insights,
Interviews
& More . . .

Meet Jetta Carleton

William C. Berkeley

JETTA CARLETON was born in 1913 in Holden, Missouri, (population: about 500) and earned a master's degree at the University of Missouri. She worked as a schoolteacher, a radio copywriter in Kansas City, and, for eight years, a television copywriter for New York City advertising agencies. She and her husband settled in Santa Fe, New Mexico, where they ran a small publishing house, The Lightning Tree. She was the author of the *New York Times* bestseller *The Moonflower Vine*. She died in 1999. ∾

The Lightning Tree

JETTA CARLETON LYON called The Lightning Tree, the private publishing firm she owned and operated with her husband, Jene, "an affair of the heart." She said the work was hard and the pay was low, but the satisfaction of keeping books alive was reward enough.

The Lyons set up their shop southeast of Santa Fe in the foothills of the Cerros Negros in 1973. They named their press for a giant ponderosa there, a landmark scarred by lightning. Jene, who had worked as a production manager for New York publishing firms, was a genius with printing equipment and served The Lightning Tree as pressman, Linotype operator, and hand compositor, in addition to his duties as designer and bookkeeper.

Having enjoyed some success as a novelist, Jetta used her literary skills to read manuscripts, proofread galleys, and do some rewriting. Until 1991, The Lightning Tree produced an eclectic list of titles, including books of poetry, regional history, bibliographies, and cookbooks, all designed and set in type by Jene.

The foregoing description, which accompanied the exhibit Lasting Impressions: The Private Presses of New Mexico, *was written by Pamela S. Smith, retired director of The Press at the Palace of the Governors, Santa Fe, and author of* Passions in Print: Private Press Artistry in New Mexico, 1834–Present. *Reprinted with permission of Pamela S. Smith.* ❧

> 66 [Jetta] said the work was hard and the pay was low, but the satisfaction of keeping books alive was reward enough. 99

Jetta Carleton and *Clair de Lune*

JETTA CARLETON'S FIRST NOVEL, *The Moonflower Vine*, was a critical and commercial success when it was first published in 1962. Although the novel eventually fell out of print, it nevertheless enjoyed a cult-like following of reverent readers, among them the novelist Jane Smiley. In 2009, after Ms. Smiley included it in a list of one hundred classic novels, Harper Perennial reissued *The Moonflower Vine*. Once again it attracted enthusiastic reviews and brisk sales. Jetta Carleton joined the company of those rare writers, like Harper Lee and Ralph Ellison, whose one and only novel is discovered anew generation after generation.

But there were still more discoveries to be made. Jetta had long been working on a second novel, *Clair de Lune*. Her family thought the manuscript had been swept away, along with most of her other papers, by a tornado—a bit of Missouri irony Jetta surely would have loved. After the reissue of *The Moonflower Vine*, a small Colorado newspaper published an interview with an old friend of Jetta's who had recently read the manuscript of *Clair de Lune*. Dedicated sleuthing led the family's literary agent, Denise Shannon, to Santa Fe, New Mexico, and to Joan Daw, a close friend in Jetta's later years.

Over the course of their twenty-year friendship, Jetta had been working on one or another draft of the novel. During that same period she and her husband ran a small press called The Lightning Tree. "It was a lot of work, and sometimes it was a lot of fun," she wrote of the press. "But mostly it was staying with it, month in, month out, with no real vacation. In spite of fatigue and tedium, machinery that malfunctions, walls that melt down, books that won't sell, frustration, boredom, disappointments, you stay with it." It seems that she nursed along her second novel with the same dedication and wry pleasure. At the time of her death in 1999, Jetta bequeathed the manuscript of *Clair de Lune* to Daw and her daughter.

Jetta may have spent decades taking the novel apart and putting it back together, but the paradoxical result is an enchanting freshness of style and inventive characterization. Though set in a very particular time and place, *Clair de Lune* is a classic coming-of-age story. Unlike many novels that center on female protagonists—indeed, unlike *The Moonflower Vine*—the story of *Clair de Lune* does not revolve around romantic love. Though there is a romance, it is incidental to the central theme of a young woman becoming who she is, who she must be.

Like *The Moonflower Vine*, *Clair de Lune* is set in Jetta Carleton's home territory of southern Missouri, but it is a formal departure from *Moonflower*, which shifted between the points of views of the several members of the Soames family. *Clair de Lune* is told from only ▶

> 66 Jetta may have spent decades taking the novel apart and putting it back together, but the paradoxical result is an enchanting freshness of style and inventive characterization. 99

two perspectives: the author's, who writes an informal prologue and epilogue and introduces each of the novel's three movements, and twenty-five-year-old Allen Liles's, to whom she handed part of her own story, "altered to fit."

Though Allen has never been out of Missouri, she has, like any serious reader, traveled far in her imagination—to the salons of Paris, the Italy of Byron, and, perhaps most momentously, to Greenwich Village: the Greenwich Village that is "much farther away from southern Missouri than it measured on a map." The measure of that distance is evident in the characters who populate the junior college where she takes her first teaching job. Each represents a future comically remote from the one Allen desires. Mrs. DeWitt Medgar is a sour, skeptical soul who finds everything about Allen suspect, starting with her name. Dr. Ansel, Ph.D., a man "who knew what he knew and loved it greatly," is still ball-and-chained to his widowed mother. The teachers Verna, Mae Dell, and Gladys form a veritable chorus of forsaken dreams and lives measured out in coffee spoons. And then there's Miss Maxine Boatwright, young, pretty, socially prominent, and already engaged. Maxine is everything a young woman might aspire to be in this small city: a well-married member of the country club set. In the daytime Allen is just another of their company, if slightly unusual: she is devoted to her teaching, passionate about contemporary

66 Though Allen has never been out of Missouri, she has, like any serious reader, traveled far in her imagination. 99

literature, and acclimating herself to the demands of her new station in life. In the evenings, alone, she "dream[s] herself forward" into quite another future.

At the opening of the second movement of the novel—what I think of as its "Clair de Lune" movement— the author writes: "But the night, as Thoreau reminds us, is a very different season. And it was a different creature who—on those spring nights when spring had barely appeared, so shivering and dissembling that only the very prescient could tell it was there at all— ran down the steps from Miss Liles's apartment, leaving behind the trappings of the day. . . ."

Here we see exactly how much of Jetta's own youthful "nightcrawling" she's given to Allen. In a letter to her agent in 1972, she wrote: "I've been obsessed lately by the sudden realization that a good part of my youth—between 16, say, and 28—was lived most joyously after dark. . . . My goodness, what a lot of larking about we used to do in the middle of the night! I can remember prancing up and down the big wide clean back alleys of Joplin, Missouri, on spring nights when the air was full of the scent of mock orange; and through empty parks and graveyards and along country roads. And we were always going into places, for godsake! I waded in more fountains, sat in the laps of more statues in public places, climbed astride more bronze horses, than anyone else I've ever known. And all of it in the wee hours, ▶

66 In the evenings, alone, [Allen] 'dream[s] herself forward' into quite another future. 99

without anyone to stop us, and without a trace of fear."

The larking is launched when Allen discovers her true kin in the two young men who attend her literary seminar, George and Toby. Under the moonlight, the three explore the "chosen landscape" of the soul—listening to music, discussing literature, declaiming poetry and playacting, and soon giving in to full blown "lunacy," gallivanting around town, eating sweets and drinking beer, and waltzing in the park. With these friends, only a few years younger than she, Allen feels brilliant and completely engaged, and for a while she manages a fragile balance between daytime decorum and nighttime daring.

Inevitably, Allen's trespasses become the cynosure of gossip and speculation. With a mixture of mortification, shame, and confused pride, Allen faces the moral, social, and financial implications of her nighttime self. Back and forth she goes, from the determination to keep her position at the school to the lure of larger dreams, the woman she knows herself to be, and the larger world she longs to join. She is not undone by fear but refined by it.

The last scene masterfully enacts the suffocating tension between Allen's two choices. Finally, she is compelled to make a bold, irrevocable move—quite a daring one for any young woman, especially one living in post-Depression, small-town Missouri.

Jetta Carleton was herself such daring soul, moving from Missouri to New

66 Under the moonlight, the three explore the 'chosen landscape' of the soul . . . soon giving in to full blown 'lunacy.' 99

York, where she worked as a television advertising copywriter. Creating Allen Liles from a distance of more than fifty years, she is able to dramatize the dilemma her character faces with a light touch, bring her characters to life in a sentence or two, and portray each of them with a clear-eyed compassion born of experiencing much more than dreams. Jetta's philosophy is Epicurean, finding the highest virtue in happiness and friendship. How rare it is for a novel to celebrate "the chosen landscape of the soul," the enchantment of moonlit spring evenings, and the importance of good old-fashioned fun.

Since Jetta's novel was still a work in progress when she died, Joan Daw and her agent, Denise Shannon, asked me to edit the manuscript, to address some inconsistencies of sequence and characterization, and to clarify a few phrases likely to perplex a twenty-first-century reader. I have used my lightest editorial touch and done my best to honor what I believe were Jetta Carleton's intentions.

I expect *Clair de Lune*, like *The Moonflower Vine*, will meet with enduring success, especially among young readers. It is, at its heart, a novel that encourages idealism—a quality, as Jetta Carleton says of innocence, that seems in short supply these days. ❧

> " Jetta's philosophy is Epicurean, finding the highest virtue in happiness and friendship. "

Ann Patty
October 2011

The Moonflower Vine: A Neglected Book

The following is Brad Bigelow's review of The Moonflower Vine. *The review appeared on NeglectedBooks.com, December 23, 2006.*

I READ *THE MOONFLOWER VINE* after coming across Jane Smiley's discussion of it in her *13 Ways of Looking at the Novel*. It wasn't so much what Smiley had to say about it as that it was essentially the only genuinely little-known novel she saw fit to include in her list of one hundred great novels. In there amongst *Wuthering Heights*, *Moby-Dick*, and *Ulysses* was this book with a completely unfamiliar title and by a completely unfamiliar author. To see a neglected book rate such high-profile coverage alone made it worth a try.

I can't say that *The Moonflower Vine* would have stood much chance of a second look from me had it not come with such a sterling recommendation. Its marketing, back when it was picked as a Literary Guild selection and condensed in a Reader's Digest edition, was definitely aimed at a feminine audience, and its first paperback edition featured a small picture of a big, strong, dark-haired man embracing a delicate young woman—the sort of image that's become the cliché of gauzy romantic novels.

As Bo Diddley sang, though, you can't

66 Its marketing, back when it was picked as a Literary Guild selection and condensed in a Reader's Digest edition, was definitely aimed at a feminine audience. **99**

judge a book by looking at the cover. There's barely a lick of romance in the whole of *The Moonflower Vine*. Carleton grew up on a Missouri farm perhaps not too unlike that described in her novel, and no farm family that survives a hard winter or a bad harvest has much romanticism left in its veins. The pragmatism of farm life is multiplied by the stern morality of the Midwest Methodist, with its clear-cut sense of right and wrong (and none of the Southern Baptist's taste for a little melodramatic backsliding).

The Moonflower Vine is a multidimensional tale of the lives of Matthew Soames; his wife, Callie; and their four daughters, Jessica, Leonie, Mathy, and Mary Jo. Mary Jo is probably closest in profile to Carleton herself. The youngest of the girls, she is roughly the same age as Carleton and, like her, left rural Missouri for a career in the world of television in New York. She narrates the introductory section of the book, which takes place one summer Sunday when the daughters (with the exception of Mathy, who dies before the age of twenty) have come back to the family farm for a visit. This section is gentle, lightly comic, and bucolic in its description of rustic pleasures such as skinny-dipping in the creek.

The rest of the book, however, is related in the third person. Starting with Jessica, it deals in turn with each of the other members of the family—Matthew, who struggles throughout ▶

> 66 Carleton grew up on a Missouri farm perhaps not too unlike that described in her novel, and no farm family that survives a hard winter or a bad harvest has much romanticism left in its veins. 99

his career as a teacher and principal of a small-town school with a lust for bright young women in his classes; Mathy, the family rebel, who elopes with a barnstorming pilot; Leonie, the dutiful daughter, who never quite manages to find her right place in the world; and finally, Callie, the mother, whose brief moment of adultery mirrors her husband's own private sin.

Sin is a constant presence in the book. Everyone in the family, with the possible exception of Mary Jo, commits one or more sins, in their own eyes or those of the community, that prevents any form of love expressed in the book from being completely unequivocal. Matthew never fully forgives Mathy for quitting school and running off with one of the local renegades, nor Jessica for marrying a drifter Matthew takes on briefly as a hired hand. The Soameses are a God-fearing family, stalwart members of the Methodist Church, very much Old Testament Christians.

At the same time, though, progress makes its own changes in their lives. While Matthew and Callie refuse to install indoor plumbing, planes, trains, and automobiles all bring the outside world a little closer to their doorstep. Jessica and her new groom catch a train for his family home in southern Missouri—genuine hillbilly country—

❝ Sin is a constant presence in the book. ❞

and though he dies less than a year later, she remains with his people thereafter. Ed, one of Matthew's old students, returns to town with an old biplane and proceeds to sweep daughter Mathy off her feet, only to kill her a year or two afterward in a crash landing. Sometime later, Leonie takes a trip to Kansas City, meets a somewhat reformed Ed, and eventually decides to marry him.

Though *The Moonflower Vine* is full of lush descriptions of the trees, birds, flowers, and plants that fill the Soameses' world, it's very much a Midwestern, rather than Southern, novel. The comedy and tragedy are always moderated with a spare sense of realism. Missouri is, after all, the "Show Me" state—skepticism prevents any of the characters from leaping headlong into any of their passions for more than a moment or two. Or, rather, it makes them look before leaping, if leap they do.

As the reviews of *The Moonflower Vine* on Amazon.com demonstrate, this novel, though long out of print, continues to hold a fond place in the hearts of readers who've discovered it.

Brad Bigelow edits and maintains the Neglected Books Page (www .neglectedbooks.com), which features reviews, articles, and dozens of lists of fine but forgotten books and authors. He also edits the Space Age Pop Music ▶

> ❝ Missouri is, after all, the 'Show Me' state—skepticism prevents any of the characters from leaping headlong into any of their passions for more than a moment or two. ❞

The Moonflower Vine:
A Neglected Book *(continued)*

Page (www.spaceagepop.com), which pays attention to music most people prefer to ignore. After serving with the U.S. Air Force for twenty-five years, he now works for NATO and lives outside Brussels, Belgium. ⌒

Don't miss the next book by your favorite author. Sign up now for AuthorTracker by visiting www.AuthorTracker.com.